William Douglas Morrison

Juvenile Offenders

William Douglas Morrison

Juvenile Offenders

ISBN/EAN: 9783337366919

Printed in Europe, USA, Canada, Australia, Japan

Cover: Foto ©Andreas Hilbeck / pixelio.de

More available books at **www.hansebooks.com**

BY

W. DOUGLAS MORRISON

AUTHOR OF

CRIME AND ITS CAUSES, THE JEWS UNDER THE ROMANS, ETC.

NEW YORK

D. APPLETON AND COMPANY

1897

PREFACE.

I HAVE had occasion to point out publicly from time to time that one of the formidable problems confronting civilised communities at the close of the' present century is the problem of habitual crime. It is perfectly well known to every serious student of criminal questions, both at home and abroad, that the proportion of habitual criminals in the criminal population is steadily on the increase and was never so high as it is now. In almost every official document dealing with penal administration this unsatisfactory state of things is both admitted and deplored. In France, Germany, and Italy the proportion of old offenders who come before the criminal courts is constantly growing, while in England matters are just as bad. This is made perfectly clear by the report of the Committee on the Identification of Habitual Criminals. "From a table compiled for the use of that committee it appeared that in Lancashire, the West Riding of Yorkshire, and Staffordshire about 70 per cent. of the prisoners tried were known to have been previously convicted ; in Liverpool, Birmingham, and Bradford, 79 per cent. ;

and in Norfolk and Suffolk, 61 per cent.; while in London the proportion was only 47 per cent. The committee arrived at the conclusion that in London the proportion of habital criminals who were arrested but escaped detection was much larger than in other districts, and that, speaking generally, a certain proportion of old offenders, small in some districts, considerable in others, escape identification altogether." This passage is a quotation from the revised Criminal Returns for England and Wales, and more than justifies every statement which it has fallen to me to make upon the subject.[1]

What does this enormous percentage of old offenders among the criminal population mean? It means that, as far as the bulk of the criminal population is concerned, penal law and penal administration have completely broken down. The supreme, if not the only, object of a properly constituted penal system is to prevent the offender who has been once convicted from repeating the offence. If a penal system fails in this primary and fundamental object in three cases out of four—and this is what the returns teach us is happening at the present moment—

---

[1] Up to the last two years these Criminal Returns were in a very backward and unsatisfactory condition. The appearance of an article by the writer in the columns of *Mind* for 1892 led to their revision. An article in the *Fortnightly Review* for 1894 also led to an official inquiry into prison administration. At the termination of this inquiry the following letter was addressed to me by one of its most distinguished members: "Now that we have reported I cannot let the opportunity pass without saying how deeply I think, that not only the Prisons' Committee, but the whole English public, are in your debt. You have been the real instrument in bringing about what I hope will be a very great change for the better."

the time has come for reconsidering the principles on which existing penal methods are based. As long as these methods remain in their present condition of inefficiency the community will have to endure the loss, disquietude, and danger arising from the existence in its midst of a compact and formidable body of habitual criminals; it will have to go on spending millions per annum in protecting itself against them. It is to be recollected that when a penal system fails to prevent the offender from repeating the offence, the inevitable result is that a vast and expensive body of police is required to protect society against him when he is at liberty. What the habitual criminal costs the community when in prison is a mere trifle to what he costs when he is free to roam the streets. He can be kept in prisons for four or five hundred thousand pounds a year; when at liberty he costs in police protection alone between four and five millions.

In the present volume I have endeavoured to show how habitual crime may be diminished by better methods of dealing with juvenile offenders. A wide experience of the criminal population convinces me that the habitual offender, the man who takes to crime as a trade, as a rule begins young. Unless a man has acquired criminal habits in early life it is comparatively seldom that he degenerates into an habitual criminal. The criminal population may be roughly divided into two classes: the habitual offender and the occasional offender. There is a borderland where the distinction between these two classes is practically obliterated. But in the main they constitute two distinct divisions of the criminal population, and it is not often that the occasional criminal degenerates into the habitual criminal unless he acquires criminal habits in early youth. As a rule the fatal transition from the one class to the other takes place during the period of immaturity. It follows from these facts that one of the most effective methods of dealing with habitual crime is to prevent the juvenile offender from acquiring confirmed criminal habits.

How is this to be accomplished? This question can only be answered after an inquiry into the conditions which produce the juvenile delinquent. Crime among the juvenile population is produced by certain conditions, and all attempts at dealing with it is only groping in the dark until we know what these conditions are.

In accordance with this view I have devoted the first part of the present volume to an examination of the conditions which produce the juvenile offender. In a preliminary survey of the extent of juvenile crime among civilised communities, I have pointed out that the problem of juvenile crime is not diminishing in magnitude. Whether we look at home or abroad, whether we consult the criminal returns of the Old World or the New, we invariably find juvenile criminality exhibiting a distinct tendency to increase. It is a problem which is not confined to any single community : it is confronting the whole family of nations ; it is arising out of conditions which are common to civilisation.

The upshot of this preliminary chapter naturally

leads us to ask what these conditions are. These conditions I have divided into two fundamental classes : individual and social., The principal individual conditions are the sex, the age, the bodily and mental characteristics of the juvenile offender ; the most important social conditions are parental and economic circumstances. Juvenile crime arises out of the adverse individual or social conditions of the juvenile offender, or out of both sets of conditions acting in combination. Such is the conclusion at which I arrive after a wide survey of the personal and social circumstances of the juvenile delinquent population.

After arriving at the principal causes which produce juvenile delinquency, the next and most obvious step to take is to see how far it is possible to minimise and remove these causes. It is a commonplace which hardly requires to be repeated, that before we can remove an effect we must first remove its cause. In the second part of this volume I have endeavoured to show how existing methods of dealing with juvenile offenders may be better adapted to the purpose of diminishing the causes which produce juvenile crime. In discussing the value of punitive methods I have been compelled to point out that these methods, although to a certain extent inevitable, are of comparatively little service as instruments of social security. The worthlessness of purely punitive methods arises from the fact that the tendency of these methods is to aggravate and intensify the adverse individual and social conditions which turn the juvenile into a criminal. It follows as certainly as night follows day that if punitive methods are aggravating the conditions which make a youth a criminal the application of these methods, instead of doing him any good, will add force and volume to his criminal tendencies and will assist in transforming him from an occasional into an habitual criminal. Society must aim at securing the maximum of determent with the minimum of punishment.

It is to ameliorative methods of treatment that we must look for the best results in dealing with juvenile delinquency. The supreme object of these methods is to minimise, or, if possible, remove the adverse individual and social conditions out of which juvenile crime arises. In so far as ameliorative methods are successful in taking away or diminishing the force of these adverse conditions, in so far they will be successful in diminishing the proportion of juveniles who ultimately harden into habitual criminals.

Ameliorative methods of dealing with the individual offender will accomplish much, but it must be borne in mind that these efforts do not touch the general conditions out of which juvenile crime arises. These general conditions are the unhappy individual and social circumstances in which a considerable proportion of the juvenile population are born and have to live. It is to an amelioration of the adverse conditions of life among large sections of the juvenile population that we must look for a mitigation of the problem of juvenile crime. So long as great numbers of the general juvenile population are the offspring of degenerate and degraded parents, and have to grow up in an atmosphere of moral and material wretchedness, we shall always have a high percentage of juvenile crime. It is in these wretched and degenerate conditions of existence that juvenile delinquency has its origin, and it will always continue to flourish till these conditions are ameliorated.

The task of ameliorating these adverse conditions is one which devolves on the forces of civilisation in Church and State. Hitherto Christian charity has in the main directed its beneficent energies towards the alleviation of individual miseries. In the future its efforts must be more and more directed towards removing the causes by which these miseries are produced. It is when Christian charity enters upon this great task that it is fulfilling its highest mission in the world.

W. D. M.

WANDSWORTH PRISON, LONDON.
October, 1896.

CONTENTS.

PART I.

THE CONDITIONS OF JUVENILE CRIME.

CHAPTER III.

CHAPTER IV.

CHAPTER V.

CHAPTER VI.

CHAPTER VII.

Heredity and surroundings—Influence of imitation—Influence of the family—Illegitimacy—Illegitimates in industrial school population—Mortality among illegitimate
children—Illegitimates in reformatory schools—Social
effect of illegitimacy—Relations between illegitimacy and
crime—Illegitimacy is lowest where crime is highest—
Relation between density of population and illegitimacy—
Relation between density of population and crime—Relation between illegitimacy and crime—Relation between
pauperism and illegitimacy—Causes of this relation—Relation between orphanhood and juvenile crime—Juvenile
offenders without father and mother—Small percentage of
totally orphaned children in industrial schools—Juvenile
offenders who have lost their fathers—The mothers of
fatherless children — Motherless children — Motherless
children in industrial schools—More motherless than
fatherless children in industrial schools—Causes of this
disparity—Deserted children among juvenile offenders—
Desertion by the father : by the mother—The treatment
of deserted children—Children of criminal parentage—
Parental condition of reformatory school children and
juvenile prisoners—Effect of removing adverse parental
conditions in reducing juvenile crime—Juvenile offenders
with both parents alive—Character of the parents.

CHAPTER VIII.

Economic condition of orphaned and deserted children—
Economic condition of illegitimate and partially orphaned
children—Children dependent on their mothers only—
Economic condition of juvenile offenders with both
parents alive—Contributions of parents to maintenance
of juvenile offenders—Economic condition of juvenile
prisoners—Juvenile prisoners without homes—Municipal
homes for homeless boys—Juveniles in large cities—Occupations of juvenile offenders—Relation between occupation and crime—Relation between unskilled labour and

---

PART II.

THE TREATMENT OF JUVENILE CRIME.

CHAPTER IX.

CHAPTER X.

CHAPTER XIII.

PART I.

THE CONDITIONS OF JUVENILE CRIME.

CHAPTER I.

6 2 0 2

THE EXTENT OF JUVENILE CRIME.

General observations on criminal returns—Extent of crime only approximately known—The most comprehensive record of crime is cases reported to the police—Criminal returns of various countries : Australian, English, French, Italian, German—Value of criminal returns : value of cases tried, of convictions, of reports to police—Exactitude of criminal returns depends on attitude of population towards the criminal law— Illustrations of this principle in Ireland, United States, Italy— Movement of juvenile crime in civilised communities—Growth of humane feeling makes it difficult to estimate the tendencies of juvenile crime—Juvenile crime on the Continent—Juvenile crime in England—Relation between prison population and juvenile crime—Effect of voluntary homes in reducing prison population—Latest returns relating to juvenile crime in England—Juvenile crime in the United States.

IT is impossible to measure the exact proportions of juvenile crime among civilised communities owing to the inevitable imperfection of all official returns relating to the criminal conditions of the population. These returns, however carefully they may be drawn up, can only include offences which come within the knowledge of the judicial and police authorities, and it is hardly necessary to remark that a considerable

number of offences of almost every description are
constantly being committed which do not reach the
ears of the authorities at all. Many a crime is perpetrated of which no one is aware except the person
who committed it. Many offenders are not prosecuted even when they are detected : cases of criminal
illegality which are well known to private individuals
are in many instances never publicly reported to the
police. In all these circumstances the offences which
have taken place leave no public record behind them.
They are passed over in silence in all the official
statistics of crime. The amount of crime committed,
whether by juveniles or adults, is always largely in
excess of the amount of crime recorded in the most
complete and elaborate public returns. The silence,
stealth, and secrecy, which play so essential a part in
almost all the operations of criminal offenders, must
always have the effect of preventing the State from
arriving at an exact estimate of the full extent of
crime. On this grave subject, as well as on other
matters of the utmost social importance, we must be
contented with approximations. It is, however, to be
recollected that these approximations, though falling
short of absolute accuracy, are of the greatest value
for all practical purposes.

The number of criminal cases annually reported to
the police constitutes the most comprehensive account
of the criminal condition of a community. In some
of the Australian colonies, as, for instance, New South
Wales, a record is kept and published of all offences
which come under the cognisance of the police. In
England and Wales a similar record is published of

all serious or indictable offences reported to the police. On the other hand, offences of a non-indictable character are not recorded. In most continental states no record is kept of offences committed or reported to the authorities unless the offender is arrested and tried. In France and Italy the criminal returns are based upon the number of cases tried ; in Germany these returns are based upon the number of persons convicted. It may be laid down as a general principle that criminal returns increase in accuracy in proportion as criminal proceedings develop. Criminal returns relating to the number of offences reported to the police are more comprehensive but not so accurate as criminal returns relating to the number of persons tried. A certain proportion of cases reported to the police are of such a frivolous character that it is unnecessary to bring them into a court of justice. Cases, again, in which convictions are obtained are a more accurate representation of the actual facts than cases which are merely tried. It is only after the offender has been brought before a court of justice, and the whole facts of the case submitted to the rigorous test of legal proof, that it is possible to say with an approach to exactitude in what the offence has consisted, or whether an offence has been committed at all. As criminal returns diminish in comprehensiveness, they increase in accuracy. When a community is living under normal social and political conditions the most accurate, although the least comprehensive, test of the extent of crime within it is the number of persons convicted from year to year. When, on the other hand, the social and political conditions of a community are not normal—when, for example, considerable sections of the community are actively hostile to the law—then the value of conviction ceases to be a sound test, and the value of trials or cases reported to the police increases in significance. The reason of this is obvious. It is exceedingly difficult to procure convictions when the population is out of sympathy with the law. When circumstances of this character arise juries will not find the prisoner guilty, no matter how strong the evidence may be against him; witnesses will not come forward, even if they have seen the offence committed. Ireland furnishes an interesting example of the effect of social and political conditions on the import of criminal statistics. As far as ordinary crime is concerned the Irish returns relating to convictions are a trustworthy test of its extent and seriousness. This arises from the fact that as far as regards ordinary crime the Irish population is in sympathy with the law. But there is one class of offences in which the Irish returns relating to convictions cannot be accepted as an approximate measure of their prevalence in the community: I mean agrarian offences. Where it is a question of agrarian offences the Irish people as a body are more or less hostile to the law. As a result of this condition of the public mind it is exceedingly difficult to get evidence in connection with these offences; it is also exceedingly difficult to get juries to convict. Convictions accordingly lose their ordinary value as a test of the extent of agrarian crime. In such circumstances the best test is the number of offences reported to the police. What holds good with

respect to agrarian offences in Ireland holds equally
good with respect to the crimes committed by lynchers
in the United States and the robberies and assassina-
tions committed by secret societies in Italy. In short,
the relative value of the returns of crime depends on
the attitude of the population towards the criminal law.

Contenting ourselves with these general observations on the character of criminal returns, we may
now proceed to ask what these returns teach us as to
the prevalence of juvenile crime. In the first place,
is juvenile delinquency increasing or decreasing
amongst civilised communities? This is an apparently simple question, yet it is not an easy one to
answer. The difficulty of answering it arises from
the fact that the attitude of the public mind and
the attitude of the judicial mind towards juvenile
offenders has been and is still undergoing important
modifications in the direction of greater leniency
and indulgence. The result of this is that there is
less inclination on the part of the public to prosecute
than used to be the case; and when prosecutions do
take place there is a distinct tendency to mitigate the
seriousness of the charges preferred against the young.
When the weakness, the inexperience, the immaturity
of youth are taken into consideration, the tendency
towards greater humanity in dealing with the young
must be pronounced a wholesome one. But the
effect of this new development of humane feeling is
to make the task of ascertaining whether juvenile
crime is moving upwards or downwards a difficult
and complex operation. In cases where the movement is downwards the decrease may be apparent

rather than real. It is a movement which may be accounted for by a more humane condition of the public mind and more humane methods of criminal procedure.

Unfortunately, there are very few communities at the present time in which juvenile delinquency is exhibiting this downward tendency. In France the number of juvenile offenders under sixteen, as well as the number between sixteen and twenty-one, is unquestionably increasing. In Belgium, owing to the fact that the statistics relating to the age of offenders are somewhat imperfect, it is difficult to say what direction juvenile crime is taking. In 1891 the reformatory schools of Belgium (*maisons de réforme*) were changed into charitable institutions (*maisons de bienfaisance*), and received neglected children as well as juvenile offenders. It is therefore impossible to estimate the proportions of juvenile crime in Belgium by a reference to the number of inmates committed to these establishments. Article 25 of the law of 1891 increases the difficulty of comparing the past and present of Belgium with respect to juvenile crime. According to the provisions of this Article children under sixteen who have committed comparatively slight offences cannot be committed to prison ; they must either be liberated altogether or placed in the hands of the authorities for educational treatment. In Italy, under the old penal code, juvenile offenders are classified into three distinct groups. All children under fourteen years of age are included in the first group, all juveniles between fourteen and eighteen are included in the second, and all youths between eighteen and twenty-one are included in the third. In each of these groups there is a distinct increase of juvenile delinquency. The only statistics relating to Switzerland are the number of juveniles committed to correctional establishments. These public institutions —ten in number—are so full that it was recently impossible to admit many of the cases committed to them by the criminal tribunals. In spite of this increase Dr. Guillaume, the head of the statistical bureau at Berne, inclines to the opinion that juvenile crime is not increasing, although he at the same time confesses that it is not diminishing. In Norway the changes in criminal law which have taken place in recent years make it difficult to estimate the movement of juvenile crime. In Sweden a similar difficulty is experienced owing to the operation of chapter iv. of the law of 1890 relating to the treatment of juvenile offenders. In Holland juvenile delinquency among children under sixteen years of age has doubled within the last twenty years. In Russia the number of juveniles between fourteen and twenty-one years of age convicted before courts of assizes and judges of the peace is increasing faster than the growth of population, and was never so high as it is at present. In Hungary, whether we confine our view to the numbers of juvenile offenders under sixteen, or extend it so as to include all juvenile offenders up to the age of twenty, we find the youthful population exhibiting exactly the same criminal tendencies as in other countries. Both members of the dual monarchy have the same complaint to make as to the upward movement of juvenile crime. In

Austria a large number of cases of petty theft, false
pretences, and offences of a somewhat similar description, are not included in the criminal returns. Offences
of this character are very prevalent among the youthful population. The Austrian returns relating to
juvenile crime must therefore be regarded as very far
from being either complete or even comprehensive.
But, incomplete as they are, they still tell the same tale
as the returns of other civilised communities. From
year to year, almost without interruption, the number
of young offenders continues to increase. German
criminal statistics include many of the minor offences
which are excluded from the Austrian, and consequently enable us to measure the movement of crime
in the German empire with greater precision. But
the comprehensiveness of the returns, instead of
modifying our opinion as to the growth of juvenile
crime on the continent of Europe, is calculated to
deepen the conviction that it has assumed the proportions of a general phenomenon. Whilst crime among
the adult population in Germany has increased
between 25 and 30 per cent. within the last ten
years, juvenile crime has increased more than 50.
per cent. Our review of the criminal condition
of the European populations across the Channel has
been a fairly wide one, and wherever we look we are
confronted with the fact that the moral status of the
juvenile population, as far as it can be exemplified in
the statistics of crime, is the reverse of satisfactory.

It has for many years been customary to look at
England as the one bright spot on the European
horizon, and continental observers, when bewailing

the criminal tendencies of the juvenile population among themselves, have at the same time held us up as the one state in the sisterhood of nations in which juvenile delinquency was steadily on the decline. England was placed upon this pedestal in consequence of the steady and practically uninterrupted decrease of the juvenile population in prisons under the age of sixteen. Since the admission of the working classes to the franchise in 1867 the number of children under the age of sixteen committed to prison has been continually diminishing, and there is no sign that the process has even yet become exhausted. The number of juveniles committed to prison at the present time do not amount to a third of the numbers annually committed about thirty years ago. This is in some respects a very remarkable fact, whatever explanation we may ultimately arrive at as to its real significance. It has been usual to assume that only one explanation of the decrease of the juvenile prison population was possible. The falling off of the commitments of juveniles to prison was assumed to be coincident with a diminution of the proportions of juvenile crime. This explanation was so often put forward, and remained so long unquestioned, that it ultimately came to be accepted as an indisputable axiom.

Constant contact with considerable sections of the prison population, as well as observation of the change of attitude which was coming over the criminal courts in their dealings with convicted men, forced some of us to the conclusion that the movement of the prison population was a very untrustworthy test of the

general movement of crime. In articles in various
periodicals I had occasion to point out that the
increase or decrease of the prison population depended upon many other circumstances besides the
increase or decrease of crime. The size of the prison
population depends in the first place on the duration
of sentences. If it is a growing tendency of the
criminal courts to diminish the length of sentences,
the criminal population, other conditions being
similar, will diminish in the same ratio. If a man
is sentenced to twelve months' imprisonment for an
offence of the same character as used to be visited
with a sentence of five years' penal servitude, the
population in penal servitude is bound to diminish.
But in these circumstances the decrease of the penal
servitude population is not a proof of the decrease of
crime. It is a proof of the growing spirit of mildness
which is entering into the administration of the
criminal law. In the same way if a person is merely
fined or called upon to find sureties for good
behaviour for the same offence which used to carry
with it a sentence of imprisonment, the prison population will diminish. But here again the diminution
of the prison population in no sense implies a corresponding decrease of crime. It merely shows that
judges and magistrates are losing faith in the efficacy
of the jail, and are coming round to the belief that
other and more humane methods are just as effective
for keeping the population within the sphere of law.
The fact that sentences are diminishing in length, the
fact that imprisonment is being more and more supplanted by other forms of punishment, the fact that

the prison population is not an approximately accurate test of the growth or decline of crime is now universally admitted. They are even incorporated in the revised criminal statistics of England and Wales. When these obvious facts were put before the public a few years ago by me, in the pages of the *Nineteenth Century*, I was attacked in unexpected quarters, as has been said, "with a bitterness almost amounting to ferocity."

If the prison population as a whole cannot be accepted as a test of the dimensions of crime, far less can the number of juveniles in prison, or committed to prison, be taken as measuring the extent of juvenile delinquency. If there is one thing more conspicuous than another in connection with the administration of criminal law, it is the constantly increasing unwillingness of judges and magistrates to commit children to prison. The Chief Constable of Staffordshire, in an interesting pamphlet on the Fluctuations of Crime, gives the following example of this reluctance : " I have before me," he says, " particulars of a young lad who was seven times convicted of felony without being committed to prison, and it was only on the eighth conviction that he was committed to prison as a preliminary to treatment in a reformatory." This is not an isolated and exceptional case Many other instances of a similar character might easily be given if it were necessary to add further force to a fact which is sufficiently notorious. The action of the judiciary in connection with the imprisonment of children finds a parallel in the action of the executive. It is not so very long since the prisons of England used to contain within their walls a large number of children under fourteen years of age. At the present time whenever a child under fourteen is committed to prison, even if merely on remand, the fact must at once be communicated to the executive, unless the child is under detention preliminary to his transfer to a reformatory school. In recent years the law itself has been altered in the direction of minimising the number of juveniles in prison. According to the provisions of the Reformatory Schools Act of 1893 it is no longer obligatory to send a juvenile to prison before committing him to detention in a reformatory. Before the passing of this Act all children sentenced to reformatories had to be committed to prison for a certain period. The Act of 1893 has wisely abolished this ridiculous arrangement, and at the present time about 70 per cent. of the children sent to reformatories are transferred to these institutions without being subjected to preliminary imprisonment. It will thus be seen that the judiciary, the executive, and the legislature are all acting in concert· with the object of reducing the juvenile prison population to the lowest possible minimum. Under such a powerful combination of circumstances the decrease of the prison population under the age of sixteen comes within the category of facts which admit of simple explanation.

Other agencies in addition to those just mentioned have likewise been at work in reducing the proportions of the juvenile prison population. Within the last twenty years in particular a vast amount of philanthropic effort has been expended in the founding of voluntary homes for the class of children who used to find their way into prison. These voluntary homes are products of private charity; they receive no assistance whatever from the State, and are absolutely unconnected with it. Some of these institutions, such as Dr. Barnardo's Homes and the Church of England Society for providing Homes for Waifs and Strays, deal with dependent and delinquent children on a vast scale. Other institutions of a similar character confine their operations within more modest limits. But all of them are actively occupied in the beneficent work of saving the young, and were it not for the magnificent efforts which they have put forth, and which they are now putting forth with unabated energy and devotion, England would occupy a very much worse position with respect to crime of all kinds than it does to-day. It is exceedingly difficult to say how many of these voluntary homes are at present in existence. No less than 120 of them are in connection with an excellent society known as the Reformatory and Refuge Union. But the homes in connection with this society do not by any means exhaust the list; they only serve to show what a vast amount of voluntary activity is at present being exhibited in the task of rescuing the young from a condition of dependence and crime.

Inasmuch as the juvenile prison population, owing to the circumstances which have just been mentioned, sheds so very little light on the movement of juvenile crime in England, we must look for information on this important question in other directions. Unfortunately it is impossible to obtain information of a

3

satisfactory character covering a considerable period
of time. Prior to the publication of the English
Judicial Statistics for 1893 no information was
accessible relating to the number of juveniles tried or
convicted before the criminal courts. All that can
be done in the direction of ascertaining whether
juvenile crime has been increasing is to consult the
returns dealing with the number of juveniles sent to
prison, the number sentenced to be whipped, and the
number ordered to be detained in reformatory and
industrial schools. These returns, it is to be recollected, do not take account of the numbers (increasing
in later years) who are discharged under the provisions of the Summary Jurisdiction Act, or the numbers punished by the imposition of a fine, or the
numbers dealt with under the First Offenders Act,
or the numbers handed over to voluntary homes and
police-court missions. On the other hand, the returns
include a certain number of children committed under
the Education Act; but this Act is often utilised by
humane magistrates as a merciful substitute for the
more severe provisions of the criminal law. Notwithstanding the incompleteness and inadequacy of
the figures relating to the number of juveniles
imprisoned, whipped, and sent to correctional institutions as a test of the movement of juvenile delinquency, these returns, as far as they are of any value
at all, show that the number of juvenile offenders has
increased within the last thirty years. That the
increase is not greater than the growth of population
is to a large extent to be attributed to the efforts of
the various institutions which have sprung up in
recent years for alleviating the lot of the young.

When we pass away from the rather unsatisfactory attempt to compare the present with the past, and proceed to examine the latest returns relating to juvenile delinquency, we find ourselves on surer ground. For some years past the thankless task has devolved upon me of pointing out the imperfections of our criminal statistics, and the backward position which they occupied as compared with official publications of a similar character in France, Italy, and Germany. Happily as a result of these representations our criminal returns were taken in hand and reorganised, and we are now enabled to gauge the moral condition of the juvenile population in so far as it is revealed in the statistics of crime. Up to the present time we have only information relating to two years. It is almost needless to remark that the narrow limits of two years constitute too short a period of time for drawing conclusions either one way or the other as to the growth or decrease of juvenile crime. Exceptional social and economic circumstances produce exceptional fluctuations, and the effect of these exceptional circumstances can only be counterbalanced when we have figures before us which deal with a considerable number of years. It may not, however, be amiss to mention the opinion of the editor of the revised returns, as to the present tendencies of juvenile crime. Though the juvenile population of the English prisons has decreased, he says the results now obtained unfortunately show that this does not imply any real diminution in the amount of youthful criminality. A statement of this character at once puts an end to the idea that England occupies an exceptional position among the nations of the world with respect to juvenile crime. If it has the effect of shattering our self-complacency and compelling us to look unwelcome facts in the face it will do an immense amount of good. We shall recognise that more strenuous efforts are yet needed on the part of the individual and society in furthering the highest welfare of the young.

I cannot close this survey of the movement of juvenile crime among civilised communities without reference to the United States. All students of criminal questions owe a debt of gratitude to Mr. Frederick Wines, the special census agent, for his luminous and exhaustive official report on Crime, Pauperism, and Benevolence in the United States.[1] This report, which enumerates the prison and reformatory school population, is the only information we possess which deals with the criminal condition of the United States as a whole. In discussing the character of the English criminal returns it was pointed out that the prison and reformatory school population was a very incomplete, and in some respects inadequate, representation of the real dimensions of crime in a community. The same remark applies to the American returns relating to reformatories and prisons. The American as well as the English criminal law uses a variety of methods in addition to prisons and reformatories in the treatment

[1] Report on Crime, Pauperism, and Benevolence in the United States at the eleventh census, 1890. Part II.: General Tables. Washington, 1895.

of criminal offenders. In these circumstances it will
easily be understood that the number of offenders
under detention only affords a partial view of the full
extent of crime in the United States. But this view,
such as it is, certainly shows that the position of the
United States with respect to juvenile delinquency is
no better than the position of Europe. The population under detention in reformatory institutions is
increasing more rapidly than the growth of the community as a whole, and, as far as it is possible to see,
the juvenile population in prisons is doing the same
thing. How many juveniles in addition to those
committed to prisons and reformatories are dealt
with by fine, by admonition, by sureties for good
behaviour, by voluntary institutions, it is impossible
to tell. It is highly probable that the numbers dealt
with by these various methods are exhibiting the
same upward tendency as the population of prisons
and reformatories. Whether, then, we look at the
Old World or at the New, we find that juvenile crime
is a problem which is not decreasing in magnitude
with the march of civilisation. Every civilised community is confronted with it in a more or less
menacing form.

Much has been done, but much yet remains to be
done. The work that has been accomplished in the
past is not a ground for self-complacency and
quiescence in the present. It is, on the contrary a
stimulus to fresh exertion.

CHAPTER II.

THE DISTRIBUTION OF JUVENILE CRIME.

International distribution of juvenile crime—Difficulties of international comparison — International distribution of crimes
against the person—Crime in the north and south of Europe—
Homicide among juveniles in England and the United States—
Causes of homicide in the United States—Homicide among the
coloured population of the United States—General conditions
determining the distribution of homicide—Local distribution
of juvenile crime—Unevenness in the local distribution of
juvenile crime—The distribution of juvenile crime runs parallel
with the distribution of crime in general—Juvenile and adult
crime run together, as both proceed from the same conditions
—Density of population and crime—Effects of a dense population in producing crime—The solitary dweller in large cities—
The struggle for existence in large cities—The temptation to
cupidity in large cities—Effect of decentralisation of industry
in diminishing crime—Local distribution of pauperism and of
crime—Least crime where there is most pauperism—Poor law
administration and crime—Economic conditions and crime—
General conclusions.

IN the preceding pages we have seen that amongst
almost all civilised communities juvenile crime is
exhibiting a tendency to increase as fast as the
growth of the juvenile population, and in many
countries even faster. In some countries the real
proportions of juvenile crime have been obscured by
alterations in judicial procedure and alterations in

the treatment of juvenile offenders, but when these alterations are accounted for the fact becomes comparatively clear that little progress has as yet been made in reducing the dimensions of juvenile delinquency. It would be interesting as well as instructive if we could only get to know what countries are worst situated and what countries are best situated with respect to juvenile crime. A fact of this character would perhaps enable us to see what sort of repressive or preventive agencies are most likely to be successful in overcoming the tendencies to crime amongst the young. Unfortunately it is impossible to construct a table which would show with any degree of accuracy the comparative situation of the various civilised communities with respect to juvenile crime. The difficulty of constructing such a table does not arise so much from the want of figures as from the circumstance that the figures when confronted with one another could not be accepted as an accurate representation of the facts. The figures relating to juvenile crime, and in fact to all sorts of crime in every community, are determined by the character of the criminal law and the methods of criminal administration which prevail in that community. But it is notorious, as has already been pointed out, that in no two countries is criminal law identical, and in no two countries is it administered on the same principles or regarded with the same eyes by the populations who happen to be subject to it. As long as criminal law and administration, and the attitude of the various populations towards both, differ so widely as they do at present, all attempts at instituting comparisons must be more or less misleading. The only remarks which can be made with any degree of probability on the international aspect of juvenile crime is that offences against the person, and more particularly the crime of homicide, are greater among the juvenile populations of the south of Europe than among the juvenile populations of the north. As far as the crime of homicide is concerned the differences in criminal law are not of such a profound nature as to destroy the value of international comparisons, and these international comparisons all tend to show that juveniles in the south are more addicted to homicide than juveniles in the north. How this apparent difference between the north and the south is to be explained is an exceedingly difficult matter. The difference is attributed by some to difference of social surroundings in the shape of political, religious, marital, and economic institutions ; it is attributed by others to physiological and mental differences arising out of differences of race ; it is also attributed to social differences arising out of racial differences. The difference between the north and south of Europe in the matter of homicide among the young probably arises from diversity of racial, social, and climatic conditions combined.[1]

Whilst we are dealing with the international aspect of homicide it may be of interest to compare the amount of homicidal crime in England with its amount in the United States. In the United States

[1] See E. Ferri. "L'Omicidio nell' Anthropologia Criminale," vol. i. p. 236.

the most accurate and comprehensive returns we
have to go by are the returns relating to the offences
committed by the population committed to prison.
According to the United States census of the prison
population in 1890 it appears that there were twenty-
three children under the age of fourteen under
detention for the crime of homicide, and 388
juveniles between the ages of fifteen and eighteen
under detention for the same offence. In England,
on the other hand, according to the criminal returns
for 1893 and 1894, there were no cases of conviction
for homicide among the juvenile population under
sixteen years of age, and only six cases among the
juvenile population between sixteen and twenty-one.
If the United States returns relating to homicide
include manslaughter as well as murder it will still
be found that the numbers per million of the juvenile
population are much higher in America than in
England. In England there were only seven cases
of manslaughter in the two years 1893–4 among
children under sixteen, and eighteen cases of the same
offence among juveniles between sixteen and twenty-
one. Whatever allowances we may make for differences in judicial procedure between the two
countries, it is hardly possible to resist the conclusion
that homicide among the young, whether in the form
of murder or manslaughter, is more prevalent in
proportion to the population in the United States
than it is in England.

The difference with regard to this capital offence
may be accounted for on a variety of grounds. In
the first place it is possible that the American comes

to maturity more quickly than the Englishman. If this is the fact a child of fourteen in the United States is nearer manhood than an English child of the same age, and it is universally recognised that the nearer maturity is approached the larger is the proportion of offences against the person. Another cause of the comparative prevalence of homicide among the juvenile population of the United States is no doubt to be attributed to the large influx of emigrants in recent times from the south and south-east of Europe. It is notorious that peoples of the type of the Italians and Hungarians exhibit much less respect for human life than is to be found among the northern races. Contact with the humanising influences of American civilisation no doubt has a wholesome effect in modifying the character and temperament of the children of the emigrants from the south. But family and racial characteristics cannot be altogether obliterated by social surroundings, and it is not at all unlikely that juvenile delinquency of the most serious kind in the United States is in some measure to be set down to the boundless hospitality of her shores.

Another cause of a racial character of the comparatively high ratio of juvenile homicide in the United States is the presence of a large coloured element in the population. In proportion to its numbers the coloured population is very much more addicted to homicide than the white population. Although the coloured population only amounts to one-seventh of the inhabitants of the United States, yet it is responsible for no less than one-third of the cases of homicide. The habit of carrying arms is a social rather than a racial characteristic, and this habit has the effect of augmenting the proportions of homicide in every community which is addicted to it. As far as the United States is concerned, American civilisation is capable of ultimately absorbing the vast mass of extraneous elements which is continually seeking incorporation within it, but the criminal returns show that it has to suffer severely while the process of assimilating heterogeneous races is in operation.

A review of all the facts relating to the crime of homicide among the young would seem to show that its distribution in various countries is determined by a variety of conditions. It is determined in the first place by the comparative quickness or slowness with which the youthful population of various races reaches maturity. It is determined by the homogeneity or heterogeneity of the population. It is determined by racial and social characteristics. Some of these conditions are capable of being modified, and some are exceedingly hard to change. Social conditions, for example, are susceptible of almost infinite modification, and in so far as these conditions are modified in a healthy direction the crime of homicide will steadily diminish among the young.

An inquiry into the local distribution of juvenile crime yields more satisfactory results than an examination of its international distribution. Difficulties which are almost if not altogether insuperable in the case of international comparisons hardly exist at all in comparisons instituted between different divisions of the same community where the whole community is living under the same form of criminal law. In some countries, such as Switzerland and the United States, where each canton or each state has a criminal law peculiar to itself, comparisons between different divisions of the same country present a certain number of difficulties. But in countries such as England, France, and Germany, where the criminal code is the same and where the criminal administration is the same, very useful results may be arrived at as to the causes of crime by looking at the manner in which it is distributed in the several divisions of the country.

One of the first facts which strikes an inquirer into the criminal condition of a community is the uneven manner in which crime is distributed among the various geographical divisions of which a country is composed. The criminal map, for instance, of France shows that some departments are much more addicted to offences against the law than other departments. The criminal maps of Germany or Italy exhibiting the territorial distribution of crime tell the same tale of inequality. The criminal map of England shows that there is the widest diversity between one county and another with respect to the local ratio of offences. In the county of Cornwall, for instance, there are less than fifty indictable offences against property per hundred thousand of the population. In the county of London, on the other hand, there are more than 250 indictable offences against property per hundred thousand of the population. Such counties as Lancaster, Stafford, Warwick,

Durham, Northumberland, exhibit between four and five times as many indictable crimes against property as the Welsh counties along the sea-coast. When we look at the geographical distribution of crimes against morals, or at the geographical distribution of offences such as drunkenness, we see the most remarkable differences between one part of the country and another. In some counties crimes against morals are six times as high as they are in other counties. In the same way drunkenness is from four to six times more prevalent in the northern counties of England than in the eastern. It is unnecessary to give any additional facts to show the wide diversity which exists between one part of the country and another with respect to the prevalence of crime.

In England juvenile crime is distributed in very much the same manner as crime in general. Where crimes of violence and crimes against property reach a high ratio in proportion to the population, it will usually be found that juvenile crime is also at a high ratio in proportion to the juvenile population. In other words, juvenile crime is usually high where crime as a whole is high. The only way in which a rough estimate can be arrived at of the manner in which juvenile offences are distributed is by looking at the commitments to prison and industrial schools in the various counties of England and Wales. The annual number of committals to prison and industrial schools is not by any means an accurate test of the distribution of juvenile offences. Large numbers of juveniles are disposed of by fine, by admonition, by sureties, by corporal punishment, and the numbers disposed of by imprisonment and committal to industrial schools is only a fraction of the number of juveniles annually tried before the criminal courts. But the number of juveniles committed to prison and to correctional institutions is our only available test of the distribution of juvenile crime. According to a return drawn up by me for the Departmental Committee on Prisons, and incorporated in the Minutes of Evidence, the number of commitments to prison and to industrial schools is greatest in such districts as the metropolis, Northumberland, and Lancashire. It is likewise in these districts that crime as a whole is greatest. On the other hand, counties which disclose the lowest proportion of juvenile offenders to the population are as a rule counties which show a low percentage of crime in general. The exceptions to the rule that crime in general and juvenile crime run on parallel lines are explicable on the ground that the treatment of juvenile offenders differs in different parts of the country. In some parts fining, admonition, whipping, are largely resorted to in the treatment of juvenile offenders; in other parts magistrates are more inclined to commit to prison or to correctional institutions. When these differences of procedure are taken into account the general conclusion remains that there is an intimate connection between the local distribution of crime in general and the local distribution of juvenile crime.

The reason juvenile crime runs on parallel lines with crime as a whole is that both juvenile crime and crime as a whole proceed in the main from the same conditions. One of the first and most conspicuous of these conditions may be described as the concentration of population arising out of the concentration of manufacturing industries. All over the civilised world most crime is committed in districts which are most thickly populated. Whether we look at the criminal returns of France, Germany, or the United States, we find that, as in England, a high rate of crime is always the result of a densely aggregated population. A population of 100 persons to the square mile, if it forms part of the same nationality and is living under the same laws, is much less criminal in proportion to its numbers than a population of 500 persons to the square mile. And again, a population of 1,000 persons to the square mile is much more criminal in proportion to its numbers than a population of 500 persons to the square mile. Wales, for instance, with the exception of Glamorgan, has only a population of about 150 to the square mile. In Glamorgan the population to the square mile is between 700 and 800. The result is that the dense population of Glamorgan produces, in proportion, between three and four times as much crime as the rest of Wales. Westmoreland, with a thin population, does not produce half as much crime per thousand inhabitants as the neighbouring county of Lancaster, with a dense population. In estimating the effect of density of population on the tendency to crime it is to be remembered that social laws do not possess the rigidity and inevitability of physical laws. They are always more or less modifiable, and this holds true of the relation between density of population

and crime.   In cases, for instance, where there is little
economic stability, and where considerable sections
of the community are from time to time suddenly
plunged into distress, a sparse population may
produce more crime than a dense one.   And, on
the other hand, a comparatively dense population
with a high degree of economic stability will be less
criminally disposed than a district with few inhabitants to the square mile if these inhabitants have
to lead a precarious, unsettled economic existence.
But where economic and other social and administrative conditions are similar, a dense population in
proportion to its numbers produces a larger amount
of crime than a sparse population.

The mischievous effects of a crowded population
on the character of the individuals composing it arise
from several obvious causes.   A community of this
sort produces a large proportion of weak and ineffective people possessing very inadequate physical
equipment for successfully fighting the battle of life.
As a result of their physical deficiencies people of
this kind are unable to obtain regular employment
or to keep in work when they obtain it.   Disease and
sickness interfere with them and incapacitate them,
and they are driven down to the very lowest social
stratum if they do not happen to have been born in
it.   A juvenile in this position, although he may not
have any strong criminal instincts, is sorely tempted
to enter upon a criminal career.   The ordinary
avenues of honest industry are closed against him
owing to his bodily infirmities ; the precarious means
by which he procures a bare existence sometimes

completely fail him. The comparative impunity with which offences may be perpetrated in large cities emboldens him, and even if he is caught and convicted imprisonment is a mode of punishment he does not keenly feel. Towns also contain a larger percentage of orphan children than the country districts, and a larger percentage of young people who lose their parents as they are entering upon the most critical period of life. This arises from the circumstance that the mortality of the towns is higher than the mortality of the rural districts. Nothing is more disastrous than the loss of parental care in early life, and there can be no manner of doubt that the proportions of juvenile delinquency in our large cities is considerably swollen by this cause alone. Even when the parents do not die a good many of our city children have to leave the parental roof when quite young owing to deficiency of bedroom accommodation. Such children are compelled to take up their abode in the common lodging-house. Here they find themselves in the society of vagrants, thieves, and the lowest scum of the community. In the midst of such surroundings it is no wonder that many of them are submerged and lost.

A considerable number of juveniles from the country also fall when they enter upon town life. The restraining eye of the village community is no longer upon them. In many cases they find themselves in a large city without friends, without family ties, and belonging to no social circle in which their conduct is either scrutinised or observed. In youth the social instincts are keen, and must in one way

4

or another be gratified, but the only method in which the solitary dweller in vast cities can do this is at the cheap music-hall and the public-house. It by no means follows that every young man who frequents these places of entertainment is to be set down as lost. On the contrary, the majority are able to set up some sort of limitation for themselves, which they rarely or ever venture to overstep. They are aware that a single week's thoughtlessness is sufficient to lose them their occupation, and perhaps to undo them for ever. The fear of these consequences acts in most cases as an effective check on the impulse to dissipation. On the other hand, unfortunately, instances are not wanting in which the lonely, unfriended existence of the country lad in a large city is the chief cause of disaster to his life. In the last century Adam Smith pointed out the perils of city life which beset the migrant from the country, and these dangers are more acute now than they were in his day. "A man of rank and fortune," he says, "is the distinguished member of a great society, who attend to every part of his conduct, and thereby oblige him to attend to every part of it himself. His authority and consideration depend very much upon the respect which this society bears to him. He dare not do anything which would disgrace or discredit him in it, and he is obliged to a very strict observation of that species of morals, whether liberal or austere, which the general consent of this society prescribes to persons of his rank and fortune. A man of low condition, on the contrary, is far from being a distinguished member of any great society.

While he remains in a country village his conduct may be attended to, and he may be obliged to attend to it himself. In this situation, and in this situation only, he may have what is called a character to lose. But as soon as he comes into a great city he is sunk in obscurity and darkness. His conduct is observed and attended to by nobody, and he is therefore very likely to neglect it himself, and to abandon himself to every sort of low profligacy and vice."

In addition to the causes already mentioned a dense population heightens the proportion of offenders to the population, inasmuch as it intensifies the struggle for existence, whilst its glare and glitter excite the desire to enjoy. Nowhere is competition so keen as in densely packed centres ; nowhere is a man so disposed to push aside his neighbour ; nowhere is consideration for others at a lower level. In a large city the old disposition to regard the stranger with suspicion, if not as an enemy, is to a large extent revived, and as each citizen is a stranger to the other the whole of the inhabitants live in an atmosphere of suspicion and distrust. These conditions of existence are destructive of social cohesion in its highest forms, and have a tendency to develop the selfish instincts till they overstep the borderland which separates selfishness from crime. Another important reason of the high percentage of juvenile offences in large cities is the cupidity excited in the young mind by the spectacle of so vast an amount of wealth around. Most of the juvenile offences committed in this country arise from cupidity, and consist of offences against property. The strongest temptation of the ordinary juvenile is the impulse to steal ; in the towns this impulse is stimulated in every street by interminable lines of shops and warehouses exhibiting all kinds of merchandise in a half-protected state. These temptations are almost irresistible to the homeless arab, the youth who is temporarily out of work, and a considerable class of children whose moral sense is either untrained or undeveloped. Opportunity is the greatest of all temptations, comparative impunity is the next, and with the combination of opportunity and impunity which exists so widely in all large centres it is no wonder that they are hotbeds of youthful crime.

From a moral point of view it is unquestionable that the decentralisation of industry is one of the most needed of present-day reforms. Cases occur from time to time in which large manufacturing establishments are transferred from the cities to the country, and wherever such transfers are practicable an immense amount of benefit immediately accrues to society in general. Some look forward to a time when it may be possible to transfer mechanical power to the remotest country districts, and in this way revive many rural industries which are at present languishing or extinct. Whether this expectation will ever become a reality it is impossible to say ; thus far the progress of mechanical invention has had the effect of concentrating our population and centralising our industries, much to the detriment of the moral and physical stamina of the race. It is highly questionable whether the enormous increase of national wealth which this century has witnessed is not being purchased at too high a price. If we compare the mortality of the industrial population which produce this wealth with the mortality of the agricultural population it at once becomes apparent that our vast national accumulations have to be paid for by a frightful shortening and sacrifice of human life. In a world such as ours, where in international matters might is right, it is highly perilous to under-mine the vitality of a nation merely in order to make its population somewhat more opulent. There is considerable reason to fear that this is the baleful process at present in operation in our midst. The true policy for a nation desirous of remaining great is to give most encouragement to those occupations which produce the most vigorous class of citizens. In the decade 1881–90 there was an annual average of 117 deaths in the towns to every 100 deaths in the country ; it is the country, accordingly, which contains the most vital elements of the population, and the supreme aim of statesmanship at the present time should be directed towards the establishment of a hardy and enterprising race upon the soil. Just now our rural classes are sunk in poverty and pauperism, but in spite of these tremendous draw-backs they are a more robust and less criminal population than the dwellers in the towns. What might they not become if these drawbacks could be to some extent removed and a modest career opened out for their latent energy and enterprise? In any case it is to measures of this character that we must look for a reduction in the proportions of youthful crime.

In the preceding remarks on the local distribution of juvenile offences it has been seen that there is evidently a close connection between juvenile crime and density of population, and it has also been shown that there is an intimate relation between the proportions of juvenile and adult crime in the several geographical divisions of England and Wales. It still remains for us to inquire whether there is the same intimate connection between the local distribution of pauperism and the local distribution of juvenile delinquency. In other words, do we find that there is a high ratio of pauperism where there is a high percentage of juvenile offenders? Were there no means of answering this important question except by consulting our own intuitions we should probably arrive at the conclusion that pauperism and juvenile crime run hand in hand, and that therefore the ratio of pauperism to the population must be high where the ratio of juvenile offences is high. This is an exceedingly plausible conclusion, but it is not justified by the official returns of the Local Government Board. According to these returns the connection between pauperism and crime, so far as it exists, does not lie upon the surface. In fact, so much is this the case that when we begin to compare the distribution of pauperism with the distribution of crime, both juvenile and adult, it immediately becomes manifest that as a rule there is least pauperism where there is most crime, and of course least crime where there is most pauperism.

Let us select a few examples of this condition of things. On the 1st of January, 1892, the number of paupers in England and Wales per thousand of the estimated population amounted to 26.2. Below this average for the whole country are the counties of Lancaster, Chester, Northumberland, Warwick, Middlesex, Durham, and several others. Now it is a remarkable circumstance that all the counties which have just been mentioned as showing a percentage of pauperism below the average, at the same time exhibit a percentage of juvenile crime, and of crime in general, above the average. On the other hand, if we look at the counties which are most burdened with pauperism, we find that a very large proportion of them are counties with a very small percentage of either juvenile or adult crime. In the counties of Norfolk, Dorset, and in North Wales, which contain more than 40 paupers per thousand of the population, there is not half as much crime of any description as exists in counties containing less than 20 paupers per thousand of the population. The county which shows the lowest percentage of pauperism is the county of Lancaster, but it is nevertheless the district which has the highest ratio of juvenile crime. The county of Norfolk has the largest number of paupers per thousand of the population, but it has a comparatively small number of juvenile offenders.

What are the most probable causes of this remarkable disparity between the ratio of pauperism and the ratio of crime? In addition to the causes already noted as producing a high rate of crime in large centres of population, the method of administering the poor law requires to be mentioned. In order to prevent wholesale imposture the guardians of the poor in our densely populated districts are obliged to administer the law to a greater or less extent on certain hard and fast principles. It is almost impossible for them to know the real antecedents of a large proportion of the applicants for relief, and one of the inevitable results of this lack of accurate information respecting the cases which come before them is that applications for poor-law relief are, as a rule, dealt with more rigidly in towns than in the country. It is therefore probable that the refusal of assistance, or the knowledge that assistance will be refused if applied for, while it has the effect of reducing the numbers on the poor rate in our large cities, has also the effect of swelling the proportions of crime in them. In the country districts, on the other hand, the poor law is administered by persons possessing an intimate knowledge of the real economic circumstances and antecedents of almost all applicants for assistance. These applicants, unlike the city poor, are not a floating population which are here to-day and somewhere else to-morrow ; they are not composed of people for the most part without a history or a settled home. Almost all of them have resided from childhood upwards in the same village or the same neighbourhood. It is easy to trace their previous history, and to acquire an accurate knowledge of their character, their habits, and the most important vicissitudes in their humble career. It would appear that this intimate and minute acquaintance with all the details and circumstances of each case is of considerable importance in connection with poor-law administration—in fact, it is probably a partial explanation of the difference in the ratio of pauperism in the agricultural districts as compared with commercial and industrial centres. Inasmuch as it leaves the greater poverty of the agricultural labourer out of account, as well as his immemorial attitude towards the poor law, this explanation is obviously of a partial character. Nevertheless it counts for something ; and, as far as crime is concerned, the fact that the distribution of poor-law relief is more general in the country than in the towns is undoubtedly to be reckoned as one among the many reasons why the country population is less criminally disposed than the urban population.

It is not, however, to be supposed that a more rigid administration of the poor-law system in the country districts will have the effect of raising the rate of crime to the same high level as exists in towns. If crime were merely a product of poverty this would no doubt be the case, but it is a well-ascertained fact that a multitude of offences against the criminal law are not the result of economic causes. Innate disposition, parental example, social surroundings, social habits, the presence of temptation and opportunity, all play a more or less prominent part in determining the extent and intensity of crime. Several of these causes operate much more powerfully in the towns than in the country. As far as the amount of crime is concerned there is accordingly every reason to believe that densely populated centres will always be at a disadvantage as compared with thinly peopled districts. Offences against the person, for instance, are very seldom the direct result of economic causes. Owing to the extensive opportunities for contact and conflict arising out of the existence of a highly concentrated population, offences of this character are more numerous in towns, in proportion to the inhabitants, than in the country. It is the same with drunkenness. The opportunities for becoming intoxicated are much greater in towns than in the country, inasmuch as the public-house is almost always closer at hand. Offences against property stand upon a somewhat similar footing. The opportunity of committing such offences, and therefore the temptation to commit them, is always greater in towns ; the consequence is that a larger number are committed by the town populations. These examples are sufficient to demonstrate that an equalisation of the economic conditions of existence as between town and country would not necessarily be followed by a corresponding equalisation of the ratio of crime.

On summarising the results of this inquiry into the local distribution of juvenile offences the following conclusions come prominently to the front. It is found, in the first place, that where there is a high rate of crime in general there is also a correspondingly high rate of juvenile crime. The principal causes of this coincidence are the corruption of the young by the old, and the fact that both adult and juvenile criminals are a product of the same personal, social, and economic circumstances. In the second place, it is found that the personal, social, and economic conditions which generate a criminal disposition and criminal habits of life are fostered to a very large extent by the herding together of the population in a few immense commercial and industrial centres. In these centres a decadent race springs up, owing to the unwholesome conditions of existence ; the struggle for life is keener and more unscrupulous ; cupidity is more highly and frequently excited ; a larger homeless population exists ; men are more in the position of strangers to each other, and offences are less easily detected. All these agencies, working together, have the effect of making large cities the principal hotbeds of delinquency. The third conclusion at which we arrive is that there is least crime where there is most pauperism. This remarkable state of things is in part to be accounted for on the ground that a wider distribution of poor-law relief has the effect of preventing the commission of certain kinds of offences, inasmuch as the relief received is sufficient to satisfy the fundamental requirements of life among that class of the community which is most tempted to become criminal. But this explanation only covers a portion of the ground. The highest ratio of pauperism is in the country districts. If the death-rate is taken as a criterion, there is not so much decadence among the rural population ; there is a smaller homeless class than in the towns ; there is more regularity of employment ; there is less chance of character being vitiated ; there are fewer excitements to cupidity, and there is a greater probability that the offender will be arrested and brought to justice.

It follows from these conclusions that the most effective methods of combating juvenile delinquency consist in improving the hygienic surroundings of the inhabitants of the towns, so as to make the urban population more effective instruments for fighting the battle of life in an honest way, and, in the second place, in so ameliorating the economic condition of the rural population that they will not be tempted to forsake the comparative wholesomeness of the country for the temptations and vicissitudes of the town.

CHAPTER III.

SEX AND JUVENILE CRIME.

Necessity for studying the conditions which produce crime—Why penal laws fail—Conditions which produce crime of two kinds : individual and social—Individual conditions—The effect of sex on crime—Relation between male and female crime among juveniles under sixteen—Among juveniles under twenty-one—Among juveniles in reformatories—Among juveniles in industrial schools—Sex and juvenile crime in the United States—Causes of the unequal distribution of crime among the sexes : 1. The law more lenient to females than to males; 2. Social and economic conditions of the sexes differ ; 3. Biological conditions of the sexes differ—Effect of sex on the nature of crime—The character of female offenders—The offence as an index of the character of the offender—The habit of offending as an index of character—Value of knowing previous character in dealing with juveniles—Summary of conclusions.

IN the preceding chapters we have inquired into the extent and local distribution of juvenile delinquency. Our next step will consist of an inquiry into the individual conditions of the juvenile delinquent. Crime of all kinds is a product of certain antecedent conditions residing partly in the individual and partly in his surroundings. All attempts at dealing with criminal problems which take no account of the conditions which tend to produce the criminal population are predestined to failure. One of the

principal reasons our penal laws have hitherto been
so ineffective in diminishing the proportions of crime
is that these laws have practically ignored the individual and social conditions on which the movement
of crime depends. An enactment directed against
a certain kind of crime will in the end have comparatively little effect in diminishing its amount if
the antecedent conditions which produce the crime
remain untouched. In the same manner a mode of
punishment directed against a certain form of crime
will do no good if the punishment has the effect of
intensifying and aggravating the adverse individual
and social conditions of the person who has committed the offence. In order to reduce the proportions of crime we must first of all diminish the
adverse conditions which produce it. In these
circumstances the first thing to do is to ascertain
what the individual and social conditions are which
produce the criminal population. If we know what
these conditions are we shall be in a position to
see how far they are capable of being removed or
minimised. In the same proportion as they can
be removed or minimised the criminal population
will decrease. *Cessante causa, cessat effectus.*

Let us look, in the first place, at the individual
conditions on which juvenile crime depends. These
conditions may be comprehensively described as
consisting of sex, age, body, and mind. Before
dealing with these conditions in detail it must be
recollected that juvenile crime is never the result
of a single individual cause, or even of a combination
of them. Juvenile crime, as well as crime of all

kinds, is the result of individual and social conditions acting in combination. In discussing juvenile crime the conditions which produce it are separated and looked at singly for purposes of exposition, but they are not to be considered as separated in reality. In each particular crime one condition may be more prominent than another, but at the same time the crime is the result of a combination of conditions. As sex is the most fundamental of all individual distinctions, let us deal first with the effect of sex on juvenile crime. How is juvenile crime distributed among the two sexes? We can get an answer to this question in a variety of ways. In the first place we may consult the police returns relating to the number of juvenile criminals at large under sixteen years of age. As an accurate representation of the actual number of juvenile offenders at large these returns possess exceedingly little value. At the same time they are useful as a means of ascertaining in what proportions crime is distributed among the sexes. The causes which invalidate their accuracy as a trustworthy statement of the numbers of the criminal classes at large do not come into operation as far as the sex of these classes is concerned. For this reason the proportion of males to females among the juveniles reported by the police as habitual offenders is of considerable utility as a test of the effect of sex on crime. According to the police about 85 per cent. of the habitual offenders under sixteen are males, and 15 per cent. females. If these returns are to be accepted as approximately accurate —and they are supported by other returns which are less open to question—the effect of sex on the tendency to commit or abstain from crime is very conspicuous. The accident of sex and the attributes of sex make it between five and six times more likely that a boy will become a criminal than a girl. A fact of this kind is conclusive evidence that human conduct is to some extent determined by causes which lie outside the control of the individual. Sex is one of these causes.

When we examine the returns relating to the sex of offenders convicted under the age of twenty-one, and which are of a more accurate character than the police returns, we find that crime is distributed among the sexes in the proportion of thirteen females to eighty-seven males. In reformatory institutions crime is distributed among the sexes in the proportion of twelve females to eighty-eight males. In industrial schools the distribution of the population according to sex is somewhat different. In these institutions there are twenty-four females to seventy-six males. The relatively high ratio of females to males in industrial schools is to be attributed to the character of the offences for which large numbers of children are committed to industrial establishments. These offences are in a great many cases of a passive rather than an active character. It is for this reason that the proportion of girls in industrial schools is so much higher than the proportion of girls in reformatory schools. In the United States the juvenile population of the reformatories is divided by sex in much the same proportions as the juvenile population in industrial schools in Great Britain. According to the results of the census of 1890, 22 per cent. of the reformatory inmates were females, and 78 per cent. were males. The high percentage of females in the United States reformatories is owing to the fact that the American judiciary are very unwilling to commit girls to prison under the age of twenty-one. The prisons of the United States only contained 7 per cent. of female prisoners under twenty-one, while English prisons contain about 16 per cent. of females under the age of twenty-one. In other words, American magistrates commit females under age to reformatories in a great many cases where English magistrates would commit them to prison. In America the law deals more leniently with females than in England. The small number of females in prison and the high ratio in reformatories, as compared with England, is a proof of it.

The effect of sex on the disposition to obey or offend against the criminal law is manifest not only in England and the United States but all over the civilised world. In every continental country males form a larger proportion than females among juvenile offenders; and in Australia the position of affairs is precisely the same. It must, therefore, be admitted that we are not merely in presence of temporary and accidental circumstances, but are in reality confronted with a universal law. Wherever we cast our eyes this law holds good; everywhere we find that females, whether juveniles or adults, are less addicted to crime than males. How is the difference between male and female criminality to be accounted for? It is some-

5

times asserted that this difference is, after all, more apparent than real, and the foundation for this view is that female offenders are more leniently dealt with than male offenders. It must be admitted that there is a certain amount of truth in this contention. In the English criminal courts male offenders are acquitted in the proportion of one in six, whereas female offenders are acquitted in the proportion of one in four. If it is assumed, and there is every reason for assuming, that the evidence on which the criminal charge is founded is as strong in the case of women as in the case of men, it inevitably follows that the machinery of the criminal law is more indulgent to women than to men. In other words, a woman with precisely the same weight of testimony against her is much more likely to be let off than a man. It is very reasonable to suppose that the leniency of the criminal courts towards female offenders has its counterpart in the whole sphere of criminal administration and even of social life. The public are less disposed to make charges of a criminal character against the female part of the population, the police and other authorities are less inclined to make charges, and the result is that criminal statistics do not adequately represent the full dimensions of female delinquency. Admitting the justice of these contentions to the utmost, and even multiplying female offences by one-third, the fact still comes out that females are less addicted to crime than males. We are accordingly justified in saying that the indulgence of the public and the administration to female offenders will not explain the whole circumstances, although it does explain a certain part of them.

Another explanation of the difference between male and female delinquency consists in attributing the disparity to the action of social influences. Women, it is said, have fewer opportunities of becoming criminal offenders, owing to the nature of the social conditions which keep them out of contact with many of the hard realities of existence. The circle of female activity is in the majority of cases bounded by the precincts of the home. This sphere offers far fewer opportunities for the commission of criminal offences than the wide field of social and industrial life which is occupied by men. In fact, it is always found that when women enter this field in considerable numbers the percentage of female crime has a distinct tendency to increase ; the equalisation of social and economic conditions as between man and woman has the effect of bringing the proportions of male and female crime nearer to the point of equality. In the Metropolitan Police district a fourth of the offences determined summarily are committed by females ; in Manchester a third are committed by females. On the other hand, in the county of Surrey, outside the Metropolitan Police district, little more than a tenth of the summary offences are committed by females, and in the county of Lancaster little more than a seventh are committed by females. In the metropolis and in Manchester, where the economic conditions of the sexes are to some extent equalised, the result of this partial equalisation is immediately manifested in a nearer approach to equality in anti-social action. In the immediate neighbourhood of these great centres where this equalisation of social condition does not exist in the same degree, the effect is seen in the much smaller proportion of female offenders.   On these grounds it must be admitted that the extent of female crime is determined, among other things, by the social conditions of female existence, and that these conditions are on the whole more favourable to a non-criminal life than the conditions which affect men.

Nevertheless, the whole of the disparity between the criminal tendencies of the sexes is not to be explained by a reference to the disparate nature of their social functions.   Difference of social function is itself a product of biological causes, and it is to these causes that we must look for a complete explanation of the effect of sex on crime. Women are less criminal than men because their physical and mental structure is different. The effect of this difference is seen in cases where the social and economic conditions of the two sexes are almost entirely the same. Up to the age of fourteen the social and economic circumstances of the boys and girls who are committed to industrial schools are practically alike. They are brought up in the same class of home, they attend the same kind of school, they are allowed a similar amount of liberty, they live amid the same social surroundings. Yet we find that about five boys are sent to an industrial school to one girl. It is evident from this fact that social and economic causes will not explain the difference between male and female criminality ; these causes are of a still more funda-

mental character ; they are rooted in the organism
as well as its environment. According to the teachings of physiology the structure and constitution of
the female sex are of such a character as makes them
less fitted for great bodily and mental exertion than
men. The female bent of mind is less active, less
aggressive, less liable to come into conflict with the
established institutions of society, and therefore less
criminal. It follows from these facts that the effect
of sex on crime is an effect which will be permanent.
It is an effect which is not resting on transitory
causes such as education or social habits and conditions, which the march of civilisation may modify
or revolutionise ; it is resting on foundations anterior
both to civilisation and humanity, and will continue
to manifest itself as long as the race endures.

The effect of sex on the nature of adult crime is
perfectly obvious. All offences requiring the exercise
of muscular force and mental daring are to a pre-
ponderating extent the work of men, while offences
in which masculine qualities are not required are
considerably participated in by women. The annals
of juvenile delinquency reveal a very similar condition of things. Of all the females committed to
reformatory schools in the year 1894 only two were
sent for offences against the person, and a very small
fraction for offences against property with violence.
On the other hand, several boys were committed to
these institutions for offences against the person, and
a fair percentage for burglary and housebreaking.
The offences in which girls reach more nearly to the
level of boys are fraud, the unlawful possession of

property, and domestic theft. Offences of this character are, partly for social reasons and partly for
biological, more apt to be committed by girls. The
social danger arising from the commission of offences
against the person by girls is practically non-existent,
and the same may be said with respect to offences
against property with violence. Petty theft and
vagrancy. constitute the great bulk of delinquency
among female juveniles. The nature of the offences
committed by girls sent to reformatories in the
United States is very much the same as the nature
of the offences committed by girls in England. The
only difference is that there is perhaps a somewhat
larger proportion of crimes of violence, owing to the
fact that reformatories are used for females who
have reached maturity, whilst in England they are
only used for girls under sixteen.

It must not be supposed that the character of
females committed to reformatory and industrial
schools is better than the character of boys. The
lighter nature of the offences for which girls are as a
rule committed is apt to produce the impression that
the criminal bent is less pronounced in them than in
boys, but as a matter of fact this impression is an
erroneous one. The very circumstance that girls do
not in general commit such serious offences as boys
has the effect in a multitude of cases of causing these
offences to be condoned and overlooked. Very often
this method of treatment is more or less successful,
but in those instances where it happens to fail the
ultimate result is that a girl is a more hardened
offender than a boy before she is committed to an

industrial or reformatory institution. She enjoys a
longer period of comparative impunity; she has
accordingly more time to form criminal habits, and
when ultimately taken in hand by reformative
agencies her character has become considerably
depraved. In addition to this the criminal character
of an offender is not always to be estimated by the
nature of the offence. A very serious offence is
sometimes committed by a juvenile whose character
is by no means deeply penetrated by criminal instincts and impulses, whereas, on the other hand, we
often witness a strongly marked criminal disposition
in juveniles convicted of comparatively trivial offences.
The nature of an offence for which a juvenile is
convicted must not in most cases be considered by
itself as a satisfactory index of character and disposition. The character of the offender is manifested
much more accurately by the habit of offending than
by the nature of the offence. It is true that criminal
statistics do not show that girls have contracted
criminal habits before committal to reformatory and
industrial schools to a larger extent than boys, but
the statistics of previous convictions are at present
exceedingly imperfect, and are practically worthless
as a test of the previous career of the juvenile
offender. But even if these statistics were correct,
they would only relate the number of times a female
offender had come before the magistrate and been
convicted. They would still be silent respecting the
number of times the offender had not been taken
before a magistrate at all, but had been pardoned on
the score of sex and youth.

That the habit of offending is, as a rule, more
deeply seated among incriminated girls than boys,
and that the character of such girls is therefore
worse, although the nature of their offences is lighter,
may be seen by looking at the relative percentage
of boys and girls who do badly after discharge
from reformatory and industrial schools. In the
three years 1888–90, out of a total of 4,258 juveniles
of both sexes liberated from reformatory schools,
79 per cent. of the boys are reported as doing well,
but only 76 per cent of the girls. The remaining
cases were unknown or doubtful, or had been again
convicted. The number of juveniles liberated from
industrial schools during the three years 1888–90
amounted to 11,396. Out of this number 86 per
cent. of the boys were doing well and 83 per cent. of
the girls. It is thus evident that both in reformatory
and industrial institutions the number of girls who
fail after they leave them is in excess of the boys.
As I can see no reason why there should be a greater
innate difficulty in reforming girls than boys, and as
the social conditions amid which both sexes are
placed after discharge are perhaps more favourable
to girls than to boys, the only conclusion to be drawn
from the larger percentage of failures among girls is
the conclusion that, as a rule, they have become more
habituated to crime before regenerative influences are
brought to bear upon them, and are therefore more
difficult to reclaim.

At present an accurate record of the past career of
juvenile offenders is not kept, on the ground, no doubt,
that it is not worth while to preserve an account of

the trivial offences of the young. From a superficial
point of view this method, or rather want of method,
has a good deal to commend it, but looked at in the
light of the future welfare of the child it is often
productive of disastrous consequences. The result
of a defective system of registering recidivism is that
many children develop into habitual offenders without the knowledge of the magistrates who are called
upon from time to time to deal with them. Offences
which have become a habit are accordingly regarded
as first offences, and in many instances the offender
passes through a prolonged period of impunity, which
has the ultimate effect of leading to a career of
habitual crime. For reasons which have already
been referred to this period of comparative impunity
is usually more prolonged in the case of girls than
in the case of boys, and although it is more humane
for the moment it is sometimes more disastrous in
the end. The treatment of the young should be
regulated in accordance with the assured results of
experience, and one of the most assured of these
results is that the custom of allowing a longer period
of impunity to a girl than a boy makes it more difficult to improve the character of the former when this
task has at last to be taken in hand. The evil effects
of too prolonged impunity is seen not only in the
percentage of failures among girls who pass through
our reformatory and industrial schools, but also in the
high ratio of incorrigible girls among the inmates of
these institutions. One of the witnesses before the
Reformatory and Industrial Schools Commission
estimated the number of incorrigibles at her school

as amounting to from 8 to 10 per cent. At none of the reformatories for male children is the percentage so high. This in all probability is to be attributed to the fact that the reformation of boys is undertaken before they have become so much habituated to crime. In the interest of the youthful population, and especially in the interest of girls, it is of vital importance that as accurate a record as possible should be kept of their previous conduct. The existence of such a record would be more or less of a key to the permanent dispositions of the offender; it would help the magistrates to distinguish between transitory ebullitions and abiding tendencies; it would enable them to send the right class of children to reformative institutions, and it would prevent many children from being sent to these institutions at all.

A summary review of this inquiry into the effect of sex on juvenile delinquency shows in the first place that girls are less liable to come within the clutches of the criminal law than boys. It also shows that this state of things exists not only in England and the United States, but all over the civilised world. The causes of this difference in the criminal disposition of the two sexes are not to be explained by the fact that females are more leniently dealt with than males, or that the difference is a product of different social conditions. Both of these causes operate to a certain extent in minimising the statistics of female offences; the first has the effect of making these offences appear smaller than they really are, while the second has the effect of actually keeping down their number. But the action of these two causes,

whether looked at individually or in combination, is
not sufficient to account for all the facts. After
making a most ample allowance for the part played
by administrative leniency on the one hand and
social conditions on the other, it still remains obvious
and incontestable that juveniles of the male sex
constitute the bulk of youthful offenders. A complete explanation of this phenomenon must be sought
for in the biological differences which exist between
the sexes. These differences are both mental and
physical, they are individual and not social, they are
fundamental and not transitory, and will always
exercise a paramount influence over human action.
These biological differences affect not only the
amount of crime committed by the two sexes, but
also its nature ; boys commit a larger proportion of
serious offences against person and property than
girls. Nevertheless, it is not to be inferred from this
circumstance that the disposition of the less serious
offender is less criminal; on the contrary, the evidence
of statistics and the experience of reformatory school-
managers agree in showing that female offenders are
rather more likely to descend into the ranks of
habitual criminals than male offenders. In our view
this condition of things arises largely from the fact
that females are, as a rule, later in being subjected to
reformative discipline than males, with the ultimate
result that this discipline is less effective when at last
it has to be resorted to. It is therefore no real kindness to female children when they exhibit symptoms
of habitual delinquency to allow these symptoms to
develop unheeded. It is of course easy to make too

much of petty offences like vagrancy and trifling thefts, but it is also easy to make too little. It is not what these offences are in the present, but what they portend in the future, which is the essential point for consideration. All available evidence forces us to the conclusion that the habitual repetition of petty offences is the preliminary preparation for the commission of great ones. In order to avoid the greater evil it is imperative to deal with the lesser. It is the most real kindness to the child to deal with it whilst it is in the corrigible stage ; once this stage is passed the most self-sacrificing efforts are of no avail, and a human life is irretrievably ruined. This matter affects the interests of society as vitally as the interests of the individual. The utmost care should accordingly be bestowed upon ascertaining whether a petty offence is an isolated act or whether it is one of a series ; at present a want of accurate knowledge on these points is often followed by deplorable conse-quences when the offender arrives at maturity and possesses the power as well as the will to do mischief.

CHAPTER IV.

AGE AND JUVENILE CRIME.

IN the preceding chapter the effect of sex on the disposition to crime among the juvenile population has been discussed ; it now remains for us to consider the effect of age. The testimony of criminal statistics all over the world is unanimous in attributing a supreme measure of importance to the part played by age in determining the amount and nature of criminality. Each period of life has its dominant mental and physical characteristics, and these characteristics are manifested in anti-social as well as in social forms. The period of life which may be described as the age of growth and development is a period in which the senses are in a condition of comparative maturity unaccompanied by a corresponding ripeness of the physical and intellectual powers.´ This period extends from childhood till the approach of manhood ; it is a time when the individual is passing through the long and complicated process of adjustment to social surroundings. Most of the juvenile population are to a great extent amenable to this process ; at the same time there are a considerable number of intractable cases, and this intractability sometimes assumes a form which brings the refractory individual within the operation of the criminal law. In very early life inadaptability to social surroundings usually shows itself in the shape of truancy, vagrancy, wandering habits—in short, a disposition to revert to the nomadic stage of civilisation. The greater the demand made by society on the child, such as the demand in the present century that he shall regularly attend an elementary school, the more clearly is the extent of this nomadic instinct brought to light. Of course in all cases where parental supervision is of an efficient character the wandering impulse is usually corrected and extinguished, but when there is little or no parental supervision a child of nomadic tendencies is apt to be picked up by the police as a vagrant, and in this way to make its first acquaintance with the criminal law.

A disposition to evade parental and scholastic authority, showing itself in vagrant habits, may be considered as being in many cases an initial step towards the complete evolution of an anti-social life.

It is a step which can be taken, and is often taken, by children of surprisingly tender years; it is the first offence against social order which the very young can commit. As growth and development proceed, and if there is no corresponding process of adjustment to external circumstances, the tendency to revert to the nomadic and to rebel against the industrial stage of civilisation is joined by the tendency to rebel against the arrangements of society respecting property. We have now the young thief as well as the young vagrant. Each stage of growth is accompanied by fresh dangers, and the critical period between boyhood and youth produces the offender against the person. This is a period of profound physiological change; dormant instincts and emotions begin to waken into life, necessitating the exercise of restraint upon a more extensive scale. Many a juvenile who has unconsciously succeeded in adjusting himself to surrounding social conditions up to this critical stage, is unable to battle against the new instincts which then stir within him, and he becomes an offender against the person.

The tendency to crime is intensified at this age by new social conditions as well as by biological alterations within the personality. It is at this period of life that the sphere of contact with the outer world is immeasurably enlarged. Hitherto social existence had been confined within the limits of the home and the school; it now begins to embrace the boundless field of industrial life. In this field contact with outward conditions is multiplied a hundredfold; the juvenile enters what is practically a new

world—a world of intensified effort and struggle, a
world with a severer code of discipline, where the
difficulty of adjustment to external circumstances is
harder to effect.   Many a juvenile who has passed
successfully through the discipline of the home and
the school, as well as the discipline entailed upon him
by the instincts of approaching manhood, is unable to
adjust himself to the demands of industrial life.   In
some cases this inability arises from the hard conditions of industrial life itself, in some cases it arises
from defective physical organisation on the part of
the youth, in some cases it arises from the incapacity
of the immature mind to control the matured senses,
but from whatever of these causes or combination of
them the inability proceeds, its ultimate result is to
produce a vagrant or an offender against property, or
perhaps a combination of both.

It will thus be seen that the evolution of criminal
characteristics follows in the main the evolution of
the organism, and is largely dependent upon its
growth and development.   In the early stages of life
the first anti-social impulse which comes into collision
with the criminal law is the vagrant instinct; next
comes the instinct which manifests itself in offences
against property; finally comes the instinct which
shows itself in offences against the person.   In
mentioning anti-social impulses in this order it is
not to be understood that this is the order in which
they arise and assume a definite shape in the human
mind.   As a matter of fact such is not the case.   The
disposition to use personal violence or the disposition
to steal may show itself in the child before the vagrant

spirit comes to light, but the use of personal violence by the very young is seldom followed by consequences which necessitate the action of the criminal law. The same remark applies to offences against property. In cases of petty theft or personal violence by children the criminal law is not required, but it is bound to take cognisance of cases of vagrancy, and it is for this reason, and for this reason only, that vagrancy stands first on the list of offences committed by the young.

When the period of growth and development has reached its climax, and the individual enters upon the second stage of life—the period of maturity—his anti-social enterprises closely correspond with the stage of existence which he has attained. . In maturity the physical and mental powers are at their highest pitch of vigour, criminal impulses have become solidified into criminal habits, personal and social circumstances exercise a more powerful influence ; the sphere of opportunity is enlarged ; life altogether has become more complex ; the individual touches society at a great many more points. As a result of this wide-reaching combination of individual and social circumstances the period of early maturity is the time when the population is most addicted to crime. Among different races maturity is reached at different ages. Accordingly, international criminal statistics do not show that each age produces the same proportion of offences. In some countries where the population reach maturity at a comparatively early age, crime is greater in extent at an earlier age than in other countries where the juvenile

6

is later in reaching manhood. It is the stage of maturity, and not merely the number of years a person has lived, which determines the amount as well as the character of crime.

In European communities, if we include all kinds of offences, the most criminal age is between twenty and thirty. What we find in Europe we also find in Australia and the United States. In the colony of New South Wales, for instance, the number of offenders apprehended in 1890 for all kinds of offences under the age of twenty amounted to 3,372 ; the number apprehended between the ages of twenty and forty amounted to 22,174, the number apprehended over forty dropped to 13,022. In the United States, if the prison population is to be taken as a test of the amount of crime among the population at various periods of life, the most criminal age is between twenty and twenty-four. At the census of 1890 the number of prisoners in the United States prisons under the age of fourteen amounted to 711 ; between fifteen and nineteen the number in prison increased to 8,984 ; between twenty and twenty-four the numbers in prison leapt up to 19,705 ; between twenty-five and twenty-nine the numbers begin to diminish (16,348), and steadily continue to decrease with the advance of age. In England the annual number of convictions for all kinds of offences of a criminal character follows very much the same course as in Australia and the United States. In the year 1894 the number of children convicted under the age of twelve amounted to 2,450. Between the ages of twelve and sixteen the number of convictions rose to 10,161. Between sixteen and twenty-one the number of convictions still continues to rise, and reach a total of 31,139. Between twenty-one and thirty convictions reach their highest level, and attain a total of 69,280. In looking at these statistics it is necessary to remember that the difference between the amount of crime in the five years from sixteen to twenty-one, and the ten years from twenty-one to thirty, is not so great as at first sight appears. The ages between sixteen and twenty-one only include a period of five years, whereas the ages between twenty-one and thirty include a period of ten years. The ratio of convictions to the population between sixteen and twenty-one amounts to about 20 per thousand, the ratio of convictions to the population between twenty-one and thirty is about 30 per thousand.

The effect of age on the number of juvenile offences is also exemplified in the returns relating to industrial and reformatory schools. On looking at the totals for all classes of industrial schools it will be seen that the numbers increase year by year from infancy upwards until the age of twelve. When the age of twelve is reached the industrial school population begins to diminish. A smaller number of children are committed to these institutions between twelve and fourteen than between the ages of ten and twelve. The diminution in the number of committals to industrial schools after the age of twelve has been passed is entirely due to an alteration in the method of dealing with juveniles over twelve. After the age of twelve has been passed the reformatory school begins

to take the place of the industrial school, and whipping
as a mode of punishment is more frequently resorted
to. The decrease in the number of children committed to industrial schools after the age of twelve
is not a contradiction of the principle that offences
increase as maturity is approached. It is merely an
exemplification of the fact that methods of punishment are to some extent determined by the age of
the offender. We see another instance of the same
fact in connection with the population of reformatory institutions. Fewer juveniles are committed to
reformatory schools at the age of fifteen than at the
age of fourteen. The reason of this is that after the
age of fourteen magistrates are less reluctant to
commit juveniles to prison, or to pass a sentence
of corporal punishment. Where we perceive any
apparent drop in the continuous growth of crime
in the years between youth and manhood, it is
practically certain that this drop is only apparent. A
full investigation of the circumstances will reveal the
fact that we have to do with an alteration of judicial
procedure and not with a decrease of criminality.

The character as well as the amount of juvenile
crime is largely determined by the age of the offender.
English industrial schools, truant schools, and day
industrial schools contain offenders of the youngest
type. When we examine the nature of the offences
for which juveniles are committed to these institutions it will be found that more than one-half of
them are sent to industrial schools for offences of
what may be comprehensively described as of a
nomadic character. All cases of persistent non-

attendance at an elementary school belong to this class. All children belong to this class who are sent to industrial schools for begging, wandering, frequenting the company of thieves and abandoned women. Children who are convicted of being intractable and incorrigible at home, and children who are sent to industrial schools as refractory paupers, in most cases belong to the nomadic class of juveniles. In addition to children of nomadic habits industrial schools also contain a considerable proportion of children convicted of petty theft, or of some other offence punishable with imprisonment. The number of children committed to industrial schools on account of petty theft is always larger than appears in the returns. In many cases of this character the charge is reduced to some slighter offence, in the interests of the child's future welfare, and many cases of petty theft appear in the returns as cases of intractability, or wandering, or truancy from school.

Children cannot be committed to industrial schools over the age of fourteen, or detained in them over the age of sixteen. In reformatory schools, on the other hand, children may be committed up to the age of sixteen and detained till the age of nineteen. Until recently they might be detained till the age of twenty-one. But an Act was passed a few years ago, which is usually known as Lord Leigh's Act, which limited the age of detention to nineteen. The fact to be observed is that the children committed to reformatory schools are a somewhat older class of juveniles than the children sent to industrial schools. The result of this superiority in age is that the reformatory

school population is composed of offenders of a somewhat more criminal character than the industrial
school population.   Very few children, for example,
in industrial schools are charged with indictable
offences.   In reformatory schools, on the other hand,
almost half of the inmates are convicted of indictable
offences.   Whether an offence will be dealt with on
indictment, or by summary proceedings, is to a considerable extent determined by the age of the offender.
This fact must be taken into consideration in comparing the gravity of offences committed by reformatory school children with the offences committed by
children in industrial schools.   But, even after making
every possible allowance on the ground of age, it is
incontestable that the older children in reformatory
schools are, on the whole, sent to these institutions for
more serious offences than the children committed to
industrial schools.   We have already seen that at
least half of the industrial school population are committed for offences in the nature of vagrancy.   Only
about a tenth of the reformatory school population
are convicted for offences of this description.   The
great bulk of the reformatory school inmates are
committed for offences against property.   Sometimes
these offences merely take the form of malicious
damage to property, and properly belong to the
category of offences engendered by the spirit of
mischief, rather than by the desire to steal.   But
most of the offences against property committed by
the reformatory school population are cases of theft
in one or other of its various forms.   Sometimes the
theft is simple larceny, sometimes it is pocket-picking,

sometimes it is the embezzlement of money, some-times it is obtaining money by false pretences. A certain number of juveniles under sixteen are also convicted of offences against property with violence, such as shopbreaking, housebreaking, and burglary. But the percentage of these more serious crimes is exceedingly small among the reformatory school population. Crimes of this description require a greater amount of physical and mental power than is usually to be found among juveniles under the age of sixteen.

It is also chiefly owing to this lack of power that offences against the person are not numerous among the reformatory school population in England and Wales. An exceedingly small proportion of juveniles in reformatory institutions are committed for common assaults, or aggravated assaults, or assaults on females, or the more serious crime of manslaughter. As a matter of fact, the great bulk of the inmates of these establishments may be described as vagrants and young thieves. The principal difference between the population of the reformatory and industrial schools is that in the latter the vagrants preponderate and in the former the thieves ; the principal reason for this difference is that industrial schools contain younger children than reformatory schools, and that vagrancy precedes theft in the evolution of crime.

In dealing with the nature of the offences com-mitted by juveniles in industrial and reformatory institutions it is to be recollected that these children do not by any means comprise the whole of the

juvenile delinquent population. Large numbers of
juveniles are annually convicted by the criminal
courts who are not sentenced to a period of detention in correctional establishments. It is also to
be recollected that a juvenile does not become a man
after the age of sixteen, as our English criminal law
so fatuously supposes. In order therefore to get a
full view of the nature of juvenile crime among the
population up to the age of civil maturity, that is to
say, the age of twenty-one, we must look at the
returns relating to the number of persons annually
convicted up to that age. Let us examine these
returns in the order of their seriousness, to see what
they tell us with respect to' the nature of juvenile
delinquency. The most serious cases tried in this
country are cases tried before courts of assizes and
quarter sessions, and cases of an indictable character
tried before courts of summary jurisdiction. In the
year 1894, 26 children in every 100,000 of the juvenile
population under the age of twelve were convicted of
indictable offences. Between the ages of twelve and
sixteen years 261 in every 100,000 of the juvenile
population between these ages were convicted of
indictable offences. Between the ages of sixteen
and twenty-one years 330 in every 100,000 of the
juvenile population of the same age were convicted
of indictable offences. It will be seen from these
statistics that juvenile crime steadily increases in
amount the nearer maturity is approached. It also
increases in seriousness. Crimes of violence against
the person are not half so numerous among children
under sixteen as they are among youths between.

sixteen and twenty-one. Crimes against morals are between three and four times more numerous among youths between sixteen and twenty-one than among the juvenile population under sixteen. When we pass from crimes of violence against the person to the consideration of crimes of violence against property, we get almost exactly the same results. Crimes in the nature of burglary, housebreaking and shop-breaking, and the like, are four times more frequent among youths over sixteen than among juveniles under that age. When we descend to the lighter kinds of offences against property, that is to say, offences which juveniles under sixteen are not pre-vented by physical impediments from committing, the vast difference in the proportion of crime between juveniles under sixteen and juveniles over sixteen at once disappears. The juvenile under sixteen is almost as much addicted to simple theft as the juvenile who is on the verge of manhood.

Let us now look at the effect of age on offences of a summary character. These offences, it is hardly necessary to remark, are in the main of a less serious nature than indictable offences. They consist princi-pally of offences against the person, offences against the licensing laws, the labour laws, police regulations, the vagrancy acts, and municipal regulations of various kinds. Offences of this description form by far the largest number of offences committed from year to year. For one offence of an indictable character which is committed about a dozen offences of a summary character are committed. Juveniles under sixteen form a very small proportion of the class

of offenders convicted of summary offences. This
arises to some extent from the fact that they are not
in a position to commit summary offences of certain
kinds. The most numerous class of summary offences
are offences against the liqour laws in the shape of
drunkenness. In the year 1894 there were over
98,000 convictions for drunkenness alone. This
amounted to one-half of the total summary convictions in cases of a criminal character. The question
of the relation between intemperance and crime is a
very interesting one, and it is often answered by
saying that if there were no drunkenness there would
be no delinquency. It is hardly possible for any one
who looks at the connection between age and crime
to take up this extreme position. Among children
under the age of sixteen it may be said, if the criminal
returns are to be taken as a test, that such a thing as
intemperance hardly exists. In 1894, in a total of
nearly 100,000 convictions for being drunk, only
about forty cases occurred among children under
sixteen. Among the adult population between the
ages of thirty and forty more than 50,000 convictions
for drunkenness occurred. According to the theory
that drink and crime inevitably go together, we ought
to find the population between the ages of thirty and
forty committing a great many more offences of an
indictable character than the population under the
age of sixteen. But as a matter of fact we do not
find anything of the sort. Among juveniles under
sixteen who are not addicted to the habit of drink
there are 261 indictable offenders to every 100,000
of the juvenile population under sixteen. On the

other hand, among the population between thirty and
forty who are largely addicted to drink there are only
200 indictable offenders to every 100,000 of the
population of a similar age. In other words, there
is less indictable crime among the drunken than
among the sober section of the population. Let us
take another instance. The population between the
ages of thirty and forty is seven times as much
addicted to the habit of intemperance as the population between the ages of sixteen and twenty-one,
but the comparatively sober population between
sixteen and twenty-one is much more addicted to
indictable crime. Between sixteen and twenty-one
there are 330 convictions per annum for indictable
offences per 100,000 of the population; between
thirty and forty there are, as has just been said, only
200 convictions per annum.

Before drawing paradoxical conclusions from these
figures it is as well to bear in mind that they do not
represent all the facts of the case. In the first place
it must be recollected that although juveniles are not
seriously addicted to drink, and are seriously addicted
to crime, yet juveniles addicted to crime are often the
product, or in part the product, of intemperate surroundings. When we inquire into the character of
the parents of juvenile offenders it is frequently found
that they are people of drunken habits. The children
of people of intemperate habits are more or less likely
to be degraded and demoralised by their parents. It
is not the drunken habits of the children themselves,
but the drunken habits of the parents, which in many
cases produce crime among the children. Although

intemperance is not directly responsible for juvenile crime it is often indirectly responsible. It has a tendency to create the atmosphere in the midst of which criminality is generated. I have never seen any returns relating to the extent to which intemperance prevails in England among the parents of juvenile offenders. I do not know that such returns exist. The information derived from young prisoners themselves as to the habits of their parents, when they have parents, is not altogether to be depended on. Some of these juveniles are inclined to exaggerate the evil ways of their parents in order to palliate their own offences, whilst others are disposed to make their parents out to be much better than they really are. Assuming that the exaggerations of the one class are counterbalanced by the concealments of the other, I should say, after analysing a large number of cases, that from 15 to 20 per cent. of the juvenile prison population are descended from parents who are considerably addicted to drink. This is no doubt a considerable percentage, but it cannot be said to account for more than a fifth of the cases of juvenile crime in England.

In the United States it would appear that drunkenness among parents is a more frequent contributory cause of crime than it is in England. This at least seems to be the case if the returns of the New York State Reformatory are to be accepted as a fair test of the parental conditions of juvenile offenders in America as a whole. According to the returns of this reformatory drunkenness can be clearly traced in no less than 38 per cent. of the ancestors of the inmates. I do not know whether the word "ancestry" which is used in the returns means merely father and mother or also more distant relatives. From the contents of other portions of the report it appears to mean father and mother only. Drunkenness among the parents of 38 per cent. of the prisoners in the reformatory is a high and a serious percentage. It shows that the demoralising influence of drink is apt to destroy the future of the child as well as the character of the parent. Yet it must be pointed out that it leaves no less than 62 per cent. of the cases in New York State Reformatory entirely unaccounted for on the ground of drink among the parents. We must, I am afraid, be prepared to accept it as a fact that juvenile crime cannot be explained by a reference to the one word drink. It is perfectly legitimate to point out the strong bonds of con- nection between drink and crime. But when the question of the relation between drink and crime is looked at from a perfectly dispassionate point of view it becomes as clear as noonday that the habit of intemperance alone will not explain the tendency to violate the criminal law. We have already seen that pauperism alone will not explain crime; we now see that drunkenness alone will not explain it. Both of these conditions contribute sometimes directly and some- times indirectly to increase the volume of criminality. They are social diseases of such an acute character as are bound to manifest themselves in violations of the criminal law. But to attribute all cases of crime either to the one cause or to the other is to overlook facts as large as mountains, and as easily discernible.

Before concluding our observations on the relation between age and crime it will be of interest to ascertain, if possible, to what extent crime becomes a habit among the young. An offence which is merely a transitory and unrepeated incident in the life of a juvenile is not nearly so serious from the point of view of social security as an offence which is one of a series committed by the same offender. A solitary and unrepeated offence is usually the product of a set of individual and social circumstances of a peculiar and extraordinary character. Circumstances of this description probably never recur in the life of an individual, and as the circumstances do not recur the offence does not recur. The offence, as a matter of fact, is an untoward and hateful incident; it is not the outcome of the dominant characteristics of the individual; it is the deplorable product of an abnormal moment when the individual is temporarily unbalanced by the operation of an exceptional set of conditions without him or within him. It is as unfair to judge the character of a man by an isolated offence of this kind as it would be to estimate his capacity for walking by the fact that in exceedingly difficult circumstances he once stumbled and fell. On the other hand, when an offence is one of a series, when it is being habitually committed, it is a pretty sure indication that either the character of the individual is abnormal, or that his circumstances are abnormal, or that, as often happens, both circumstances and character are abnormal. A person in this condition becomes a serious social danger; he has acquired the habit of crime by the adverse conditions of his existence; criminal conduct becomes a part of his ordinary self, and he exhibits it at every favourable opportunity.

We have, unfortunately, no means of ascertaining the exact proportions of habitual offenders among the juvenile delinquent population as a whole. Our only information upon this important point, as far as England is concerned, is information relating to the previous convictions of juveniles committed to reformatory schools. According to the returns for 1894 dealing with this subject, it appears that considerably more than one-half (64 per cent.) of the offenders admitted to reformatories had been convicted of crime more than once. In 462 cases the convictions were second convictions, in 222 cases they were third convictions, in 96 cases they were fourth convictions, in 46 cases the juveniles had been from five to ten times convicted. But these official returns of previous convictions are not by any means exhaustive. They do not reveal the full extent to which crime has tended to become a habit among the reformatory school population. The imperfection of these returns arises from two circumstances. In the first place it very often happens that the previous conviction is not recorded, and in the second place the absence of a previous conviction is not a proof that the juvenile is a first offender. All that the absence of a previous conviction in many cases implies is that the offender has hitherto succeeded in escaping detection. He may have committed a great many offences before he was finally detected and brought before the criminal courts, but in the eye of the law he is reckoned as a first offender. When a young offender is questioned as to the details of his former career it is very soon seen that the official record of his previous history is a very inadequate test of his real character and antecedents. The reports of the Philanthropic Society's farm school at Redhill for the year 1891 contains an interesting illustration of the incompleteness of public returns relating to the previous history of young offenders committed to that institution. In the year 1891 thirty-three of the fresh arrivals had no previous convictions recorded against their names. As far as the criminal law was acquainted with them they were first offenders. But when these thirty-three juveniles came to be examined by the experienced secretary of the Philanthropic Society it was discovered that all of them had committed offences in addition to the offence for which they were actually discovered and convicted; that many of them had been previously convicted, but the previous conviction was unrecorded; and that at least 24 per cent. of them had been in voluntary homes and truant schools before being ultimately committed to the reformatory. In a word, all these juveniles, although young in years, were rapidly acquiring the habit of crime. These thirty-three cases are so useful as affording an indication of the nature of juvenile crime, as well as of the manner in which crime becomes a habit among the young, that they are here reproduced.

No. 1, aged 15.—Convicted of stealing jewellery from his father's house. He admits having previously robbed his father of a watch, which he pawned for twenty shillings. The jewellery, £2 16s. in value, he sold for eleven shillings, a part of which he spent at the Varieties Theatre, Hoxton. He had been out of work and in bad company for more than a year.

No. 2, aged 15.—Convicted of stealing a pair of boots from a shop. He has been locked up for being on enclosed premises; has been twice to a truant school and birched there; and has been concerned with others in robbing bakers' shops, &c.

No. 3, aged 14.—Convicted of stealing four gallons of apples from a granary, which was entered by means of keys stolen from a neighbouring shop. He is one of a gang of four who have been constantly thieving for some time past. Three years ago he was found guilty of a similar offence, and cautioned; two days after he helped to rob a carrier's cart. He also admits other thefts.

No. 4, aged 15.—Convicted of being found on enclosed premises and attempting to rob a shop till. He had been locked up three times for stealing apples, for vagrancy, and wilful damage, but was cautioned and discharged. He admits frequent thieving and keeping bad company.

No. 5, aged 15.—Convicted of unlawful possession of old iron. He had been previously charged with stealing carrots, but the prosecutor was paid twenty shillings not to appear. He had also been charged with stealing iron, but was let off with a caution. He admitted having committed many other thefts, and having associated with convicted lads who would "steal anything."

No. 6.—Convicted of stealing sweets from a shop. When eight years old was charged with a similar

7

offence and dismissed on account of his youth. Admits thieving from shops ever since ; at first led by older boys, and has latterly himself induced his juniors to go with him. This was the case in the offence for which he was committed to the reformatory ; two younger lads were also concerned in it, and all had deliberately planned the robbery.

No. 7, aged 15.—Convicted of embezzlement. Two other cases of embezzling his master's money were proved at the same time, and his master gave him a very bad character.

No. 8.—Convicted of stealing a postal order from a letter. Admits having opened several other letters and stolen at least two orders previously. In the last instance he forged the signature of the clerk of the Poor Law Union, of which he was an inmate, to obtain the money.

No. 9, aged 14.—Convicted of burglariously stealing a pair of shoes from a shop window. Admits at least three previous thefts within the last six months.

No. 10, aged 15.—Convicted of stealing a basket of egg-cups. Has been an habitual thief for at least twelve months. Admits frequent thefts from shops.

No. 11.—Convicted of stealing jackets on two occasions ; of stealing £1 4s. and a penknife ; of stealing 10s. and two sheets. He had been for some time suspected by the police, and admits other thefts of money, fruit, &c.

No. 12. aged 13.—Convicted of stealing a dress and jacket, value £1 10s., from his sister. He has been previously charged before the magistrates, but dismissed with a caution. Admits numerous other thefts from shops, &c.

No. 13, aged 15.—Convicted of embezzlement. Had previously been charged with embezzlement of £2 15s., was sent by the magistrate to a voluntary home in London. Nine months afterwards again convicted of embezzlement, and again sent by the magistrate to the same voluntary home. About a week after was again charged and convicted.

No. 14.—Convicted of stealing zinc to the value of £1 7s. Had been charged with robbing a till and acquitted. Admits previous thefts and keeping bad company.

No. 15, aged 14.—Convicted of stealing groceries from a cart. Once remanded for a week for stealing pigeons. Admits thieving off and on for upwards of three years, and had been to a truant school.

No. 16, aged 15.—Convicted of stealing a watch. Has been connected with thieving companions and previously locked up.

No. 17, aged 15.—Convicted as a rogue and vagabond for attempting to pick pockets. Was apprehended in the company of a convicted thief, and had absconded from a boys' institution, where he bore a bad character.

No. 18, aged 12.—Convicted of breaking into a counting-house and stealing £6 9s. Had been keeping bad company and admits continually thieving. Once stole a boat at night and took it to Shoreham, where he sold it for £3.

No. 19, aged 13.—Convicted of indecent assault. Admits thieving and being in bad company for the last eighteen months.

No. 20, aged 11½.—Convicted with No. 19 of indecent assault. Had been keeping bad company, and had been under bad home influences.

No. 21, aged 15.—Convicted of stealing a live duck. Had been locked up and discharged for stealing meat ; admits habitual thefts for upwards of a year.

No. 22, aged 15.—Convicted of embezzlement from his master. Once taken to the police station for repeated thefts and forgery ; has robbed various masters for two years past ; has also forged his mother's name and robbed her.

No. 23, aged 14.—Convicted of vagrancy. Admits having been several times in custody for stealing.

No. 24, aged 15.—Convicted of theft from a shop. One of a gang known as the "Forty Thieves," leaders of which have been sent to the reformatory ship *Cornwall* and elsewhere. Once before in custody for theft, but not prosecuted ; was concerned in a robbery of £15 from a baker's shop, and admits robbing tills, &c., for three years past.

No. 25, aged 14.—Convicted of stealing from his master. For the last two years he has been in bad company and connected with numerous thefts.

No. 26, aged 13.—Convicted of being on enclosed premises for an unlawful purpose. Once charged with stealing papers, but dismissed with a caution ; for two years past has frequented the company of thieves and bad companions.

No. 27, aged 13.—Convicted with No. 26 for the same offence. Once charged with wilful damage and cautioned ; has been three times at a truant school.

No. 28, aged 15.—Convicted of embezzlement. Admits having robbed his employers for at least eight months.

No. 29, aged 14.—Convicted of stealing £58 from a house; stole £5 the year before, and has robbed his family for five years or more.

No. 30, aged 14.—Convicted of stealing eight brooches, valued at £15. Previously remanded for stealing apples; had been sent to a boys' home for robbing a chapel, and has lived by thieving and begging for four years.

No. 31, aged 11½.—Convicted of cruelty to a pig. Admits habitually thieving and associating with young thieves.

No. 32, aged 14.—Convicted of stealing £3 from his master. Had previously been remanded for stealing muzzles, was sent to a voluntary home, where he remained twelve months; was then found a place in a school, where he sold the books and kept the money.

No. 33, aged 14.—Convicted of stealing his master's money. Had frequently robbed his mother, and admits being in the habit of thieving, gambling, and keeping bad company.

If the offenders committed to Redhill Reformatory School are a type of the class of juveniles committed to reformatory schools generally, it is evident that the great bulk of them are on the way to become habitual criminals, and are only stopped short by being committed to correctional institutions.

According to the drift of the present chapter, which we shall now proceed to sum up, the form which

juvenile crime assumes is to a very large extent
dependent on the degree of maturity which the
offender has attained. The very young offender is
prevented by physiological incompleteness from being
anything but a vagrant or a petty thief, and we
accordingly find that in the overwhelming majority of
cases the very young commence their criminal career
as vagabonds and petty thieves. Mental and
physical immaturity makes it impossible for them to
be serious offenders either against person or property ;
their conduct is determined by biological conditions,
and these put an effectual bar to anything in the
shape of serious crime. As the mental and bodily
faculties of the young approach their full development
the capacity for committing crime increases at the
same ratio, and the offences of juveniles verging upon
manhood assume a closer resemblance to adult crime.
On the whole, however, juvenile crime always remains
less grave in character than adult crime, but it must
not be regarded as of less moment on this account. We
have already pointed out how very quickly the erring
juvenile evolves into an habitual offender, and it is the
habitual offender who constitutes the greatest danger
to society. The habitual offender is the criminal
expert, the criminal by profession, the person who
makes a living by criminal devices, and one of such
men will commit more offences in a year than twenty
occasional offenders. An offender of the professional
sort will also effect his escape in a surprisingly large
proportion of instances, and although he is undoubtedly caught from time to time, he generally
manages to secure the services of able counsel to

defend him, and even if he is convicted the punishment inflicted is seldom calculated to induce him to
abandon his criminal mode of life. In many cases it
is perhaps questionable whether the old offender has
the power within him to abandon his sinister career ;
it is the life he has led from a child ; it is the only
kind of life he is thoroughly at home in ; every fibre
of his mind has become adapted to it, and the life of
an orderly, well-conducted citizen is irksome to him
in the extreme. A criminal of this type almost
invariably begins his career in early youth. He
begins it as a vagrant and petty plunderer of odds
and ends, but he finishes his apprenticeship as the
expert burglar and pickpocket who in time of stress
does not stick at taking human life. It is therefore
most essential in the interests of society, and also in
the interests of the individual, that juveniles who are
exhibiting a pronounced tendency to degenerate into
criminal habits should be carefully dealt with before
these habits have had time to become confirmed.
Once the mind has acquired a rigid criminal bent, the
task of reformation becomes difficult in the extreme.
But if the task of reformation is undertaken before
criminal tendencies have become solidified into fixed
criminal habits, it is certain, if properly conducted, to
lead to a satisfactory amount of success.

CHAPTER V.

THE PHYSICAL CONDITION OF JUVENILE OFFENDERS.

Official reports on the physical condition of delinquent juveniles—
Death and mortal illness rate in juvenile institutions—Mortality
in industrial schools—Death rate among boys—Mortal illness
rate—Death rate of industrial school girls—Mortal illness rate—
Difference in the death rate among boys and girls in industrial
schools—Rejections on the ground of disease—Proportion of
children in industrial schools descended from short-lived
parents—Stature of industrial school children—Weight of
industrial school children—Dr. Warner's inquiries as to industrial school children—Conclusions as to physical condition of
industrial school children—Physical condition of reformatory
school children—Death and illness rates—Ratio of orphans—
Physical condition of juvenile prisoners—Physical inferiority
as a cause of crime.

IN considering the effect of sex and age on the
criminal disposition of the population we have in
reality been estimating, in no small measure, the
action of the physical organism on human conduct.
In the course of our investigations into the relations
between sex and crime it was pointed out that the
differences between male and female crime, in extent
as well as in nature, were in a large degree to be
accounted for by the disparities which exist between
the bodily constitution of the two sexes. In the same

manner it was pointed out in dealing with the effect of age on crime that the state of development at which the human organism had arrived exercised a decisive influence on the anti-social tendencies of the individual. Both sex and age are expressions intended to represent certain biological conditions, and when it is shown that sex and age have a considerable effect on the criminal tendencies of the race, this is only another way of stating that biological conditions are directly and indirectly an important factor in determining the course of human action. But sex and age do not exhaust the conditions which require to be taken into consideration in our treatment of the problems of crime. It is probable that certain conditions of a more or less pathological character may also play an important part in moving the springs of conduct in a criminal direction. In order to ascertain whether this surmise is justified or not let us compare (as far as the materials at our disposal will permit) the bodily condition of juvenile offenders with the bodily state of juveniles of a similar age who have not appeared before the criminal courts. In the annual reports of the inspector of reformatory and industrial schools for Great Britain we have sometimes general statements to the effect that many of the children admitted to these institutions are enfeebled by hereditary maladies or by poverty and starvation, but nowhere are statistics given to exhibit the extent of this enfeeblement.

In the absence of precise information in the official returns respecting the physical condition of juveniles committed to reformatory and industrial schools, it devolves upon us to attempt to elucidate this important matter by utilising all the available material which indirectly bears upon it. Of the various elements of which this material is composed it is probable that the death and mortal illness rate is one of the most important. If it is found that there is a greater amount of mortality among juvenile offenders than among the general population of a corresponding age, the existence of this fact is of itself a strong presumption that the army of juvenile offenders is composed of many feeble and debilitated members. What, then, is the present rate of mortality in our industrial schools? How does it stand as compared with the rate of mortality among juveniles at large? An answer to these questions will help to bring our inquiries to a definite issue. Let us deal first with the death rate among boys in English industrial schools. The death rate among industrial school boys in England amounted to an annual average of 4·0 per thousand in the five years 1887–91. The ages at which children are admitted into industrial schools range between five and fifteen. It is true that fourteen is the highest age at which a juvenile is legally admissible, but in reality considerable numbers are admitted who have passed that period of life. On the other hand, sixteen is the highest age at which an industrial school child can be detained without its own consent. These being the circumstances of the case, it may be stated with a reasonable degree of accuracy that the age of children in industrial schools ranges between five and fifteen ; the death rate among the boys of this population is, as has been said, 4·2 annually in every thousand. Now what is the death rate among boys between the ages of five and fifteen in the population of England taken as a whole, and for a similar period of time? According to the Registrar-General's report it appears that during the five years 1887–91 the yearly average death rate between five and fifteen was 3·7 per thousand of the boy population.

But the rate of mortality among the inmates of industrial institutions is in reality considerably higher than the returns actually disclose. According to the thirty-third report of the inspector of reformatory schools no child is discharged from these establishments whose state of health gives reasonable hope that he may recover with proper care. It may therefore be considered that all children dismissed from industrial schools on account of illness are children who are likely to die. They are sent away because their recovery is looked upon as hopeless. In these circumstances it is very essential to ascertain what proportion of the population of our industrial schools are annually sent away in a moribund condition. It is only after this fact has been brought to light, and the moribund rate added to the death rate, that the actual rate of mortality in industrial schools can be ascertained. According to the returns it appears that during the five years 1887–91 an annual average of 4·7 per thousand of the male industrial school population were discharged in a moribund condition. Therefore if those children who die after discharge outside the walls of industrial schools are added to the numbers who die inside the walls, it will be found that

the actual death rate of industrial school inmates
is about 9 per thousand. The death rate of the
general juvenile population of a similar age is, as has
already been stated, only 3·7 per thousand—that is
to say, the real death rate among industrial school
children is fully twice as high as the death rate
among children of a similar age outside. Facts of
this character are conclusive evidence that, so far as
the death rate among young offenders is a criterion
of their physical condition, these offenders are inferior
physically to the general population of a similar age.

After this inquiry into the death and moribund rate
of industrial school boys it now behoves us to take
up another branch of the same subject and to deal
with the physical condition of industrial school girls
as it is exhibited in the annual ratio of deaths and
discharges on account of mortal illness. For the
purposes of this investigation we shall select the same
period of time as was selected in the case of boys, that
is to say, the five years 1887–91. During these five
years the annual average death rate in the ranks of
English industrial school girls amounted to 8·4 per
thousand. The ages at which girls are admitted to
industrial schools are the same as the ages of admission for boys, that is to say, between five and fourteen.
The age of discharge is also the same, that is to say,
sixteen. For the purpose of comparing the death
rate in English girls' industrial schools with the death
rate of the female population of a similar age, we shall
adopt exactly the same method as has already been
adopted in the case of boys : we will compare the
rate of mortality in girls' industrial schools with the

rate of mortality among the girl population of England and Wales between five and fifteen. During the five years 1887-91 the rate of female mortality between the ages of five and fifteen amounted to a yearly average of 3·8 per thousand. The average mortality in girls' industrial schools in England and Wales is therefore fully twice as high as it is among the outside population.

From the death rate let us now proceed to the number discharged from female industrial schools in England on account of mortal illness. During the five years 1887-91 the annual average discharged as diseased amounted to 3·9 per thousand. If these moribund children are added to the numbers who actually die within the walls of industrial institutions it raises the rate of mortality among the female industrial school population to an annual average of over 12 per thousand. It is manifest from these figures that the rate of mortality among female offenders committed to industrial schools is immensely higher than the rate of mortality among female children of a similar age in the general population. This excessive mortality is not, it is to be hoped, to be attributed to anything in the shape of harsh treatment. It is probable that the majority of girls in industrial schools are much better treated than they had ever been outside. The most probable explanation of the facts is that the physical condition of these children was defective to start with, and the high death rate among them is one of the ways in which this defective physical condition exhibits itself.

In the course of this inquiry it has been seen that

the death and moribund rate in boys' industrial schools
amounts to an annual average of 9 per thousand,
whilst in girls' industrial schools the death and moribund rate amounts to 12 per thousand.   Why is the
rate so much higher among girls than among boys ?
The death rate of boys and girls in the general population during the period we have selected for comparison is almost exactly the same.   What then can
be the reason why girls committed to industrial
schools are more apt to die than boys ?   It is probable that one of the causes of the difference in the
rate of mortality among female as compared with
male industrial school children is owing to the circumstance that female children committed to industrial schools are less frequently rejected on account
of physical infirmity than is the case with boys sent
to similar institutions.   It is an understood principle
among industrial school authorities that children
manifestly unfitted for industrial training are not to
be accepted ; it accordingly happens that a certain
percentage of cases are annually rejected on the
ground that the children are too weak and feeble to
derive any substantial benefit from the course of
industrial training provided for the inmates of these
institutions.   Our industrial school returns are perfectly silent as to the percentage of rejections on the
score of disease and debility.   A return of this kind
ought to be furnished to the public.   When a magistrate, in the exercise of his discretion, decides that a
child coming before him is to be detained for a certain
specified period in an industrial school, it is imperative that he as well as the general public should know

what actually does become of that child. As far as the general public are concerned it is certain that at the present moment they do not possess this information ; the child is committed by the magistrate to the school, but whether he is actually admitted is a matter which we have at present no ready means of verifying. In these circumstances it is impossible to say what percentage of boys is rejected and what percentage of girls, but it is probable that a larger number of boys are refused admission by reason of physical weakness than girls, and if this be the case it at once explains the difference in the rate of mortality between boys and girls in our industrial institutions. If a larger percentage of physically enfeebled female children are admitted than is the case with boys, it follows as a matter of course that there will be a higher rate of mortality among them. This inquiry into the disparity between the death and disease rate of industrial school boys and girls inclines us to the conclusion that the death rate among girls is in all likelihood the most accurate test of the extent of mortality among juvenile offenders of tender years, and it illustrates the serious amount of bodily decadence which prevails among juveniles addicted to crime.

In addition to the test afforded by the death and mortal illness rate a valuable criterion is to be found in the ratio of orphans in the industrial school population. Premature death, when not produced by violence, is a sure sign of feeble vitality, and if it is ascertained to be the fact that a considerable proportion of industrial school children have lost one or both parents, this fact may be accepted as a fairly accurate indirect proof that these children are descended from a degenerate stock. Marriage usually takes place at a comparatively early age among that section of the community whose children find their way into industrial schools. The parents of industrial school children do not require to be long lived in order to see their families arrive at maturity, and they must be very short lived indeed if they die before their children have attained the age of fourteen.

To what extent are the inmates of industrial schools sprung from short-lived parents? In order to answer this question we shall take the number of children admitted during the five years 1887–91 who have lost one or both parents. In the period which has just been mentioned 21,357 children of both sexes were received into English and Scotch industrial schools (excluding day industrial schools), and of this number no fewer than 8,377 had either one or both parents dead. In other words, 39 in every 100 of the inmates of our industrial schools are either totally or partially orphaned. The fact that the ratio of orphans in industrial schools is so high is a sure sign that these children are the offspring of a decadent stock ; and inasmuch as the weaknesses of the parent are very frequently handed down to the child, we must expect to find a large number of the delinquent population in industrial schools burdened with diseased and debilitated constitutions.

Hitherto we have been dealing with facts and inferences drawn from the industrial school population as a whole ; let us supplement this material with more detailed information respecting the physical condition of industrial school inmates in some of the schools. The stature of a child is as a rule a fairly effective test of its physical condition. If a child is puny and undergrown it may safely be accepted as a sign that it has been living under conditions unfavourable to vitality, or that it has inherited these conditions from its parents. Among industrial school children both of these conditions are usually present. Some years ago a committee was appointed by the British Association for the purpose of collecting observations of a systematic character as to the height, weight, and other physical characteristics of the inhabitants of the British Isles. The results of this inquiry were published in the year 1883. Among other information the report of the committee contains a table showing the relative statures of boys between eleven and twelve in the general population and in industrial schools. Among the general population boys in public schools are the tallest for their age ; next in order of height are boys in middle-class schools ; after them the children in elementary schools and military asylums ; last of all are the children in industrial schools. Between the children in public schools and the children in industrial schools there is a difference of no less than five inches. The total number of children measured is not very large, and observation on a somewhat wider scale might produce slightly different results. It is probable that the differences would be comparatively minute ; in all observations of this nature it is remarkable how little the ultimate result is affected by increasing the

8

numbers submitted to examination. According to
the report of the Committee on the Mental and
Physical Conditions of Childhood the proportion of
abnormally small children in industrial schools is
higher than among any other class of English
children. This Committee examined about two
thousand children in these institutions. As far,
then, as stature is concerned we may very safely
conclude that industrial school children are considerably below the average of the juvenile population in the general community. And in so far as
defective stature is a criterion of physical degeneracy,
it is unquestionable that the delinquent population in
industrial institutions suffer from defects of development.

Another very valuable index of the physical condition of the industrial school population is weight.
In this respect all classes of the ordinary population
of a similar age surpass the industrial school inmates.
According to the report of the Anthropometric Committee of the British Association (1883) industrial
school boys of the age of fourteen are nearly seven
inches shorter of stature and 24¾ pounds lighter in
weight than juveniles of the same age in the general
population. Whether we compare the children in
industrial schools with the general population of all
classes, or with any class in particular, it will be
found in every instance that as regards weight these
juveniles are distinctly inferior to every other section
of the youthful population. A large proportion of
industrial school boys and girls are, as has been
pointed out in a preceding chapter, drawn from the

towns ; and if these children are normally developed we should expect them to come up to the standard of town children of the artisan classes. But both in height and weight they fall considerably short of this standard. No matter what year we select, between six and sixteen the industrial school child is always below the average. It is the same with females as with males. Often inferior in weight as well as in stature to the class from which he springs, the juvenile offender in our industrial schools must accordingly be set down as, in many cases, a decadent member of the community, not only from a moral, but also from a physical point of view.

The recent researches of Dr. Warner as to the physical and mental condition of children confirm the report of the committee of the British Association with respect to industrial school children. Dr. Warner found that, with the exception of children in Irish schools, there is a larger percentage of abnormal children in industrial schools than in any other class of schools. Dr. Warner examined nearly two thousand children of both sexes in industrial schools in London and the country, and of this number 591, or rather more than 29 per cent., presented physical or mental defects. In English day schools the number of children who were either physically or mentally defective only amounted to 17 per cent. The defects noted by Dr. Warner consisted of smallness of stature, smallness of head, affections of the eye, affections of the nervous system, defects of development, excessive paleness or thinness, and mental dulness.

Let us now summarise the results of this inquiry

into the physical condition of offenders between the ages of six and sixteen committed to industrial institutions. It has been pointed out that our only means of testing the physical condition of the total population of these institutions is by comparing the death and mortal illness rate which prevails in them with the death rate of the general community of a similar age. The application of this criterion discloses the fact that the death rate in the general male population between five and fifteen amounts, for the period under examination, to 3·7 per thousand ; on the other hand, the death and mortal illness rate in boys' industrial schools is as high as 9 per thousand. The death rate of girls between five and fifteen in the general population is 3·8 per thousand ; the death and disease rate of girls in the industrial school population is 12 per thousand. From this vast difference in the ratio of mortality between the outside population and the inmates of industrial schools we arrive at the conclusion that the industrial school population is composed of a much higher percentage of juveniles of feeble frames and feeble vitality than the population as a whole. Our next conclusion is not based on an examination of the whole of the industrial school population ; it is based on an examination of the inmates of certain selected schools. This conclusion is that both as regards height and weight the children in industrial schools are inferior to children in the general population, no matter from what class these children are drawn. Passing from height and weight to anomalies as a whole, our next conclusion is that, with the exception of children in Irish schools, the inmates of our in-industrial institutions present a higher percentage of physical and mental shortcomings than school children taken as a whole. According to Dr. Warner, and speaking in round numbers, no less than thirty industrial school children in every hundred are more or less defective either mentally or physically. Coupling this fact with the additional fact that 39 per cent. of the entire industrial school population are without one or both parents, it is reasonable to conclude that a considerable proportion of these children are the victims of hereditary or acquired infirmity.

Up to the present we have been dealing with the bodily condition of young offenders under sixteen years of age. Let us enter upon another branch of the same subject, and find out what we can about the physical state of juveniles up to the age of maturity. Information upon this point is to a certain extent available in the returns relating to reformatory schools. At the present time the population of these institutions is mainly composed of juveniles between the ages of ten and twenty. The number sent to reformatories under the age of ten is now so small that they will not materially affect the result of our inquiries. In our examination of the physical condition of the industrial school population it will be recollected that the death and mortal illness rate was taken as the first test. A similar method will be followed with respect to the inmates of reformatory schools. The death and mortal illness rate in refor-matory institutions will be compared with the ratio

of mortality among the general population of a corresponding period of life. The amount of mortality
among boys in the general population between the
ages of ten and twenty for the five years 1887–91
was at the rate of 3·4 per thousand. The vast bulk
of the inhabitants of our reformatories range between
the ages of ten and twenty; the death and mortal
illness rate among this population for the five years
1887–91 will supply us with materials for forming
a tolerably accurate comparison between them and
the outside community. For the five years just mentioned the annual average of deaths in boys' reformatory schools amounted to 4·2 per thousand, and
the annual average of inmates discharged on account
of mortal disease amounted to 4·2 per thousand.
According to these figures, if the discharges on
account of mortal illness are added, the death rate
among reformatory boys is fully twice as high as the
mortality among the general community. Very similar
results are obtained by comparing the rate of mortality among reformatory school girls with the average
mortality of the female population in general of a
like age. For the five years 1887–91 the yearly
rate of mortality among the female members of the
general community between the ages of ten and
twenty amounted to 3·5 per thousand. During the
same period the yearly death rate in girls' reformatories amounted to 5·0 per thousand; the discharges on account of mortal disease were 7.0 per
thousand. If the actual deaths and the discharges
from mortal illness are added together it will be
found that the mortality among the female refor-

matory school population is between three and four times as high as the mortality among the ordinary female population of a similar age. In so far, then, as the rate of mortality is to be accepted as a criterion of the physical state of juveniles committed to reformatories, it must be concluded that there is a much higher proportion of feeble youth of both sexes in these institutions than in the outside world. As regards the amount of mortality among all classes of juvenile offenders the reformatory returns harmonise with the returns from industrial schools. In the light of these returns it is evident that from childhood up to manhood the delinquent population loses a higher proportion of its numbers than the juvenile population as a whole. As a class juvenile offenders are distinctly more degenerate than the rest of the community.

The death rate among reformatory school inmates is not the only test of the decadent condition of many of these youthful offenders. As in the case of industrial schools we are able to estimate this condition in an indirect manner by looking at the proportion of juveniles in reformatories who have lost one or both parents at the time of their committal. According to the returns for the five years 1887-91 the number of young people under the age of sixteen who had lost one or both parents when admitted to reformatories amounted to a yearly average of 33 per cent. In round numbers one in every three is descended at least from one parent, and in many cases from both parents who have died young. It is reasonable to infer from this fact that a very considerable percentage of the inmates of reformatory

schools are the offspring of a degenerate race either
on the father's or the mother's side, and the high
mortality in reformatories is sufficient to show that
in many cases the physical infirmities of the parents
have been handed down to the children.

Juveniles in prisons, as far as it is possible to arrive
at the facts, are very similar in their physical characteristics to juveniles committed to reformatory schools.
In a return dealing with the social and physical condition of a hundred juvenile prisoners between the
ages of sixteen and eighteen prepared by me for the
Departmental Committee on Prisons, it was shown
that the average stature of these young people was
from one to two inches lower than the average stature
of town artisans of a similar age. It was between
three and four inches lower than the average stature
of the general population of a similar age. The
average weight of these juvenile offenders was also
inferior to the average weight of the town population
of a similar age, as well as of the population as a
whole of a similar age. The parental condition of
these juveniles also sheds light upon the sort of
stock from which they spring. Almost one-third
of them (32 per cent.) had one or both parents
dead. Whether we look at the physical conditions
of the juvenile population in prisons, in reformatory
schools, or in industrial schools, we are always confronted with a similar set of facts. We find in each
case that the delinquent population of these establishments is on the whole composed of a larger percentage of inferior physical material than the general
population.

Many important conclusions may be drawn from these facts. At present we shall content ourselves with mentioning only one.

It is very obvious that the defective physical capacity which exists among one-half of the juvenile prison population must have a detrimental effect upon their industrial career. All these young people are members of a class who have to live by the labour of their hands. Bone and muscle is their stock-in-trade. If they are deficient in these indispensable requisites they are in the position of a shopman who is offering inferior articles for sale. Intending customers will pass them by and make their purchases elsewhere. Although inferiority in weight and stature is by no means an infallible index of physical incapacity, yet it is the rough-and-ready test which usually obtains in the labour market, and deficiencies in this respect are adverse to a workman's chances of getting employment. Just as the biological law of natural selection has a tendency to exterminate the weak, so has what may be called the economic law of industrial selection a similar tendency to exclude the apparently feeble from the labours, and therefore from the rewards, of industrial life. One of the consequences of this exclusion, whether partial or total, is that the victims of it are never properly incorporated in the army of labour. They hang upon its outskirts, and are compelled to live by picking up what the ordinary artisan has left behind. At best this is a very precarious kind of existence, and at the worst it ceases to yield a livelihood in any shape. When matters take this turn the decadent juvenile, even if he has no pronounced criminal bent of mind, is very apt to drift into criminal courses.   Two alternatives are before him—the life of a pauper or the life of a criminal.   In some cases the pauper life is temporarily adopted, in other cases crime is resorted to, and not infrequently we find a combination of both.   The results of personal experience among large numbers of juvenile offenders, as well as the evidence just furnished by statistical investigations, have for many years confirmed me in the opinion that among the many causes which produce a criminal life the physical inferiority of the offender is one of the most important.

CHAPTER VI.

THE MENTAL CONDITION OF JUVENILE OFFENDERS.

Difficulties of the subject—Methods of inquiry—Relation between physical and mental condition—Connection between bodily and mental degeneration — Mental heredity of juvenile offenders—Mental condition of parents of juvenile offenders —Mental acquirements of juvenile offenders—Parental control of juvenile offenders—Effect of adverse circumstances on character—Mental surroundings of juvenile offenders—Mental characteristics of juvenile offenders.

I N entering upon an inquiry into the mental condition of juvenile offenders it is well to remember
that mental powers and capacities cannot be gauged
with the same accuracy as physical. Mental states ,
are invisible and impalpable ; they belong to the
world of immaterial realities ; we cannot weigh and
measure them in the same fashion as we are able to
weigh and measure the bones and muscles which
compose the material substance of the human organisation. Mental conditions, in addition to being much
more difficult to gauge than physical conditions, are
also more difficult to compare. The average standard
of stature is known with comparative ease and accuracy, and it is not hard to ascertain whether a certain

section of the community rises above it or falls below
it. But the average standards of character and intelligence are not easy to estimate, and it becomes
a matter of corresponding difficulty to show in what
relation a definite portion of the population stands
towards these standards. In any estimate of the
mental condition of juvenile offenders we must
therefore be content with approximations of a more
or less accurate nature. On the one hand we must
not forget that they are only approximations, and on
the other these approximations must not be under-
estimated because they have no pretension to be
mathematically exact.

There are several ways in which the mental condition of juvenile offenders admits of examination.
The co-relation, sympathy and dependence which
exist between body and mind is exceedingly intimate,
and the intimacy of this connection enables us to
arrive at some sort of results respecting mental
conditions as the outcome of inquiries into concomi-
tant physical conditions. In the next place, mental
conditions may be illustrated by inquiries into
mental inheritance. The mental faculties of the
offspring tend to resemble the mental faculties of
the parent. Whatever light can be obtained as to
the mental faculties of the parents of juvenile
offenders will be of value to us in our attempts to
appraise the mental faculties of these juveniles themselves. Finally, if the result of our inquiry into the
mental condition of juvenile offenders on the lines
just indicated leads us to the conclusion that they
are in some respects abnormally constituted, it will

be our business to ascertain in what these abnormalities consist. That is to say, we shall try to ascertain in what respect and to what extent the mind of the juvenile offender varies from minds of the ordinary type.

First, then, What does the physical condition of juvenile offenders teach us as to their mental condition? With respect to physical condition it has been pointed out in the preceding chapter that the mortality among juveniles in reformatory and industrial schools is higher than the mortality among the general population of a similar age. It has also been pointed out that the juvenile prison population, as a whole, are under the average height and under the average weight of the general community at the same period of life. Lastly, it has been shown that a high percentage of these juveniles are descended from such a feeble stock, that over 30 per cent. of the industrial school, reformatory school, and prison population have lost one or both parents in early life. Therefore, whether we look at these juveniles from the point of view of parentage, or from the point of view of actual physical condition, the conclusion is in each case forced upon us that a high percentage of the youthful delinquent population is more feebly developed on the physical side, and more liable to succumb to the attacks of disease than juveniles of a similar age in the general community. In other words, the physical basis of mental life is in a worse condition amongst juvenile offenders as a body than amongst the ordinary population at the same stage of existence.

What do these facts respecting the physical state of juvenile offenders teach us as to their mental state. Let us admit at the outset that bodily vigour is not always to be accepted as an accurate criterion of mental vigour ; neither is bodily enfeeblement always to be looked upon as a proof of mental incapacity. Instances are not wanting to show that individuals may be possessed of a vigorous and well-compacted frame, and yet fall below the usual level of character and intelligence.   And on the other hand there are cases in which considerable mental capacity is accompanied by defective bodily development.   While duly recognising these facts, and assigning them the fullest possible significance, it must nevertheless be maintained that bodily degeneration has a tendency to produce mental degeneration, and that there is often a concomitance between the two.   The concomitance, as we have just stated, is not by any means universal, but it is sufficiently frequent to show that there is a connection between bodily and physical development.

We now come to the further question, In what does the connection and sympathy between body and mind consist?   This is a question to which a complete answer cannot in the present state of knowledge be given.   All that we can say with certainty is that there is a wide-extending co-relation between physical and mental processes.   Whether this co-relation holds good in every case—whether, that is to say, every physical process has its corresponding mental counterpart, and every mental process its corresponding physical counterpart—is a matter which it is exceedingly difficult to decide. But whether the co-relation of psycho-physical processes is of universal validity or not, it is sufficiently valid to establish the fact that where bodily processes are enfeebled mental processes are generally enfeebled too. It is perfectly true that some parts of the organism are more intimately concerned in mental processes than other parts. This is the case in particular with the brain and the nerves. But the nervous system is in turn placed in the closest relationship with the organs of movement, the organs of sense, and the vegetative organs. It affects them and is affected by them : hence it follows that a healthy condition of mind is not dependent merely on the nervous system, but on all the organs which constitute the human frame. In other words, the body as a whole is the seat and physical basis of mind, and it is incorrect to speak of mind as being exclusively centred in any of its parts. In cases, therefore, in which the seat of mind is unsound, in cases where it is badly nourished and imperfectly developed, we have, in accordance with the psycho-physical law of co-relation between bodily and mental processes a dull and undeveloped conscious life. A large percentage of juvenile offenders are, as we have seen, in this condition of imperfect development and depressed vitality. If we estimate their mental competence by the physical basis on which it reposes, we are led to the conclusion that at least a third of these juveniles are below the average healthy standard in general mental power.

The next step in our examination of the mental

condition of juvenile offenders consists in inquiring
into the mental condition of the parents. The fact
is notorious that bodily characteristics are handed
down from parent to child. Not only is there a
general resemblance between the physical aspect of
parents and offspring, there is often a reappearance
of minute peculiarities, features, and idiosyncrasies.
The similarity between parents and offspring is not
to be wondered at, seeing that the essential material
of which the offspring is constituted owes its origin
to the parents. This similarity is not confined to
physical characteristics ; mental characteristics as
well as physical conformation are a legacy from the
parents to the child. Mental inheritance is as real
as bodily inheritance. Our innate constitutional
congenital qualities of mind are as much a product
of inheritance as our constitutional qualities of body.
Accordingly, an acquaintance with the mental condition of the parents of juvenile offenders will teach
us something as to the mental condition of their
children.

A very good way of testing the mental condition
of the parents on the moral side is to look at the
number of cases in which the parents fail to fulfil
the elementary duties of parenthood. Parents fail
to perform these elementary duties when they are
criminals, when they desert their offspring, when they
leave them uncontrolled. Of the number of young
offenders committed to reformatories in the year 1891
there were, as near as it is possible to calculate, 32 per
cent. descended on one or both sides from parents who
neglected to control them, or deserted them, or were

in prison for crime. In so far, then, as moral defects
are a product of heredity, and in so far as parents
transmit these defects to their offspring, 32 per cent.
of the juvenile offenders in reformatories are more
or less in danger of having inherited obtuseness of
moral sentiment. Another test of the defective
moral status of the parents of juvenile offenders
committed to reformatories is to be found in the
meagre educational acquirements of these young
people. Seventeen in every hundred of the juveniles
sent to reformatory schools in 1891 were unable to
read or write, and seventy in every hundred could
only read or write imperfectly. That is to say, only
13 per cent. of the children sent to reformatories had
received an ordinary school board education. The
defective state of education among reformatory school
inmates which these statistics reveal is in some
measure to be attributed to the defective mental
capacity of the children themselves. But deficiency
in ordinary mental capacity is only a partial explanation of the facts. There can be no doubt that many
of these children are wholly ignorant or badly educated owing to parental neglect. And in so far as
neglect to bestow the elements of education on the
child is to be taken as a sign of moral obliquity in
the parent, it is unquestionable that at least 50 per
cent. of the parents of juvenile offenders are in this
condition. According to the doctrine of mental
inheritance, parents often hand down their moral
defects in a more or less pronounced form to many
of their children. (We may therefore say on the
grounds of heredity that a considerable proportion

9

of juvenile offenders come into the world with defective moral instincts, and that their deficiencies in
this respect, combined with external circumstances
of a more or less unfavourable character, have the
effect of making these juveniles what they are.

One more lesson as to the mental condition of
juvenile offenders may yet be learnt by examining
the mental condition of the parents. A fairly good
test of the mental capacity of parents is to be found
in the amount of success which attends their efforts
to control their offspring. If parents lose control
so completely over their children before they reach
the age of sixteen, and in most cases before the age
of fourteen, that these children become criminal
offenders, this circumstance is sufficient to show that
such parents possess very little force of will and
character. As a rule parents have an overwhelming
hold upon the minds and even on the conduct of the
young. But this is a rule which does not apply as
far as the parents of a large proportion of delinquent
children are concerned. Many of these children are
living under the parental roof, and ostensibly under
parental control, at the moment of their fall. But the
exercise of parental authority is so ineffectual that
these children nevertheless become thieves or vagabonds. As a matter of fact, in the year 1891, 44
per cent of the juveniles committed to reformatories
were living at home, and had both parents alive. No
doubt cases arise from time to time when the most
strong-minded and solicitous of parents find it extremely difficult to keep a wayward child upon the
normal path, and allowances must necessarily be

made for the existence of this fact. But the number of incorrigible children among the reformatory school population is extremely small, and, according to the returns, does not amount to more than between seven and eight per thousand. The failure of the parents to control these juveniles must not therefore be set down in the vast mass of instances to any innate unconquerable incorrigibility on the part of the offender ; the blame must be attributed to the inertia, to the want of will and want of character of the parents. The doctrine of heredity teaches us to believe this mental inertia, this defect of will and character, is transmissible, and is frequently transmitted from the parents to the child. Incapacity to control the child is exhibited, as we have just stated, among 44 per cent of the parents of juveniles in reformatories, and this mental condition is reproduced among these juveniles in the shape of incapacity to control themselves. In other words, the weakness of will in the parent reappears in the child in the form of an absence of power to resist criminal instincts and impulses.

Before proceeding any further in this inquiry it will be well to summarise what has already been set forth. It was shown in the first place that, though physical condition was not an absolutely accurate test of mental condition, it was nevertheless a fairly good all-round criterion to go by. Estimating the mental competence of juvenile offenders by this criterion, it was seen that about a third of the juvenile criminal population would be below the average in general mental power. In the second

place, estimating the mental competence of criminal
children by the mental status of the parents, it was
shown that almost all these children were descended
from parents who were either mentally or morally
unqualified to perform the elementary duties of
parenthood. The precise degree in which this condition of mental and moral incompetence descends
from parent to child depends on the answer which
is finally given to certain fundamental problems in
biology which are still a subject of debate. It
depends, for instance, on how far the mental characteristics of the child are the result of immediate
inheritance from the parents as distinguished from
more remote relations. It depends also on whether
acquired qualities or defects in the parent are transmissible as well as congenital qualities and defects.
But though we do not know the exact degree in
which human characteristics are transmitted, we
know at least that this transmission does take place
in a more or less manifest form. We know that like
has a tendency to beget like, and that, as a matter
of fact, the children of morally and mentally incompetent parents are often mentally and morally
incompetent as well. In so far, then, as a knowledge
of the mental organisation of juvenile offenders can
be gathered from an application to their case of the
laws of heredity and psycho-physics our general
conclusion is that a high percentage of them are
below an efficient standard in general mental power.

What the mental condition of a person will be is,
as we have seen, partly determined. by the physical
basis on which all mental life reposes ; it is partly

determined by the mental characteristics which he
inherits ; and it is partly determined by the mental
surroundings amidst which he lives and acts. The
effect of bodily inferiority and mental inheritance on
the mental condition of juvenile offenders has just
been dealt with ; it now remains for us to inquire
into the effect upon them of mental surroundings. It
is to be observed, in the first place, that we are born
into the world with a fundamental mental disposition
which constitutes the basis of our future character.
The essential traits of which the basis of our character is composed can never be eradicated ; these
traits are born with us and abide with us to the last.
Nevertheless, the inalienable elements in our mental
life are always profoundly modified by the mental
surroundings in which they are exercised. In this
respect, as in so many other respects, there is a
considerable similarity between mental and bodily
organisation. Nature has bestowed upon us from
birth certain characteristics of figure and feature
which we always retain, no matter what circumstances we are placed in. At the same time these
ineradicable physical characteristics are powerfully
affected by the action of our surroundings. When
the physical organisation has to develop into maturity under unhealthy conditions, such · as bad air,
impure water, inadequate food and clothing, it will
be a degenerate product, even if free from inferiority
to start with. And when the mental organisation
has to develop under unhealthy mental conditions,
we have an inferior mental product.

It follows from what has just been stated that we

must look at the surroundings in which the mind of
the juvenile offender is developed, in order to arrive
at a complete estimate of his mental organisation.
The earliest, the most pervasive mental surroundings
of a child consist of the modes of thought and
feeling of the family circle in which it lives. In the
majority of cases the mental characteristics of the
parents when not inherited by the children are
acquired by them. The characteristics of the parents
constitute a large part of the mental food of the
child, and are incorporated into its mental life in as
organic a fashion as physical nourishment is incorporated into our physical life. The mental characteristics of the parents of most juvenile offenders
have already been described as consisting of mental
incompetence or moral obliquity. It is therefore
in an atmosphere of mental incompetence or moral
obliquity, and usually in a combination of both, that
the mind of the juvenile offender receives its earliest
impressions of the external world. It is in this
atmosphere that the process of interaction between
the mind and its surroundings, which we are accustomed to call mental development, takes place.
What form mental development will ultimately
assume is usually dependent on the nature of the
surroundings in which the mind is exercised. If its
exercise consists largely of contact and communion
with the incompetent and vicious it will tend to
absorb and reproduce the defects it lives amongst.
Cases, of course, occur in which a native bent of
mind rises superior to the action of surrounding
agencies. But these cases are the exception; as a

rule the mental organism is moulded by the mental attitude and mental habits of its environment, and incorporates them into itself. Accordingly, if we are to judge the mental condition of the juvenile offender by the mental environment in which he passes the most critical period of life, as far as the formation of character is concerned, we are led to the conclusion that this mental condition must be abnormal.

In what do the mental anomalies of juvenile offenders consist? In some cases mental anomaly shows itself in defects of intellect, in other cases in defects of feeling, and in other cases in defects of volition. Very often the juvenile offender is defective in each of these mental functions; we have a feebly developed intellect combined with bluntness of feeling and instability of will. Among offenders who are intellectually abnormal, the powers of perception and retention are of an inferior order, and the juvenile becomes an offender against the law as much from stupidity as design. Among offenders who are alert enough mentally, and even above the average in this respect, there is often an absence of feeling which is truly remarkable. In some instances children of this description have never enjoyed the humanising influence of parental affection; their feelings, even when normal to begin with, have become withered and hardened by brutality and neglect. Such children are well aware of the nature of a criminal conduct, but it is not in any way repugnant to them on that account. It is from their ranks that the most dangerous class of habitual criminals are drawn. On the other hand, children of feeble wills are often gifted with genuine sensibilities, and when they fall it is because they are led away by others. When several juveniles are involved in the same offence, some children of the class we have just mentioned are sure to be found amongst them. These children are generally below the average in intellect as well as in will, and are good or bad according to the circumstances in which they happen to be placed.

In the course of this inquiry into the mental condition of juvenile offenders we have been implicitly led into an examination of the manner in which it has originated. An explicit statement on the subject will now be opportune. The defective mental equipment of juvenile offenders as a class originates either in a defective physical basis of mental life or in inherited mental incompetence, or in the evil effects of abnormal mental surroundings. In every case one or other of these three sets of causes is at work, and very frequently all of them are at work. In order to reduce the proportions of juvenile crime, these causes must first be minimised ; owing to the constitution of human nature it is vain to hope for their extinction either in the immediate or remote future. Nevertheless, we may venture to believe that the various factors which tend to produce a criminal life among the young are capable of being confined within much narrower limits than exist at present. The material and moral conditions of existence from which the young criminal springs, and by which he is moulded, are susceptible of improvement in a multitude of directions, and offer an inviting field for the exercise of enlightened and discriminate social effort. In proportion as these material and moral conditions are improved juvenile crime will diminish, and so long as they remain stationary juvenile crime will do the same. In the past society has spent too much time and money in sharpening and perfecting merely repressive agencies in the shape of prisons and police, and far too little time and money in investigating the conditions which produce the criminal and reducing them to a minimum. It is not our intention to assert that repressive agencies are useless, and that they do not have their place in the organisation of civilised life. But we cannot expect these agencies to produce results for which they are not adapted; they cannot place a healthy mind in a healthy body, or create a more highly moralised atmosphere for the young. Juvenile crime arises from the absence of these two requisites; prisons and police do not supply them, and never can. In all matters of hygiene we act upon the principle that the only way to get rid of epidemics is to remove the conditions which produce them. If a disease is arising from impurities in the water supply, or from defects of drainage, the only way to get rid of it is to remove these insanitary conditions. To build hospitals will relieve the sufferers, but cannot touch the roots of the disease. Exactly the same principle must be acted upon in order to diminish the proportions of crime. All methods of repression occupy a position somewhat analogous to hospitals. They leave the evil untouched at its roots, and therefore do comparatively little to minimise it. A thorough system of social hygiene endeavours to remove the conditions which produce the evil, and in so far as it is successful in removing these conditions the evil itself is removed.

NOTE.—The mental condition of juvenile offenders is here dealt with mainly from a statistical point of view. For fuller details the reader may consult " Die Charakterfehler des Kindes," von Dr. F. Scholz. Leipzig: E. H. Mayer, 1891 ; " Pädagogische Pathologie," von L. Strümpell. Leipzig, 1892 ; "The Neuroses of Development," by Dr. Clouston ; "Lectures on Mental Faculty," by Dr. Warner ; "Comptes-rendus du IV. Congrès international d'Anthropologie criminelle." Genève, 1896 ; " Minorenni Delinquenti Saggio di Psicologia Criminale," di Cav. L. Ferriani.   Milano, 1895.

CHAPTER VII.

THE PARENTAL CONDITION OF JUVENILE OFFENDERS.

Heredity and surroundings—Influence of imitation—Influence of the family—Illegitimacy—Illegitimates in industrial school population—Mortality among illegitimate children—Illegitimates in reformatory schools—Social effect of illegitimacy—Relations between illegitimacy and crime—Illegitimacy is lowest where crime is highest—Relation between density of population and illegitimacy—Relation between density of population and crime —Relation between illegitimacy and crime—Relation between pauperism and illegitimacy—Causes of this relation—Relation between orphanhood and juvenile crime—Juvenile offenders without father and mother—Small percentage of totally orphaned children in industrial schools—Juvenile offenders who have lost their fathers—The mothers of fatherless children—Motherless children — Motherless children in industrial schools — More motherless than fatherless children in industrial schools—Causes of this disparity—Deserted children among juvenile offenders —Desertion by the father : by the mother—The treatment of deserted children—Children of criminal parentage—Parental condition of reformatory school children and juvenile prisoners —Effect of removing adverse parental conditions in reducing juvenile crime—Juvenile offenders with both parents alive— Character of the parents.

In the two preceding chapters I have endeavoured to exhibit some of the results arising out of an examination of the physical and mental condition of juvenile offenders, and attention has been directed to the effect of these two conditions when they are of an abnormal character on the production of abnormal forms of conduct. In the course of such an inquiry it was impossible to avoid incidental reference to the influence of social conditions on physical and mental characteristics. In these incidental references it was shown that social conditions play a most conspicuous part in shaping the hereditary and congenital tendencies of the individual. It accordingly devolves upon us to discuss these social conditions in a more direct and detailed manner, and to trace their probable effect on the lives of the juvenile delinquent population. The opinion was held by John Stuart Mill, and before him by some thinkers of equal eminence, that the differences which exist between man and man are almost entirely to be attributed to differences of upbringing and social surroundings. On this supposition, if two persons are brought up in exactly the same surroundings, they will display the same mental and moral qualities or defects, and the only reason we do not find this to be the case in actual life is that no two persons, even in the same family, are subjected to precisely the same set of social conditions. Since the death of Mill a considerable amount of light has been shed upon the facts of heredity, and the claims which he urges on behalf of the omnipotence of social surroundings upon human life and character are now seen to be excessive.

The results of all recent research point to the conclusion that human beings are born into the world with a distinct bent of temperament and character which will always manifest itself in some form, no matter what process of training the individual is called upon to undergo. But the ultimate shape which inherited characteristics will assume is largely dependent on the sort of social conditions in which human development takes place. If human development takes place under wholesome social conditions, inborn characteristics of an anti-social nature may in many cases be rendered comparatively innocuous or even be completely overcome ; and, on the other hand, when development takes place under unwholesome social conditions anti-social tendencies are immensely aggravated, and are frequently generated where they do not originally exist.

As far as regards childhood and early youth the most important set of social surroundings lie within the domestic circle. The family is the primary social unit, and in the early years of childhood it is the only external agency which exercises a decisive influence on life and conduct. The depth and intensity of family influence it is impossible to measure, inasmuch as there is no accurate means of ascertaining where heredity cn·ls and imitation begins. But among social circumstances which have a hand in determining the future of the individual it is enough for our present purpose to recognise that the family is the chief. On this account our inquiry into the social circumstances of youthful offenders will most naturally begin with an examination of their parental condition.

Perhaps the most important fact relating to the

parental condition of a child is the answer to the
question whether it was born in or out of wedlock.
Let us see, then, what the returns relating to juvenile
offenders tell us upon this point. We shall deal, in
the first place, with the percentage of illegitimate
children in the industrial school population of
England and Wales. According to the returns for
a period of five years (1887–91) the number of
illegitimate children of both sexes committed to
Protestant and Roman Catholic industrial schools
was at the rate of 50 per thousand, or 5 per cent.
In order to arrive at the precise import of these
figures it is necessary to compare them with the rate
of illegitimacy among the general population. If it
is found, after taking all modifying circumstances
into consideration, that illegitimates form a larger
proportion of the industrial school population than
of the general population, we are led to the conclusion that illegitimacy has a tendency to produce
a higher ratio of delinquency than the condition of
children born in lawful wedlock. If, on the other
hand, it is the fact that the numbers of legitimate
and illegitimate children in industrial schools correspond as nearly as possible with their numbers in
the general community, it follows that illegitimacy,
whatever may be its evils in other respects, is not
an important factor in the production of juvenile
offenders. In the light of these preliminary observations let us now ascertain what the Registrar-
General has to tell us respecting the rate of illegitimacy in the general population. According to the
Registrar-General's returns the yearly average rate

of illegitimate births among the English population between the years 1831–91 amounted to fifty-seven illegitimate births to every thousand legitimate births. In recent years, however, the illegitimate birth rate has been decreasing, and if a period is taken roughly corresponding with the time when most of the inmates in industrial schools during the years 1887–91 were born, that is so say, the quinquennium 1881–85, it will be found that the rate of illegitimacy in England amounted to forty-eight illegitimate to one thousand legitimate births. It has already been pointed out that the illegitimate rate in industrial schools is 50 per thousand ; therefore the proportion of illegitimates in industrial schools is slightly higher than the proportion of illegitimate births.

If an inference were drawn from these facts as they stand it would be to the effect that the children of illegitimate unions do not contribute a much larger ratio to the industrial school population than is contributed by the children of legitimate unions, and that illegitimacy is not a predominant condition in the production of juvenile offenders of the youngest class. But before drawing any inference of this nature one important consideration must be taken into account, and that is the high rate of mortality among illegitimate as compared with legitimate children. I am not aware of the existence of statistics of quite recent date bearing upon the rate of mortality among illegitimate children in England. The most recent figures dealing with this matter were collected by the Registrar-General in 1875. At that time a considerable amount of valuable information was gathered from certain specified districts, in order to exhibit the ratio of mortality among illegitimate children as compared with legitimate. It will be seen that this information is nearly twenty years old, and that it does not embrace the whole country. In these circumstances fresh statistics of a more comprehensive character and of more recent origin would be more satisfactory, but until these figures are forthcoming we must be content to assume that the death rate among illegitimate infants, as compared with legitimate, is substantially the same at the present time as it was in 1875. According to the Registrar-General's tables the death rate among illegitimate infants is in some places four times as high as the death rate among the legitimates, and taking the mean of the twenty-four districts selected for purposes of comparison, the illegitimate death rate is more than twice as high as the legitimate death rate.

On the assumption that these figures still represent the facts with approximate accuracy, and there is every reason to suppose they do, it is very unlikely that the number of illegitimate children alive in England over five years of age amounts at the outside to more than 40 per thousand of the juvenile population over five. But in industrial schools we see that this class of children number 50 per thousand of the inmates, that is to say, illegitimates form rather more than their due proportion of the population of these institutions.

Before commenting upon this fact let us widen the basis of our inquiry into the relation between illegitimacy and juvenile offences. Juvenile offenders, as we already know, besides being committed to industrial schools, are often sent to other institutions, such as private homes, prisons, and reformatories. Respecting the rate of illegitimates in voluntary homes and prisons we are in complete ignorance, inasmuch as no record is kept of it. On the other hand, the number and proportion of illegitimates in reformatory schools are tabulated in the same manner as in industrial schools. What, then, is the ratio of illegitimates as compared with legitimates in reformatories. As far as can be ascertained the number of offenders of illegitimate birth committed to English reformatory schools in the quinquennium 1887–91 amounted to 20 per thousand. This ratio is considerably smaller than the ratio committed to industrial schools. It is also very much smaller than the rate of illegitimacy in the general population, which amounted to 48 per thousand. Of course allowance must be made for the fact that the death rate of illegitimates is much higher than the death rate among children born in wedlock. But even after ample allowance has been made for the effect of this circumstance in diminishing the percentage of illegitimate children of reformatory school age, we have still to admit that illegitimate children are not so likely to be committed to reformatories as legitimate. And in so far as committal to a reformatory is to be accepted as a test of criminal tendencies, illegitimates are not more criminally disposed than children of lawful unions. Even if the illegitimate children in industrial and reformatory

10

schools are classed together, it will be found that in proportion to their number in the general population illegitimate children do not contribute an appreciably larger number of young offenders to these establishments than is contributed by the remaining part of the juvenile population.

These conclusions respecting the effect of illegitimacy upon conduct are so distinctly opposed to prevalent opinion, that it would be unwise to accept them without more searching examination. Current opinion as to the evils of illegitimacy is based upon the unquestionable fact that the casual union of the sexes is adverse to the moral progress of the race. In order to find anything analogous to these casual unions among the progressive races we must go back to the customs of the matriarchal age. At that stage of human development marriage did not exist. The relationships between the sexes were of a transitory character. Parentage was reckoned through the mother alone, and, as among many of the lower animals, the nurture and protection of the offspring practically depended upon the mother. It is probable, in fact, that illegitimacy is either a surviving relic of the time when the mother was the sole head and guardian of the family, or that it is something in the nature of a reversion to the primitive sex customs of the matriarchal period. In any case, whether illegitimacy is a survival of an old and primitive form of social life or a sort of reversion towards it, its existence is a menace to the more evolved type of family prevailing in the West. The leading characteristics of this type consist of a union freely entered upon by the man and the woman ; of cohesion among the members of the family ; of the observance of common rights and duties ; of a tendency towards complete equality between husband and wife ; and finally of submission on the part of the family group to the control of the state. Incidental unions and their fruits present hardly any of the characteristics just described, and are accordingly visited with social and legal disabilities which injuriously affect the mother and the child. In such circumstances it is very natural to suppose that the illegitimate child will be likely to exhibit the disadvantages connected with its birth in the shape of a greater proneness to delinquency. It is therefore highly important to know why this does not seem to be the case.

The reason illegitimates, in spite of their disadvantages of birth, and in many cases of breeding, constitute such a small percentage of the juvenile criminal population can only be explained by a reference to the general conditions which tend to produce both illegitimacy and crime. In almost every county in England and Wales where the population is thinly distributed the percentage of criminal offences is below the average, or on the borders of the average. And, on the other hand, in almost every county in England and Wales where the population is thickly studded together the rate of criminal offences tends to exceed the average. In other words, the amount of crime is dependent to an enormous extent on the number of persons to the square mile. Where the number of persons to the square mile is small the rate of crime is generally low ;

and where the number of persons to the square mile is large the rate of crime is generally high. That is the sociological law which most largely affects and regulates the proportions of crime.

Now the very same law which tends to augment the proportions of crime tends to diminish the proportions of illegitimacy. That is to say, illegitimacy tends towards a minimum in those parts of England where the population is most dense, and towards a maximum in those districts where the population is most sparse. Crime, on the other hand, as has just been noted, inclines to its maximum in densely populated centres and to its minimum in thinly peopled districts. It follows from the operation of this law that the largest percentage of illegitimate children come into the world in those parts ·of England where there is the smallest amount of crime, and the smallest percentage of illegitimate children come into the world in those centres where there is the largest amount of crime. Illegitimate children, as a whole, are accordingly placed in exceptionally favourable conditions in so far as regards criminal surroundings, and it is the presence of these exceptionally favourable conditions which accounts for the low rate of illegitimates in reformatory schools and the comparatively low rate in industrial schools.

In most counties where the favourable conditions just alluded to are not present we at once see the evil effects of illegitimacy on the conduct of the juvenile population. The counties to which I refer are counties which contain a dense population with a considerable amount of illegitimacy. In the county of Chester, for instance, the density of population is above the average, the rate of illegitimacy is also rather above the average, and the result is that illegitimates form a more than ordinary percentage of the children committed to industrial schools. In the year 1890 the rate of illegitimacy in Cheshire was 43 per thousand, but the rate of illegitimates committed to industrial schools was as high as 55 per thousand. In Lancashire we are presented with another example of the same phenomenon. In 1891 the rate of illegitimacy in Lancashire was 49 per thousand, and the ratio of illegitimates committed to industrial schools was 62 per thousand. In both these important industrial centres the percentage of illegitimates committed to industrial schools is considerably above the percentage for the whole of England. This is a state of things which points to the conclusion that illegitimate children are more criminally disposed than legitimate, when they are born and nurtured amidst a dense population, that is to say, among a population where criminals and the temptations to crime are numerous. This amounts to saying that, conditions being equal, illegitimates are more likely to become offenders than legitimates. But inasmuch as this equality of conditions does not exist, owing to the fact that the percentage of illegitimate births is highest in districts where the temptations to offend are lowest, we have the general result that, taking England as a whole, illegitimates do not contribute much, if any, more than their due proportion of offenders to the juvenile delinquent population.

Before leaving the subject of the relations between

illegitimacy and crime it will be of interest to consider why it is that the same conditions which tend to diminish the average of illegitimacy should tend to augment the rate of crime, or, to put the same proposition the other way round, why the rate of crime should tend to be low where the rate of illegitimacy tends to be high. The paramount condition which affects the rate of illegitimacy and the rate of crime, but affects it in opposite directions, is, as has been already pointed out, the rate of population to the square mile.

This being the case, the final form which our inquiry assumes is formulated in the question, Why does a rate of population which produces a high rate of illegitimacy produce a low rate of crime? An answer to this question will be found in the effect which density of population has on the social conditions of existence. It is a fact which hardly requires to be mentioned that the conditions of life in thinly peopled districts differ in a variety of respects from the conditions of life in large centres of population. The state of perpetual intercourse and contact which prevails in a crowded population, and which gives rise to such a large proportion of offences against the person, does not exist in a community where the inhabitants are distributed over a large area. In such a community the wages of the population are small as a rule, the public-houses are in most cases not so accessible, and the result is that there is a comparatively low percentage of drunkenness and of the kind of offences which spring from drink. At the same time the multitude of shops, warehouses, and fine houses which are to be found in towns, and which do so much to excite cupidity, are almost absent from the country, and there are accordingly fewer offences against property. The superiority of the country with regard to health, and the more natural conditions under which the majority of the people live, keep down the ratio of offences which spring from mental and physical degeneracy. Other causes might also be mentioned which tend to minimise the ratio of crime in sparsely peopled areas, but sufficient evidence has already been brought forward to show that the difference in the social conditions of existence in thinly peopled as compared with densely peopled districts is sufficient to account for the low rate of crime in the country as compared with the towns.

The high rate of illegitimacy in the country is also explicable by a reference to the social conditions of the rural population. The sparseness of population which tends to diminish criminal offences tends at the same time to afford facilities for the illegitimate union of the sexes which are not afforded to the same extent in towns.. This is undoubtedly one cause of the high rate of illegitimacy in rural districts as a whole. Another cause is the absence of a fallen class in the country districts. And yet another and equally important cause is the pauperised condition of a large mass of the country population. A high rate of pauperism and a high rate of illegitimacy almost invariably go hand in hand, in so far as England and Wales is concerned. During the period between 1849 and 1891 it will be observed that the rate of illegitimate births to the total number of births has,

on the whole, slowly but steadily declined. The ratio
of paupers to the population during the same period
has also slowly but steadily decreased. A further proof
of the concomitance of pauperism and illegitimacy is
exhibited in the relative prevalence of both in the
different divisions of England and Wales. In the
great majority of counties where pauperism tends
towards a maximum, illegitimacy does the same and,
on the other hand, in the majority of counties where
pauperism tends towards a minimum, illegitimacy
also follows in its train. The small number of
counties which are an exception to this rule illus-
trate the fact that pauperism is not the only condition affecting the proportions of illegitimacy, but
the vast preponderance of counties which conform to
the rule are an assurance that it is the principal
condition.

The dependence of illegitimacy on pauperism is
of a very obvious character. Among a pauperised
population economic circumstances, or, in plain
language, the inability to set up a home, constitute
a serious hindrance to the legitimate union of the
sexes. Accordingly, in such a population, unless
counteracting influences of a most powerful nature
are at work, the ratio of illegitimacy is certain to
be high. It is unquestionable that the rate of
illegitimacy in the vast proportion of the rural
districts of England and Wales would diminish considerably if the agricultural labourer were in a
better economic position, if he could more easily
found a home, if his future were more assured. The
recent reports of the Royal Commission on Labour,

respecting the condition of the agricultural labourer, make it perfectly plain that he lives far too near the borderland of pauperism, that his economic outlook is far too sombre, that his life is deficient in that element of economic stability which is such a potent factor in determining the nature of the relations between the sexes. The remarks we have just made respecting the agricultural classes apply in a mitigated form to the industrial community in the towns. It is almost certain that if the bulk of the industrial population enjoyed a greater amount of economic security the effect of this would be reflected in the growth of a higher order of relations between the sexes, and in a consequent diminution of illegitimacy. It is not, of course, contended that illegitimacy is entirely a product of adverse economic circumstances, and that the removal of these circumstances will have the effect of abolishing it. Other causes are at work in producing this evil besides causes of an economic character. But among all the causes in operation in England and Wales penury appears to be the chief, and in so far as illegitimacy is a product of penury and its attendant evils, it will tend to diminish in proportion as the most potent condition producing it is removed.

A reduction in the proportions of illegitimacy will in its turn reduce the proportions of juvenile crime. For, as has been observed, other things being equal, juveniles of illegitimate parentage are more likely to become offenders than juveniles born in wedlock. And as there is an intimate connection between the proportions of adult and juvenile crime, a reduction of the percentage of illegitimacy will have the ultimate effect of diminishing the criminal population as a whole.   Such are the conclusions to which we are led by an examination of the inter-action existing between illegitimacy and social conditions more or less closely related to it.

We shall now proceed to consider the connection between orphanhood and juvenile crime.   In connection with the physical condition of juvenile offenders we have already had occasion to refer to the circumstance that a considerable percentage of young offenders had either one or both parents dead. In the present instance it is our purpose to inquire into the effect on the juvenile population of the premature loss of parental care.

In the five years 1887–91 the number of children committed to industrial schools who had neither father nor mother at the time of their commitment amounted to 42 per thousand, or 4 per cent. It is impossible to say how large a percentage of the child population of this country are deprived of both father and mother between the ages of six and fourteen.   It is therefore impossible to say with precision what the effect on juvenile conduct is of the loss of both parents.   The only remarks to be made upon the matter are that the percentage of industrial school inmates who have lost both parents is not so high as might be anticipated.   The removal by death of both father and mother before the age of fourteen means the loss of the most effective restraints on inexperience and immaturity ; in the ordinary course of things it also means an exposure to the temptations and vicissitudes of the world before the faculties are sufficiently ripened to grapple with them. In these circumstances it is natural to conclude that juveniles who are totally orphaned will form a percentage of the criminal community altogether out of proportion to their number in the general population. As far as industrial schools are concerned this does not appear to be the case. It is probable that children totally orphaned do not supply much more than their due proportion to the population of these institutions.

The only manner in which this fact can be explained is by a reference to the action of the poor law and of private charity. In a very large number of cases children totally orphaned come under the operation of the poor law. According to the Local Government Board return for the year 1891-2, considerably more than one-half of the children in receipt of in-door relief consisted of children who were orphans or children relieved without their parents. These children are, in the majority of cases, educated in workhouse schools, or in separate poor-law schools. They come very little in contact with the outer world, and the circumstances which would bring them into collision with the criminal law. The poor law stands in the place of a parent to these children; it isolates them from the world and its temptations; it exercises such a strict supervision over them that they are hardly ever arrested as vagrants or thieves; in short, it effectively shields them from the very class of offences which come within the provisions of the Industrial Schools Acts. In these circumstances it

is not to be wondered at that orphan children form
a comparatively small percentage of the industrial
school population.   And these are not all the circumstances which require to be taken into account. Large
numbers of orphan children are looked after by
charitable institutions.   The metropolis alone contains about three hundred voluntary homes for
juveniles, and in most of these institutions orphans
have the preference.   It is to the combined operation of the poor law and voluntary homes that the
small percentage of orphans in industrial institutions
is to be attributed.

We come now to the case of children who are not
absolutely orphans, but who have lost one of their
parents.   Dealing in the first place with children
who have lost their fathers, let us see how large a
proportion of these children are annually sent to
industrial schools.   In the five years 1887–91 the
number of juveniles with no father committed to
the industrial schools of England and Scotland
amounted to 20 per cent. of the total industrial
school population.   It will thus be observed that
fatherless children constitute four times as large a
proportion of the inmates of industrial schools as
children who are totally orphans.   A partial explanation of this fact has already been given in our
account of the causes which keep down the ratio of
orphans in industrial institutions.   A few additional
circumstances require to be mentioned in order to
make this explanation more complete.   It is to be
recollected, in the first place, that the number of
children in the general population who have lost

their father only is much higher than the number who have lost both father and mother. As these children form a higher proportion of the general population, it is to be expected that they will form a higher proportion of the industrial school population. But, even after taking this circumstance into account, it is highly probable that in proportion to their numbers in the general population, children who have the misfortune to lose their fathers by death constitute more than their due share of the inmates of industrial schools. How does this come to pass? It is partly to be accounted for by the fact that many of them have inherited a feeble constitution from their deceased fathers, and are consequently impeded by physical infirmity at the outset of their industrial career. An impediment of this kind is often the precursor of juvenile offences. Another and very important cause of the high percentage of fatherless children in industrial schools is the excessive and unexpected burden which the death of the father entails on the mother. It is true that the poor law comes to the assistance of widows with young children entirely dependent upon them, and in this way a position which would otherwise be unbearable is considerably mitigated. In the year 1891–2, according to the Local Government Board returns, widows were receiving out-door relief for 107,011 children dependent upon them. But the amount of relief received by the mothers of these children is not sufficient by itself to keep up the home, and in the majority of instances the widow has to supplement the efforts of public charity by corresponding efforts of her own. Owing to the steady growth of the workshop system, and the consequent decay of home industries, widows are usually obliged to leave their children to their own devices during the greater part of the day. In normal conditions of family life the workshop system of production is probably on the whole the best, as it usually ensures a superior order of hygienic arrangements for the workers. But in the exceptional case of widows with children dependent on them, not merely for subsistence but also for maternal care, the workshop system has serious defects. The enforced absence of the mother in the factory or the workshop almost entirely deprives the family of the benefits of maternal supervision and maternal affection. The mother sees comparatively little of the children, and is therefore apt to lose some of the self-sacrificing devotion of motherhood ; whilst the children see just as little of the mother and often grow up without the hallowing and constraining influences of maternal love. A life of this kind is full of peril for the young. And the extent of this peril may be estimated, by remembering the fact that one-fifth of the industrial school population is composed of fatherless children.

We have just considered the effect of the loss of the father on the conduct of the juvenile population, we shall now investigate the effect of the loss of the mother. It is usually regarded as a greater calamity for a child to lose its mother than to lose its father. Among the well-to-do classes, where the home is properly provided for in the event of the father's premature death, the loss of the father may, in the majority of cases, be the lesser of two evils. But in cases where the home is not properly provided for in the event of death, that is to say, among almost the whole of the working-class population and among a considerable section of the well-to-do population, the premature death of the mother probably entails less serious consequences on the children than the premature death of the father. If the relative proportion of fatherless and motherless children in industrial schools is to be taken as a test, it will be found that children who are left dependent on the mother form a larger percentage of the industrial school population than children dependent on the father. In the five years 1887–91 the number of children dependent on the mother committed to industrial schools constituted, as we have already observed, 20 per cent. of the inmates; in the same five years the number of children dependent on the father constituted only 14 per cent. of the inmates. In estimating the worth of these facts it is to be recollected that there are, probably, more fatherless than motherless children in the general community, owing to the circumstance that the death rate is higher among men than among women. But the difference in the proportions of fatherless and motherless children is not nearly so high as to account for the difference in the proportions of these two classes of children in industrial schools. It must in the main be accounted for on other grounds, and some of these grounds it now devolves upon us to specify.

The first ground is economic. As a rule the father is better able to provide for the material needs of the

children than the mother, and as a result of this the
children are not obliged to attempt to do anything in
the way of increasing the household income at a very
tender age.   Mothers, on the other hand, in order to
to make both ends meet, are often compelled to make
their children earn a little in the streets and public
places, and the children are in consequence exposed
to temptations which bring them within the range of
the criminal law.   In the next place, the father, as a
rule, has more authority over children than the mother.
Many of the fatherless children committed to industrial schools are sent there because the mother
has lost all control over them.   These children are
found in the streets begging or in the company of
criminals, and the mother is utterly unable to restrain
them.   The father, on the other hand, if he is aware
of it, is usually able to prevent his children from
associating with evil companions and from falling
into vagrant habits, and the prevention of these two
evils has its effect in keeping down the percentage of
motherless children in industrial institutions.   Very
often the greatest danger to motherless children is
the re-marriage of the father.   In almost all circumstances where there are young children re-marriage
is a perilous experiment, and is very apt to introduce
division and disaster into the home.   This observation applies to the re-marriage of either parent, but
it perhaps applies with the greatest force to the re-
marriage of the father.   In many instances, though
by no means in all, the step-mother finds the children
she has to look after on entering her new home a
burden which she is glad to get rid of.   This is more

particularly the case when she has afterwards children of her own. In such a home the motherless children receive little attention, little affection, little parental care. Sometimes a prejudice against them is thrust into the father's mind. For these children the home loses all its attractions; it is a place where they are usually bullied and brow-beaten; as a sort of refuge from it they prefer the dangerous liberty of the streets. It is the existence of circumstances of this character which do much to raise the proportion of motherless juveniles in industrial schools. Such circumstances occur much more frequently when children lose their mother than when they lose their father. The number of widows who marry again is not nearly so great as the number of widowers. In 1894, of every thousand men who married 111 were widowers, while of every thousand women only 77 were widows. It deserves at the same time to be remarked that the re-marriage of widowers is steadily declining, and was never so low as it is at the present time. It is outside our purpose to inquire into the causes of this interesting social fact; it is probable that one of these causes is the growing recognition of the unhappy effects of re-marriage on the future of the young.

In addition to illegitimate children and children who have lost one or both parents, industrial schools also contain a certain proportion of juveniles who have been deserted by their parents. In the five years 1887–91 this class of children formed 6 per cent. of the industrial school population. Inasmuch as these children are left absolutely alone in the

11

world at a very tender age, it is not surprising that
a certain proportion of them should ultimately be
committed to industrial schools. Children are much
more frequently deserted by the father than the
mother. In the year 1890–91 the number of men
proceeded against in the criminal courts for deserting
or neglecting to support their family amounted to
7,029, while the number of women charged with the
same offence only amounted to 217. In many of
these proceedings the father was charged with deserting or neglecting his wife as well as his children, but,
even after taking this fact into account, it is certain
that fathers are more apt to desert their offspring
than mothers. The form which desertion frequently
takes is to leave the children in a common lodging-
house, or to leave them in charge of some one and
cease to send anything towards their support. But
sometimes the children are abandoned in the streets,
and are found begging or wandering about without
any visible means of subsistence. In cases of this
kind two alternatives are open to the authorities.
The children may be taken to the union and placed
under the protection of the poor law, or they may be
brought before the magistrates and committed to an
industrial school. Sometimes the one method is
adopted and sometimes the other, according to the
circumstances of the case or the inclination of the
authorities. On the whole, it is probably the best
plan to send deserted children to industrial schools.
When they are sent to the union the poor-law authorities often hand back the children to the heartless
parent after he has completed a term of imprisonment

for neglecting them. Sometimes the imprisonment may lead to good results, generally it does not ; and the father who has deserted his children once is almost certain to do so again. The conditions which led him to desert them in the first instance usually remain the same after his sentence of imprisonment is completed. These conditions are usually idle, drunken, callous habits, or mental unfitness to bear the entire burden of parental responsibilities. Imprisonment leaves all these conditions as active as ever, and the man who is a victim of them is quite unfit to be entrusted with the nurture of the young. While every precaution should be taken to prevent children from being deserted, and while making the deserter of them amenable to the criminal law, it admits of little doubt that society consults its best interests when deserted children are withdrawn from the control of the parent. With children once deserted the resumption of parental control means the renewal of parental cruelty and neglect, and initiation into habits of vagabondage and crime.

Besides the children in industrial schools who have been deserted by their parents, there is also a class of children whose parents are habitual criminals. In the five years 1887–91 these children formed 2 per cent. of the industrial school population. The parental condition of juveniles descended from criminal parents is such that it is easy to understand why they should be committed to industrial schools. At no period of life is the impulse to imitate so keen as in early youth, and in very many instances the child of criminal parents falls into the habits of its elders as soon as it is capable of copying them. It is of course on a small scale that these habits are imitated to begin with, but bolder enterprises are undertaken as soon as mental and physical ability will permit; and if a child of criminal parentage should escape the meshes of the law till he has acquired skill and expertness in some branch of crime, it is almost impossible to reclaim him from a criminal career. He becomes a member of the habitual criminal class, and usually remains a member of it to the last. It is fortunate for society that the cares of parenthood are largely incompatible with a life of crime. In consequence of this, criminals who have children are often anxious to get rid of them. Such children fall upon the poor law or are admitted into voluntary homes, or are disposed of in one way or another, so that the parental calling may not be unduly hampered. At other times criminals who want to be rid of their children send them out to beg, and in this way a certain proportion of them are committed to indus-trial schools. It is chiefly for these reasons that in this country the criminal calling does not descend in the majority of cases from father to son. It descends by apprenticeship, and not, as a rule, by parenthood. The exigencies of a criminal life hinder the latter method and encourage the former. This is a point which should be kept carefully in view in dealing with the hereditary aspects of crime.

Before proceeding further with our inquiries into the parental condition of the industrial school popu-lation, it will be expedient to summarise the results which have just been arrived at. A summary of these results brings out the fact that 51 per cent., or more than one-half, of the inmates of industrial schools is composed of children who are either illegitimate or have one or both parents dead, or are the offspring of criminals and parents who have deserted them. In other words, more than one-half of the population of industrial schools are in an abnormal parental condition. It is interesting to find that almost exactly the same state of things exists among the population of reformatory schools. Taking the same period for our inquiries as has been taken for industrial schools, we get very nearly the same results. In the five years 1887–91 the number of juveniles committed to reformatories who were partially or entirely orphaned, or had been deserted, or had criminals for parents, amounted to 53 per cent. It is probable that the reason the percentage of juveniles in an anomalous parental condition is rather larger among the reformatory than among the industrial school population, is to be attributed to the circumstance that reformatories accept juveniles up to the age of sixteen, while industrial schools only accept them up to the age of fourteen. In any case it will be observed that in both institutions more than one-half of the inmates are children bereft, for one cause or another, of proper parental care. There are no means of ascertaining the proportion of juveniles in prison whose parental condition is somewhat similar to the condition of the children we have already dealt with. Prison statistics do not enter into the parental circumstances of juvenile offenders. We are therefore compelled to confine our remarks upon this point to the results of inquiries in particular prisons. These inquiries must not be taken as representing the juvenile prison population as a whole. But so far as they extend they harmonise with the returns relating to industrial schools. In evidence before the Prisons Committee I had occasion to point out that in one of the largest London prisons about one-half of the juvenile prison population are either without one or both parents, or are the children of parents who have deserted them or turned them adrift. In other prisons the proportions may be somewhat different, but if the parental circumstances of imprisoned juveniles are carefully inquired into it will be found, in a very large percentage of cases, that these circumstances are anomalous in some form or another.

The general conclusions to be drawn from all that has just been gathered respecting the parental status of juvenile offenders are of a very obvious character. The first and most important of these conclusions is that the future of a child is very largely determined by the parental circumstances in which it happens to be placed. If a child is of illegitimate parentage it is more likely, other conditions being equal, to fall in the battle of life than if it were born in lawful wedlock. If a child has the misfortune to lose one or other of its parents that child is more likely to become a delinquent than would otherwise be the case. Again, if a child is the offspring of callous parents who desert it, or of criminal parents who corrupt it, its career is rendered an exceedingly hard one. On the other hand, the task of society, in the light of our conclusions respecting the parental conditions of so many juvenile offenders, is a very plain but at the same time a very difficult task. This task consists in removing, as far as it is possible to do so, the conditions which prove so disastrous to the young. Whatever tends to reduce the ratio of illegitimacy will also tend to reduce the dimensions of the juvenile criminal population. Whatever tends to reduce the death rate among adults will also reduce the number of fatherless and motherless children in the community ; and a reduction in the proportions of these children will be accompanied by a reduction of the number of juvenile offenders in prisons, reformatories, and industrial schools. Lastly, whatever tends towards the moral and spiritual elevation of the community as a whole will have its effect in diminishing the number of parents who desert and corrupt their children. And in proportion as the number of such parents diminishes so also will the number of children diminish who fall through parental desertion and parental vice.

Before bringing these inquiries into the parental condition of juvenile offenders to a termination, a few observations must be made regarding the parental circumstances of young offenders whose condition is perfectly normal as far as relates to living at home with their father and mother. It will be remembered that juveniles of this description constitute 49 per cent. of the industrial school population and 47 per cent. of the reformatory school population. There are no means of ascertaining their numbers in the prison population, but as far as we are able to gather it is quite as large as the percentage in reformatory schools. It is not the fact of being illegitimate or the fact of being orphans, or the fact of being deserted, or the fact of being descended from habitual criminal parents which has had a hand in causing this large percentage of offending juveniles to be committed to prisons, reformatories, and industrial schools. In so far as parental condition has had an effect in shaping the career of these juveniles its effect must have operated through other channels than those which have just been named. A child may have both its parents alive and it may be living under the same roof with them, but the character of the parents, although they are not habitual criminals, may be such that contact with them has a demoralising influence on the mind of the young. In the case of juvenile offenders with both parents alive our inquiries accordingly take the form of asking, What sort of character have these parents? An answer to this question will probably help us to understand why so large a proportion of young people with both parents living and presumably under parental control have fallen more or less deeply into habits of delinquency.

Let us seek an answer, in the first place, in the evidence given before the Royal Commission on Reformatory and Industrial Schools. In reply to a question by Lord Norton, a member of the Gateshead School Board said that the parents of the children committed to the Gateshead Industrial School consisted of the "refuse of the labourers in the large manufactories, men who have been thrown out of employment and who have drifted into the very lowest class of the population." In no case were the homes of these parents decent and respectable. Respecting the inmates of the Park Lane Industrial School, Liverpool, the superintendent said that "from their connection with their parents, and the sort of people that they come in contact with in the homes of their parents, I have been greatly astonished when talking to the children to find what a vast amount of vice and indecency they had listened to without being aware that there was anything wrong in it." At Bristol the Commissioners were told that the character of the parents of industrial school children was in most instances of the very lowest description. Mr. Mark Whitwill, a Bristol magistrate, who made this statement to the Commissioners, said that he could tell the "particulars of every child in the Carlton House Industrial School, and with regard to the girls he added that "there is not one single instance where I should like to send the girl back to her parents." As far as boys are concerned the character of the parents is not quite so bad, inasmuch as boys have more opportunities of getting into mischief than girls. This evidence coincides with the evidence of Mr. Trevarthen, the Secretary of the Philanthropic Society's Farm School for boys at Redhill. Mr. Trevarthen, speaking, as he admitted, with great reserve, said probably one-third of the parents of the boys in Redhill reformatory were respectable persons. A certain number of the boys committed to Redhill pass through my own hands, and as far as these boys are concerned I should be inclined to say that Mr. Trevarthen's estimate as to the proportion of them

whose parents are respectable does not err on the
side of being too low.   A certain percentage of
widows and widowers whose children are sent to
reformatories are probably free from reproach.   But
in cases where reformatory school inmates have both
parents alive I find that in nine cases out of ten one
or other of these parents is distinctly disreputable.

Perhaps no one occupies so favourable a position
for forming an accurate estimate of the character
of the parents of industrial and reformatory school
inmates as the person officially appointed to collect
the contributions of the parents of these inmates.
The duties of this official bring him into the closest
possible contact with the characters and economic
circumstances of the parents.   He sees these parents
at regular intervals for a period of years; he sees
them in their own homes and amid their domestic
surroundings ; in a word, he sees them, as far as it
is possible for an outsider to do so, as they really
are.   It was stated by Mr. Macdonald, one of those
agents, in reply to a question of the Royal Commission, that only 6 per cent. of the children in
industrial schools had homes which were morally
fit for a child to live in.   Mr. Macdonald's experience
related to the parents of Scotch children ; in some
parts of England the percentage of parents of
respectable character is rather higher than Mr.
Macdonald's estimate.   As far as regards Manchester, the chairman of the industrial schools
committee of the Manchester School Board stated
before the Commission that 68 per cent. of the
parents of industrial school children were known

to be disreputable, 14'7 per cent. were of doubtful character, and the parents of 17 per cent. were reported as well conducted. This witness then proceeded to give some interesting details respecting the character of fifty parents who came into collision with the School Board authorities for persistently neglecting their children. In these fifty cases 648 summonses were served (or an average of 13 summonses to each person), 43 warrants were issued, and 94 commitments to prison were made out. Of the 94 sentenced to imprisonment only seven were actually imprisoned : one served six terms, one five terms, three two terms, and one of them one term of imprisonment. In spite of all these thunders of the law, 33 of the fifty offenders were no better than before. As a rule the parents who go to prison are hopeless drunkards ; the remainder escape by payment of the fines. A large number of these parents are engaged in highly paid employments ; in many cases it is not poverty which hinders them from fulfilling their parental duties, it is simply vicious habits of life.

Putting all these facts together respecting the parental condition of delinquent children who have both parents alive and are living at home with them, we are forced to come to the conclusion that in a very small percentage of cases is the character of the parents fit to bear examination. At the very least eighty of them in every hundred are addicted to vicious, if not criminal, habits ; the children come into the world in a polluted moral atmosphere ; they are contaminated from their earliest infancy without being aware of it; and, although their status is normal as far as the number of their parents is concerned, it is in the highest degree abnormal when the character of these parents is taken into consideration.

CHAPTER VIII.

THE ECONOMIC CONDITION OF JUVENILE OFFENDERS.

Economic condition of orphaned and deserted children—Economic condition of illegitimate and partially orphaned children—Children dependent on their mothers only—Economic condition of juvenile offenders with both parents alive—Contributions of parents to maintenance of juvenile offenders—Economic condition of juvenile prisoners—Juvenile prisoners without homes—Municipal homes for homeless boys—Juveniles in large cities—Occupations of juvenile offenders—Relation between occupation and crime—Relation between unskilled labour and crime—Unskilled labourers and the criminal law—The nature of employment and crime—Want of employment and crime—Industrial inefficiency of the criminal population—Recapitulation.

In order to form a complete estimate of the social condition of juvenile offenders it will be expedient to supplement what has been said respecting their parental condition by a corresponding series of facts respecting their economic circumstances and economic equipment. The economic circumstances of a considerable number of juvenile offenders can be arrived at with tolerable accuracy by looking at their parental condition. In all cases where they have lost both parents by death, or are deprived of them by desertion, it may safely be inferred

that the economic circumstances of juvenile offenders
are distinctly bad. It is impossible for a juvenile
who is left alone in the world by the death or
desertion of his parents to be anything else than
miserably off if he has to depend entirely on his
own resources for the means of subsistence. Even
if he obtains some sort of employment, his earnings
are too small to keep him in decency and comfort.
But children without parents and without a home find
it exceedingly difficult to get regular and salutary
work. Most employers of young people like to
know that they have a home. They do not care
to engage a lad who has to sleep in a common
lodging-house—they know that in such places the
risk of contamination is very considerable; and if
there is room for choice, as there generally is where
work is worth having, a boy who has a home is
taken in preference to a boy without one. Thus it
comes to pass that orphaned and deserted children
have, as a rule, to pick up their living in a very
precarious manner. In large cities many of them
earn a scanty pittance as street hawkers and newspaper sellers; and when this kind of occupation
fails them, as it often does, they resort to begging,
or degenerate into thieves. Irregularity of occupation begets irregularity of habits. When manhood
arrives it is difficult to correct customs which have
become habitual in youth. The inability at the
outset of life to procure regular employment finally
developes into a want of aptitude for it. The worker
who has been compelled to live by casual employment as a youth finishes by preferring to live by

this kind of labour when he becomes a man. A large number of men of this description are drawn from the ranks of juveniles who have lost their parents or have been abandoned by them in early life. When the slightest economic depression occurs this intermittent class of workers is immediately affected by it. It is always this class which constitutes the largest section of the unemployed, and also the largest section of the prison population charged with offences against property. The casual labourer, the vagrant, the casual pauper, the petty thief, are in a large number of cases the matured product of the wretched material conditions attaching to the orphaned and deserted child. As we have already seen, children of this description comprise 10 per cent. of the population of industrial schools, and a still higher percentage of the prison population.

Children who have lost their fathers and live with widowed mothers, as well as children who are illegitimate, are in a better economic position than juvenile offenders completely deprived of parental care. They have at least a home, a shelter of some kind, and this in itself is an economic advantage in a humble way. But as a rule juvenile offenders entirely dependent on the mother are low down in the economic scale. In most cases they are indifferently clad, and in many cases they have the pinched appearance of children who have been indifferently fed. The want of proper clothing is an economic disadvantage of some importance for this class of children. It often prevents them from getting employment. Clothes, it is true, are the merest externals of respectability, but. in a great many instances these externals are the only tests employers have to go by, and a boy in rags will always be looked upon with suspicion in the labour market on this account alone.   It is not at all an uncommon thing for juveniles committed to prison to say that they cannot get work as they have no clothes, and one of the many ways in which prisoners' aid societies are of inestimable benefit to the young consists in providing them, in cases of need, with a workmanlike suit of clothes.

Another economic difficulty with children dependent upon mothers alone is that the mother is very rarely able to apprentice them to a trade.   The regularity of habits and the mental discipline involved in learning a trade constitute an excellent preparation for the duties and responsibilities of social life.   All mechanical operations of a complicated character make considerable demands upon the mental powers. They are not merely a training of the eye and the hand ; they are also an admirable exercise of all the mental faculties which a proper training of the eye and the hand necessitates.   Among juvenile offenders committed to prison and dependent upon widows very few are engaged in a skilled occupation. The mothers of these juveniles are obliged to make them adopt some sort of work which will add as much as possible to the scanty family income, and at the same time entail the least possible expenditure.   The learning of a trade is incompatible with the fulfilment of these conditions.   The children of widows are accordingly put to employments where they can most expeditiously pick up a living for themselves. Several evils flow from this. In the first place, the juvenile who earns his own living at a very early age is made prematurely independent of the parent, and soon resents the advice of those most deeply concerned in his welfare. Quarrels arise; the home is forsaken for the lodging-house; evil companionships are formed which frequently terminate in crime. In the next place, unskilled labour is usually more or less irregular, and it is exceedingly difficult for a homeless youth to tide over a period of slackness. He is in the streets in a moment, and the step is an easy one from the pavement to the prison cell. Among the circumstances which tend to make the fatherless child more likely to become an offender than the motherless, the economic disadvantages which have just been noted must be taken into account.

We now come to the economic condition of delinquent juveniles in reformatory and industrial schools who have both parents alive. In what sort of position, as far as regards the means of subsistence, do these parents stand? There are several ways in which this may be approximately estimated. As a first test let us take the percentage of parents of offenders committed to reformatory schools who are ordered by the magistrates to contribute a certain amount towards the support of their children while in these institutions. After a child has been sent to a reformatory or industrial school, notice of this fact is transmitted to a local agent of the Home Office whose duty it is to collect parental contri-

12

butions. This agent makes it his business to ascertain the circumstances of the parents, and if he
considers that they are able to pay anything towards
the maintenance of their children, he endeavours in
the first place to induce them to do so voluntarily.
But as a matter of fact very few parents will contribute except under legal compulsion, and the agent,
in order to enforce payment, is obliged to summon
them before a magistrate. In the year 1892, as
a result of this process, the parents were ordered
to contribute in 64 per cent. of the committals
to English reformatory schools. In Scotland the
parents were obliged to contribute in 24 per cent.
of the committals. The difference between England
and Scotland in the percentage of cases in which
parents are called upon to contribute is principally
owing to the fact that Scotch magistrates are much
more reluctant to order parental contributions than
English magistrates; it is not to be attributed to
a material difference in parental circumstances.

If we pass from the number called upon to contribute to the amounts actually contributed, and to
the principle on which these amounts are fixed, we
arrive at a clearer estimate of the financial capa-
bilities of the parents of juvenile offenders. Let us,
in the first place, state the principle on which the
amounts which parents have to pay are usually fixed.
If a parent's weekly income passes beyond a very
small sum he is expected to pay out of this income
a proportion equal to about a penny in the shilling.
Thus, for instance, a parent who earns twenty
shillings a week would, unless his family is large,

or unless he has other exceptional burdens, be expected to pay twenty pence a week towards the maintenance of his reformatory or industrial school child. This, then, is the general principle on which contributions are usually fixed, and it shows that although the number called upon in England to contribute is large, yet the amounts which they are able to contribute may be small. If the great bulk of the amounts contributed are under two shillings a week it is a proof that the juveniles in industrial schools come from very poor homes ; and, on the other hand, in all cases in which the contributions exceed two shillings a week there is every reason to conclude that these juveniles come from homes in which it was possible for them to have the ordinary advantages of the working-class population.

Passing from the principle regulating the amounts parents are called upon to contribute, let us now endeavour to ascertain the percentage of parents who do contribute. The annual returns issued by the inspector of reformatory and industrial schools mention the number of cases in which parents are required to contribute, but these returns omit to mention the proportion of parents who actually comply with the decisions of the court. The only information we possess relating to this important point dates from the year 1882. If this year is taken as a criterion it will be found (see note on next page, column 7) that parental contributions were made in the case of 41·5 per cent. of the inmates of reformatory schools in England and Scotland, and in 40·9 per cent. of the inmates of industrial schools.[1]   These contributions were not exclusively made by the parents of juveniles who had a father or both a father and mother alive ; some of them were made by widows.   The highest sum a parent is liable to pay for the maintenance of his child in a reformatory or industrial school is five shillings a week, and it will be seen, by looking at the subjoined table, that the amounts contributed ranged from five shillings to less than a shilling a week.   It will also be observed that the great bulk of the contributors were unable to pay as much as two shillings a week.   In the reformatory school cases only 10 per cent. were paid for at the rate of two shillings and upwards, and in the industrial school cases only 15 per cent. were paid for at the rate of two shillings a week and upwards.   Therefore, if the economic condition of reformatory and industrial school inmates is reckoned by the proportion of them paid for at the rate of two shillings a week and upwards, and if the payment of two shillings a week is to be taken as the standard of comfort, we arrive at the result that only 10 per

[1] PARENTAL CONTRIBUTIONS TO REFORMATORY AND INDUSTRIAL SCHOOLS FOR THE YEAR 1882.

		1	2	3	4	5	6	7	8	9
		5s.	4s. and upwards.	3s. and upwards.	2s. and upwards.	1s. and upwards.	Under 1s.	Total paid for.	Not paid for.	Total inmates.
ENGLAND AND SCOTLAND	Reformatories	14	15	66	573	1818	257	2743	3858	6601
	Per cent.	·2	·2	1	8·7	27·5	3·9	41·5	58·5	
	Indust.schools	20	67	301	2316	3904	600	7208	10406	17614
	Per cent.	·1	·4	1·7	13·1	22·2	3·4	40·9	59·1	

cent. of the inmates of reformatories were living under comfortable economic conditions, and only 15 per cent. of the inmates of industrial schools.

Although such a small percentage of reformatory and industrial school inmates come from homes where the economic conditions are normal, it is at the same time to be borne in mind that the parents are able to pay over two shillings a week in more than 10 or 15 per cent. of the cases committed to these institutions. But ability to pay and willingness to do so are two very different things, and many of the juveniles whose parents are most able to contribute come from the most wretched homes. The quality and comfort of a home are not to be estimated merely by the income of the person at the head of it. This person may be earning enough and more than enough for the legitimate needs of his family, but the way in which he spends it may be such as to leave them on the verge of destitution. Therefore in estimating the economic situation of juvenile offenders it is essential to look not merely at the earnings of their parents, but also at the manner in which these earnings are disposed of. A child whose father is only earning one pound a week is much better off than a child whose father is earning two pounds a week if the father of the one is steady and temperate, and the father of the other wastes half his earnings on drink. Unfortunately in not a few instances juvenile offenders are sprung from parents who spend their substance on everything except the comfort and welfare of their children. All these circumstances must be kept in view in estimating the economic condition of the child by the economic condition of its parents. And if these circumstances are duly weighed it will be found that not more than 15 per cent. of the juveniles committed to reformatory and industrial schools come from homes in which they are fairly housed, fairly fed, and fairly clad.

In a preceding chapter attention was called to the physical condition of juveniles committed to prison between the ages of sixteen and eighteen. We shall now complete this inquiry into the economic circumstances of young offenders by a survey of the manner in which these imprisoned juveniles had to live.[1] In 46 per cent. of the cases these young offenders had no settled home, and usually resorted to common lodging-houses for food and shelter. Among these young people the want of a home arose from a variety of causes. A good many were without a home because their parents were dead, and they had no relations who had the will or the ability to take partial charge of them. A certain number had no home because their parents had disappeared,

[1] Particulars of 100 Male Prisoners, aged last birthday sixteen, seventeen, and eighteen, in Wandsworth Prison, London, between June 14 and 20, 1894.

Living at Home.	Living in Lodgings.	One or both Parents Dead.	Occupations.	
			Skilled labour.	Unskilled labour.
54 per cent.	46 per cent.	32 per cent.	23 per cent.	77 per cent.

See Minutes of Evidence taken by the Departmental Committee on Prisons, vol. ii. p. 537.

or because the family had been broken up by parental strife. A fair proportion had for one reason or another been turned out of doors by their parents. It is not at all an uncommon thing among certain sections of the London population for a parent to tell his son when the age of sixteen is reached that he must go out into the world and look after himself. This is usually done when the youth is temporarily out of work. It must also be said that it is a step which is often taken owing to the fact that the son cannot keep work when he gets it, or makes himself intolerable to the other members of the family. Then again numbers have no home because they have been imprisoned. It frequently happens that parents will not have anything more to do with their children if they have been convicted of crime. On the other hand, some leave home of their own accord. This arises because they get tired of the restraints of home life, or because of cruel and dissolute parents. In some cases the home is left in consequence of the want of bedroom accommodation. Many juvenile offenders are members of families ranging from six to ten or twelve persons, and as the family increases the older members have to leave the home in order to make room for the younger ones. It is absolutely certain that in large cities a considerable amount of juvenile crime may be traced to this fact alone. The absence of proper household accommodation, arising in many instances from a reckless increase of the population, has the effect of compelling numbers of young people to resort to lodging-houses at the most critical period of their lives. According to the census returns for 1891, as analysed by Mr. Charles Booth,[1] no less than 1,294,000, or 31 in every hundred of the population of London, are too thickly packed together in their homes ; in other words, two or more of the persons composing this population have to live in one room. The overcrowded condition of such a large proportion of the inhabitants of the metropolis does not always arise from poverty : in many cases it is the consequence of high rents. But no matter by what cause this state of things is produced, it constitutes a most deplorable moral evil, and in the case of the young it is often the preliminary to an existence of vagabondage and crime.

A short time ago the London County Council started a municipal lodging-house for the homeless classes in the metropolis. When the project was first resolved upon a good deal of discussion was aroused as to the wisdom and policy of the experiment. But there is little room for doubt as to the expediency of having some sort of municipal shelter for the floating mass of homeless boys who are at present drifting hither and thither on the treacherous tide of London life. The re-housing of the overcrowded section of the London poor, if it is not, as some think, an impossible task, will be at any rate a prolonged and tremendous enterprise which this generation will not see the end of. But it is quite within the compass of municipal effort to confer an immediate benefit of immense importance upon that part of the immature population of large cities who, from one cause or another, are left without a home.

[1] See Address delivered before the Royal Statistical Society, p. 12.

The immature have claims on the consideration of the community which the mature do not possess. Immaturity, especially in large cities, is a period of great stress and trial when unsupported by parental counsel, and exposed to the casual acquaintanceships of the ordinary lodging-house. One way at least in which the perils incident to this critical period of life are within the sphere of mitigation consists in establishing a kind of municipal home for homeless juveniles, and setting it apart for them alone. Under wise and careful supervision an institution of this kind would have the effect of protecting many of the younger members of the community who have the misfortune to be without a home from the multitude of corrupting influences inseparable from the association of all ages in the ordinary lodging-house. At the present time at least three thousand homeless youths are annually discharged from the London prisons, and it is certain that many of them would never have fallen into crime at all had they not been compelled to mix with the worthless and depraved characters who frequent the common lodging-house. It is usually to these places that the professional thief and burglar goes in search of comparatively innocent accomplices ; and a short time ago the newspapers contained a typical account of the manner in which the habitual offender is able to utilise the services of the young. In one of the London suburbs a series of daring robberies occurred which had for a time baffled the efforts of the authorities. At last it was discovered that the perpetrator of these crimes adopted a very simple method of procedure. In the first place he picked up a boy in a lodging-house. This boy's business was to accompany the burglar on his expeditions and knock at the doors of the houses it was intended to rob. If he got an answer he was to ask for some one whom he knew did not live there and depart. If he received no answer it was a sign that the inmates were all out or away from home. The burglar's opportunity had now arrived : the boy's part of the work was done. He disappeared, whilst the thief broke open the door and ransacked the premises. Before falling into the hands of the thief this youth had been a lodging-house waif, and it is probable that he would not have become a criminal at all if London had contained one or two well-conducted municipal shelters exclusively for the young. As it is he and hundreds of his fellows are yearly being initiated into the devices of the habitual criminal, and end by becoming members of the criminal class.

Coming back to the juvenile offenders whose economic condition we have been examining, it was found that 77 per cent. of them had not been apprenticed to any trade. They designated themselves as labourers, dockers, hawkers, newspaper-sellers, errand boys, costermongers, and so on ; in short, they belonged to the class of casual and intermittent workers when they had not sunk into the class of habitual thieves. The proportion of these juveniles without a trade corresponds closely with the proportion of offenders of all kinds without a trade in the general prison population. The bulk of convicted offenders return themselves as labourers, but it requires to be remarked that a considerable number of prisoners who call themselves tradesmen are not tradesmen at all. When put to the test they are found to be absolutely incompetent, and many prisoners class themselves as skilled workers in the belief that it will mitigate the severity of their punishment. This belief is to a great extent based upon fact, for it is no doubt the case that certain classes of skilled artisans are always required within prison walls, and in most instances the work they have to do does not involve solitary cellular confinement. It is done in workshops or in the open air, and in such circumstances the dreadful and paralysing monotony of prison life is to a considerable extent avoided. In view of these considerations it is to be recollected that the percentage of prisoners returned as skilled workers is always in excess of the number who have actually learned a trade, so that they could earn their living by it. It is, in fact, probable that 75 per cent. of the prison population cannot earn a living in the exercise of skilled occupations.

It would be highly interesting if we were able to compare the occupations of the prison population with the occupations of the general community, so as to see in what way occupation is related to crime. It is hardly open to doubt that the nature of a man's occupation has some effect upon his conduct. A man's best energies are absorbed in his calling; it is his calling which shapes the attitude of his mind during the best part of the day and during the greater portion of his active life. Occupation ac-

cordingly begets a mental attitude, a habit of mind,
a way of looking at things which must exercise an
influence of some sort in determining human action.
Unfortunately we have no certain means of judging
how far the influence of occupation extends. In the
first place, as has just been observed, the returns as
to occupation of the prison population, whether
juvenile or adult, are not of a very accurate character, and in the next place, even if they were made
sufficiently accurate to admit of comparison, they are
not drawn up on the same lines as the occupations of
the general community, as recorded in the census
returns. It is to be hoped, when the next returns
dealing with the occupations of the prison population
are issued, that they will be constructed so as to
harmonise as far as possible with the returns of the
last census relating to the occupations of the general
population. If this were done it would perhaps be
possible to form some sort of estimate of the effect
of occupation upon the tendency to crime ; at present
all estimates of this character must be accepted in
the light of mere approximations.

In spite of the imperfection of existing materials
for estimating the effects of occupation upon the
tendency to crime, there is at least one important fact
which comes clearly into view. That fact is the high
percentage of low-skilled workers in the juvenile and
adult prison population as compared with the percentage of this class of workers in the general community. In the general community labourers of all
kinds—agricultural labourers, general labourers, road
and railway labourers—do not at the outside exceed

20 per cent. of the male population over fifteen years of age. But, as has just been observed, the proportion of labourers in the male prison population amounts to between 65 and 75 per cent. of the whole. Therefore, according to the most moderate calculations, the class of low-skilled workers is between three and four times more numerous in the prison population than in the general community. Of these workers it is the general and not the agricultural labourer who does so much to swell the returns of crime. As far as it is possible to judge from personal observation and experience, the agricultural labourer does not contribute more than his proper proportion to the ranks of the prison population : the abnormal proportion of labourers in prisons is made up of general labourers from the towns. It needs, however, to be noted that a considerable number of offenders who class themselves as labourers are in reality thieves, vagabonds, tramps, and outcasts, and the existence of this circumstance makes the general labourer appear in a worse light in the records of crime. But this circumstance does not affect the fact that it is the class which is lowest down in the ranks of industry which supplies the largest percentage of offenders committed to prison. Habitual thieves and vagabonds who return themselves as labourers are men without a trade.

We now come to the question why such a large proportion of the prison population, both juvenile and adult, is composed of labourers. One reason is that this class of the community is so low down in the economic scale that a comparatively small number of offenders belonging to it are able to purge their offences by the payment of a fine. They have therefore to submit to the alternative and go to prison in all cases, and they are very numerous, in which the penalty is a fine or imprisonment. On the other hand, skilled workers and the well-to-do almost always escape imprisonment if the sentence is accompanied by the option of a fine. But inability to pay fines, although it counts for something, is not the principal cause of the high percentage of labourers in the prison population. The principal cause undoubtedly is that the ranks of the general labourer are recruited, as a rule, from the most backward, the most impoverished, the least self-respecting class in the community. Recruits also come in considerable numbers from those who have failed at other occupations either from want of ability or from want of character, or from some circumstance which has incapacitated them from pursuing the trade they may have learned. In order to secure employment the general labourer requires little ability and no character, and as a result of this, general labour is the usual resort of persons without worldly advantages of any sort, and the last refuge of all who have failed, from whatever cause, in other branches of industrial life. It is also the only resource of a large class of juveniles who have no parents or no home, or whose parents are too poverty stricken or too dissolute to give their children a training in some skilled employment.

Finally, the nature of low-skilled labour must be reckoned as contributing to the high percentage of general labourers in the prison population. As a rule the less skilled an occupation is the more difficult it becomes to get regular work at it, and irregularity of employment is a fruitful source of crime. In addition to this evil the character of low-skilled labour is very seldom calculated to exercise a refining or humanising influence on the labourer. It generally consists of manual work of the roughest description, and the mind undoubtedly has a tendency to take its tone and temper from the nature of the materials which engage so much of its attention. In many departments of industry the introduction of machinery has had a pernicious effect on the worker as a man, inasmuch as it has almost abolished the necessity for the mental training involved in the acquirement of high mechanical skill. But in so far as machinery is being utilised for performing the roughest work of the world, it must be looked upon as an unmitigated good, and the more it can be brought into play for this purpose the better it will be for the low-skilled labourer from a moral and pro-bably also from a material point of view.

Of the juvenile offenders whose circumstances I have inquired into, it now remains to be added that 30 per cent. were at regular work when placed under arrest. It will be seen from these figures that among the juvenile population the possession of work is not a complete preventive against the commission of crime. At the same time it undoubtedly has a tendency to diminish its proportions. Juveniles engaged in a regular occupation which absorbs their time and energies during the greater portion of the

day are removed by this circumstance alone from a
host of temptations which beset the unemployed.
Moreover, destitution does not tempt them to commit
offences against property, and when juveniles in work
fall into the hands of the criminal law it is usually
for offences such as assault, gambling, drunkenness,
malicious damage, obscene language, disorderly conduct, and so on. Nevertheless a certain percentage
of juveniles in work are convicted of theft and embezzlement and sometimes of housebreaking and
burglary. But the bulk of offences of this description, when committed by juveniles at all, are committed
by juveniles out of employment. In short, occupation has the effect of altering the form which juvenile
crime assumes ; it has even the effect of diminishing
its amount, but it has not the effect of totally abolishing crime. Adverse economic conditions are no
doubt a potent factor in arousing and stimulating
criminal desires, but it is a mistake to assume that
crime is entirely a product of economic adversity. It
is one among the many conditions which produce a
criminal career, but it is not by any means the sole
condition. Whilst denying the omnipotence of
economic conditions in the production of juvenile
crime, it must, on the other hand, be emphasised that
economic remedies in the shape of steadier work and
better wages would do a great deal towards reducing
the proportions of juvenile offences against property.
Moral life, like life as a whole, stands upon a material
foundation, and if the virtues are not resting on a
material basis in the form of steady work and
adequate remuneration, they will be in most cases but

poor and sickly plants. Of course instances exist of the absence of material blessings combined with purity and elevation of character, but these instances are exceptions which cannot be cited as standards for the ordinary man. The ordinary man—that is to say, the great mass of mankind—is deteriorated when placed under abnormal economic conditions. Adverse conditions of this kind prevent him from obtaining a proper amount of physical nourishment, and physical deterioration is often the prelude to mental degeneracy. Insufficient food, insufficient shelter, insufficient clothing, degrade men in their own eyes ; they imagine, and not without reason, that they are objects of contempt to the community, and in many cases their conduct eventually falls to the same miserable level as their economic surroundings. This is more especially the case with the young. Juveniles in all ranks of life are exceedingly sensitive to public opinion, and, unless gifted with great inborn force of character, are apt to become what the world in general considers them to be.

We shall now complete our examination of the economic condition of juvenile offenders by endeavouring to show why three-fourths of them are out of work, or practically out of work, at the time of their arrest. The possession of work or the want of it is dependent upon two fundamental conditions— personal competence, and the state of trade. As a rule both these conditions operate simultaneously, and it is not very often that the loss of employment is produced by one of them alone. In depressed times it is the least efficient who are the first to lose

13

work, and it is only on those rare occasions when an industry comes to a standstill that the thoroughly competent workman is thrown completely idle. In the ranks of labour the weakest, the most unfit industrially, are always the first to fall ; the fittest, the most efficient, are always the last. In periods of great commercial prosperity almost any one can get something to do if he chooses to do it, but as soon as these exceptional circumstances begin to pass away the process of eliminating the least capable workers immediately and imperceptibly comes into operation. The least efficient are the first to be cast adrift ; the class above them follows if trade depression deepens, and the process of sacrificing the less fit continues until trade commences to revive. All of us who are engaged in the task of procuring occupation for discharged prisoners are constantly being confronted with the operation of this law. A low standard of industrial ability, and therefore a considerable difficulty of obtaining employment or of keeping it when once obtained, is as great a drawback to the discharged prisoner as the condition of the labour market. In a very considerable number of cases the discharged prisoner is below the average in industrial capacity. Employers say that he is not worth his wages, that he is irregular in his habits, that he is unsteady, that he is not to be depended upon. In these circumstances it is not to be wondered at that the discharged prisoner should fall out of work as soon as the full tide of trade begins to recede. And when he loses work he falls back instinctively upon the criminal habits of the past.

What applies to offenders in general applies with equal force to the juvenile offender. He is out of work quite as much on account of industrial inefficiency as on account of the condition of trade. As a rule the juvenile offender has received little or no industrial training, as a rule he has not been accustomed to habits of regularity, in many cases his home surroundings are against him, and it often happens that he has not the physical strength for the only kind of labour he would otherwise be competent to perform. He accordingly belongs to the class of intermittent workers who are called in during emergencies, and are got rid of at the earliest possible moment. He has no permanent occupation, he drifts from one thing to another, and is in reality never in work in the sense of having some stable occupation at which he can count on earning a regular weekly wage. From what has already been said respecting the physical and parental condition of these juvenile offenders, it is perfectly plain that the industrial inefficiency which plays so large a part in making them what they are is in most cases outside their own control. " How shall a child of the slums, ill-fed in body and mind, brought up in the industrial and moral degradation of low city life, without a chance of learning how to use hands or head and to acquire habits of steady industry, become an efficient workman? It is the bitterest portion of the lot of the poor that they are deprived of the opportunity of learning to work well. Here and there an individual may be to blame for neglected opportunities; but the poor as a class have no more chance under present conditions of acquiring efficiency than of attaining to refined artistic taste or the culminating Christian virtue of holiness." [1]

The results of this inquiry into the economic conditions of juvenile offenders may now be briefly recapitulated. As far as offenders committed to industrial and reformatory schools are concerned, it has been shown that the economic condition of those among them who are orphans, or deserted, or illegitimate, or the children of widows, is about as bad as it can be. Juveniles in this position, when of an age to do something for themselves, are too impoverished to be apprenticed to a trade ; they have to engage in irregular and low-paid occupations. Offenders committed to reformatory and industrial schools who have both parents alive are also in the main in a bad economic condition. This was shown by the fact that in only 15 per cent. of the committals to industrial schools were the parents able to pay two shillings a week towards the maintenance of their offspring. In reformatory cases the parents only paid in 10 per cent. of the cases. The great mass of industrial and reformatory school children with both parents alive are therefore in very much the same adverse economic position as the class of children who are either wholly or partially orphaned. They too have to follow the poorest paid and most fluctuating kinds of labour. When we come to consider the economic circumstances of juvenile offenders in prisons between the ages of sixteen and eighteen we

[1] J. Hobson, " Problems of Poverty."

discover a very similar state of things. Of this class
of offenders no less than 46 per cent. were homeless,
no less than 77 per cent. were low-skilled workers,
and no less than 70 per cent. had little or no employment at the time of their arrest. The figures relating
to juveniles in prison were collected in 1894–5—that
is to say, during a time of commercial depression.
Allowance must therefore be made for this circumstance. But after this allowance has been made they
certainly point to the conclusion that the economic
condition of a large contingent of the juvenile criminal
population who are entering upon manhood is a
very precarious one, inasmuch as it is so exceedingly
sensitive to the slightest movements of trade.

It has already been pointed out that other causes
besides economic conditions play their part in bend-
ing the mind toward criminal courses, and it is not to
be supposed that an improvement in economic surroundings alone will ever banish criminal propensities
from the human heart. Nevertheless it is equally
indisputable that if it were possible to effect some
permanent improvement in the economic circumstances of the most impoverished sections of the
juvenile population offences against property would
undoubtedly manifest a distinct tendency to diminish.
The only way in which it seems possible to effect this
improvement is by raising the standard of industrial
efficiency among the least favoured members of the
juvenile population. How this reform is to be
accomplished is undoubtedly a most formidable
problem. It will never be accomplished if left to the
parents of such children in cases where they have

parents.   It is a reform which must proceed from collective action on the part of the community. At present the community confines its operations to bestowing industrial training on children who have actually fallen ; it is probable that it would be a wiser, and in the end a more economic, policy to bestow a similar training on those who are likely to fall.

PART II.

THE REPRESSION OF JUVENILE CRIME.

CHAPTER IX.

ADMONITION.

Principle determining repressive methods—Classification of actual repressive methods—The selection of the proper method in each individual case—The trial of juveniles—The individual and social circumstances of the offender must be considered as well as the offence—The legal defence of children in France and Belgium—Trial of juveniles in Belgium—Trial of children in Michigan—School board agents and juvenile offenders—Work of these agents in Liverpool—English criminal courts—Admonition—Admonition an ancient custom—Admonition in England—Admonition alone—Admonition and conviction—The Massachusetts system of probation—Value of this system—The probation system in England, the Continent, and the Colonies—The Belgian system—Results of the system.

In the preceding chapters it has been our endeavour to examine several of the principal conditions which produce, or which have a tendency to produce, the juvenile offender. In the course of this examination it was discovered that the juvenile offender is a result of the adverse individual and social conditions under which he has to live. As far as adverse individual conditions are concerned, it was found, for example, in a very considerable proportion

of cases that the juvenile who comes within the arm
of the law is both mentally and physically, as well as
morally, below the average of the general youthful
population of the same age and sex. And as far as
social conditions are concerned it was likewise found
that the parental and economic circumstances of the
delinquent juvenile are in the majority of cases
exceedingly defective and abnormal. In short, the
final outcome of our inquiry was to bring home the
conviction that juvenile crime is the necessary and
natural outcome of the miserable individual and
social circumstances of the juvenile offender. It
follows from what has been said respecting the
genesis of juvenile delinquency, that the only effective
method of dealing with it so as to diminish its proportions is to remove the conditions from which it
originates as far as they are removable. Methods of
repression and prevention which do not have this
supreme end steadily and conspicuously in view will
only attain success of a temporary and fictitious
character. Methods of repression and prevention, on
the other hand, which consistently aim at eliminating
the causes which tend to turn the young into the
paths of crime are certain to be rewarded by a
reduction in the numbers of juvenile criminal population.

In the light of these principles we shall now . proceed to look at the methods of repression actually in
operation for dealing with the juvenile offender.
These methods, when we come to arrange them,
may be conveniently divided into three classes—
admonitory, punitive, and educational. Admonitory

methods deal with the offender in the form of merely
warning him against a repetition of the offence, or in
the way of putting him upon his good behaviour, by
requiring him to come up for judgment when called
upon, or putting him under surveillance. Punitive
methods of repression consist in fining the offender,
in sentencing him to corporal punishment, or in committing him for a certain time to prison. Educational
methods deal with the offender by sending him to day
industrial schools, to truant schools, to industrial and
reformatory schools, to voluntary homes, or to private
persons who are willing to receive him. The delicate
and difficult task of the magistrate lies in selecting
the proper method of treatment in each individual
case, and the only manner in which this arduous duty
can be satisfactorily performed is when the magistrate
has before him an accurate personal record of the
circumstances and antecedents of the young offender.
It does not follow, as is sometimes supposed, that two
children who have committed precisely the same
offence should be dealt with by courts of justice in
exactly the same manner. If the personal and social
circumstances of these two children are different the
decision of the court in dealing with them must be
regulated by these circumstances, and not merely by
the nature of the offence. Two children, let us say,
are equally concerned in a case of petty theft : in the
eye of the law both of them are equally guilty, but if
their circumstances differ it is not in the interests of
social security that they should both receive the same
kind of sentence. The one child, it may be, is the
son of respectable and honest parents who have

endeavoured to do their duty by their family; the
other, as frequently happens, is a child who has lost
his mother, and who has to live without supervision
of any kind owing to the callousness or drunken
habits of his father.   In the first case it may be quite
sufficient for repressive purposes to dismiss the young
offender with an admonition, or to call upon his
father to become surety for his good behaviour; in
the second case it may be necessary in the interests
of the child's future welfare, and also for the sake of
society as a whole, that the neglected juvenile should
be committed to an educational institution.   In the
one case the State may safely rely on the natural
educational agency of the home, in the other it cannot, and as a consequence it must adopt methods of
repression adapted to the unfortunate parental circumstances in which the child is placed.

In addition to illustrating the fact that it is not
necessarily in the interests of society that two
offenders equally guilty should receive precisely the
same kind of sentence, the case which has just been
mentioned also illustrates the importance of supply-
ing the magistrate with as accurate an account as
possible of the individual and social circumstances of
the young offender.   When a court of law is unacquainted with these circumstances its judgment
must be determined to a large extent by the nature
of the offence alone.   A decision of this character is
often attended with unsatisfactory results.   In order
to meet all the requirements of the case a judgment
should be based not merely upon the nature of the
offence, but also upon the circumstances of the

offender. In offences involving the trial of young people many magistrates call upon the police to supply them with all available information respecting the parental and social condition of the young offender, but it would be a great aid to the efficient administration of justice if these circumstances were always placed before the criminal courts as a matter of course by some agency existing for the express purpose. According to M. Drucker in his excellent book on the protection of children,[1] a society exists in Paris for the legal defence of children brought before the criminal courts. In the course of its existence this society has succeeded in doing an immense amount of valuable work, and has been of the greatest assistance to the courts of justice in all cases connected with the trial of children and the treatment of children pending the day of trial. In addition to bringing all the facts connected with the case before the magistrates, a society of this kind is often able to show that the juvenile is innocent of the crime laid to his charge. I am convinced, from long and watchful observation, that there is generally a greater danger of a miscarriage of justice in the case of young people than in the case of adults. Immaturity, inexperience, bewilderment, prevent a young person from being able to defend himself in a satisfactory manner, or to clear himself when he is actually innocent. Cases occur from time to time in which children who are completely innocent are detained in prison. One of these cases was reported in

[1] "Le Protection des Enfants Maltraités et Moralement Abandonnés," par Gaston Drucker. Paris, 1894.

the London press in the month of August, 1895. According to the report, an errand boy of fourteen years of age, who had been more than twelve months in his master's service, was charged with theft. He was entrusted with the delivery of a parcel to one of his master's customers, and it was charged against him that he had not delivered it. The boy maintained that he had delivered the parcel, but the circumstances were so suspicious that he was remanded to prison. In the meantime it was discovered that the parcel had been delivered, but that it had been mislaid by the people who received it. When these facts came to the knowledge of the court the magistrate dismissed the case, and justly said, "The boy is discharged without a stain on his character, and I am very sorry for what has happened." The French society for the defence of accused children was established to assist in cases of this kind, as well as in cases where the children are really guilty. Societies of a similar kind exist in Belgium, and are doing equally good work.

According to a report presented to the Fourth International Congress of Criminal Anthropology by M. Thiry, Professor of Criminal Law in the University of Liege, the greatest care is taken to see that all the circumstances relating to an incriminated juvenile offender are placed before the magistrate. Before any offender under the age of sixteen is brought before a magistrate a circular mentioning the facts of the case, the name and residence of the child and his parents, is sent to two committees for the protection of children. One of these is a committee for

assisting juveniles, and another is a committee for
the defence of children tried before the criminal
courts. These committees make all possible inquiries
into the individual and social circumstances of the
offender. When the trial comes on the committees
appear before the magistrate. The juvenile and his
parents are also present. When the case has been
heard the magistrate and the committees take
counsel together as to the best means of dealing with
the offender. A system of a somewhat similar
character prevails in the state of Michigan. But the
duties of inquiring into the antecedents of the offender
are entrusted to an official known as a county agent.
According to Mr. C. D. Randall, in the *American
Journal of Sociology*, one of these agents exists in
each county. " Their duties relate to both dependent
and delinquent children. When complaint is entered
against any boy under sixteen years, or any girl under
seventeen years, for any offence not punishable by
imprisonment for life, the court is required to notify
the county agent, who attends the court and advises
the judge as to the disposition to be made of the child
after learning the facts. This consultation in the
interest of the child often leads, especially in case of
first offences, to their return to their parents or sus-
pension of sentence. If the opinion is that the child
needs reformatory treatment it is sent to one of the
reform schools."

The officials of the school boards are the nearest
equivalents in Great Britain to the county agents in
the United States. According to Mr. Stewart, the
stipendiary magistrate for Liverpool (in a letter ad-

dressed to the *Times* newspaper, June 27, 1895), these officials are of the utmost value in dealing with juvenile offenders in that great city. " Industrial schools," he says, "are voluntary institutions ; their authorities have the right, and exercise it even when they have vacancies, to decline to receive a child committed by the courts. A remand is necessary in the vast majority of cases in order that a suitable school ready and willing to receive the child may be found, and in many cases in order that full inquiry may be made as to the surroundings and history of each child, so that the court may be satisfied that it is a fit subject for industrial school discipline. In Liverpool the necessary inquiries are made by the officials of the School Board, which body has contracts with various industrial schools for the reception on specified terms of children committed through their agency. I have never yet found the School Board refuse to adopt a case which I have recommended to them, and their intimate acquaintance with the children of this city and their surroundings is of the greatest possible service to the bench in dealing with such cases." Inquiries of the character just described undoubtedly tend to diminish the number of inappropriate sentences. If these inquiries were universal, and constituted part of a properly organised system of dealing with all young offenders, they would be productive of many beneficial results. The Summary Jurisdiction Act of 1879, as well as the Probation of First Offenders Act, contemplates the necessity for an inquiry into the character and antecedents of the young offender. But these Acts provide no machinery for carrying out these inquiries. As a matter of fact the task often falls upon the police, but as the police are bound to appear as prosecutors it is work which can be better done by agencies such as exist in Belgium and the United States.

Probably no tribunals in the world are so wel adapted for dealing effectively with young offenders as the English criminal courts. This arises from the fact that the English criminal law allows very wide powers of discretion to the magistrates and judges. In many of the continental penal codes a maximum and a minimum amount of punishment is attached to each offence, and in this manner the discretion of the judges is limited. According to the German penal code a case of serious theft may be punished by a maximum of ten years' imprisonment, but it must be punished by a minimum of three months. The practice of fixing a maximum and minimum punishment to criminal offences dates to a large extent from the eighteenth century, and was necessitated by the severity of the criminal law and the capricious manner in which it was often administered. In England the criminal law was perhaps more barbarous in its provisions, and the manner in which it was administered was probably more severe than was the case on the Continent, but the alterations which our penal statutes have undergone in the present century have not been in the direction of interfering with the almost unlimited discretion of the courts. In fact it may be said that, except in the case of a conviction for murder, the choice of sentence residing in the criminal courts of this country is of the widest possible description. Of course the freedom allowed to criminal courts entails corresponding obligations as to the manner in which it is exercised, and at no time are these obligations of a more exacting character than in those cases in which the future of the young is at stake.

These observations are preliminary to a more detailed examination of the three fundamental methods of dealing with the youthful offender to which reference has already been made. As the admonitory method in its several forms is the mildest, let us consider it first. In recent years this method has attracted a considerable amount of attention, and has succeeded in forcing itself into a somewhat prominent position. The growing conviction of the futility of short sentences of imprisonment has undoubtedly had a great deal to do with the prominence which the admonitory method has acquired within the last few years. The Belgian law of conditional condemnation was recommended to the favourable consideration of Parliament expressly on this ground. It is mainly on this account that it has been advocated by Berenger in France, by von Liszt in Germany, by Alimena in Italy, by Prins in Belgium. As far as positive law is concerned the practice of merely admonishing an offender is a practice which was well known to antiquity. It is an established maxim of Roman jurisprudence that the law shall warn before it strikes. *Moneat lex antequam feriat.* In Canon law the same principle is recognised when it is laid down that an offender is to be three times admonished. It is a principle which existed in the old penal codes of France, and it is now in operation in England, in Russia, in Italy, in some of the Swiss cantons, and in several of the German states.

One of the chief advantages of a mere admonition as it is practised in England, under the Summary Jurisdiction Act of 1879, is that it saves the juvenile offender from the brand of a conviction. In many offences of a trivial character it is most important that the court should not proceed to a conviction, inasmuch as a conviction, even if not accompanied by imprisonment, is often a serious impediment to the future career of the young. " I beg leave to point out," says a very experienced magistrate, " that a serious objection to the Probation of First Offenders Act, passed in 1887, is that its application necessarily involves a conviction, which, in the case of persons charged for the first time with offences of a trifling nature, is the very thing it seems so desirable to avoid, inasmuch as a conviction, especially for an offence imputing dishonesty, inflicts an indelible stain upon the accused person, and may be a serious obstacle to future success in life." It is to be recollected that offences involving the charge of dishonesty are often the result of immaturity. They are not a product of any deep-seated criminal propensities: they represent a transitory phase of mental and moral development, and the desire to commit them quite disappears when maturity is attained. If a child is under healthy and normal home surroundings it is usually wiser in such circumstances to refrain from convicting and to regard the ends of justice as satisfied by resorting to admonition alone.

14

When an admonition is not considered sufficient to meet the requirements of the case it may be dealt with by the method of conditional release, or conditional condemnation as it is usually called on the Continent. As has already been pointed out, this method of dealing with offenders is somewhat more severe, inasmuch as it involves a conviction. But as a court of justice may sometimes consider it necessary to mark its disapproval of criminal conduct by something more than a mere admonition, and is yet reluctant to pass a sentence of imprisonment, it is exceedingly useful to have the intermediate penalty of conditional release. The method of conditional release was first introduced in the state of Massachusetts. According to the Massachusetts system the juvenile offender, after being convicted and admonished, is placed in charge of an official who is called a probation officer, and the sentence which is passed upon him is called a sentence of probation. It is the duty of the probation officer during the time that the juvenile is under his surveillance to watch over his conduct, and if it is unsatisfactory to report the circumstances to the court. In this event other and more stringent measures are taken, such as sending the offender to an industrial school, or in extreme cases committing him to prison. As far as concerns the treatment of juveniles, one of the great advantages of the Massachusetts system is the existence of the probation officer. Owing to the existence of this officer large numbers of children who would otherwise be committed to industrial or reformatory schools are enabled to remain at home with their parents. The sentence of probation, whilst it formally places the child under the control of the probation officer, allows him at the same time to return to his home and family. In this way parental authority is respected and parental responsibility is maintained. The parent, it is true, is advised and watched over by the probation officer, and in cases where the parents are as much to blame as the children the child is protected against the weakness or unworthiness of the parent. When the probation system takes the form of restoring the child to the parent under the supervision of the probation officer, family life is maintained, family affection is preserved, the child is not removed from the ordinary conditions of social existence which are such an important preparation for its future welfare in the world. The probation system, as it is practised in the United States, is much more economical as well as more natural than the system which exists in England. In England many juvenile offenders who might easily be entrusted to the care of their parents if a proper system of supervision existed, must, as matters stand at present, be sent to industrial schools. This involves considerable expense. Within the last twenty years the expenditure on industrial schools has been steadily on the increase. Under the probation system as it is worked in the United States it is probable that expenditure would diminish instead of increasing.

The English law of 1887 relating to conditional release operates without the mediation of a probation officer. According to the English statute, when an

offender is convicted of an offence which is not
punishable with more than two years' imprisonment,
the judge or magistrate, on taking all the circumstances of the case into account, may release the
prisoner on condition that he binds himself to come
up for judgment when called upon. The circumstances which the court is expected to take into
consideration are the trivial nature of the offence,
the conditions under which it was committed, and
the youth and antecedents of the offender. If these
circumstances are of an extenuating character it is
within the power of the judge or justice, instead of
inflicting a sentence of imprisonment, to liberate the
culprit on his own recognisances, with or without
sureties, and if need be to condemn him to pay the
costs of the prosecution in whole or in part. The
law of conditional release as it exists in Belgium
differs somewhat both from the English and American
statutes. The Belgian law is narrower in its operation
inasmuch as it only affects offenders liable to a
maximum of six months' imprisonment, whereas the
English law includes offenders liable to a maximum
of two years. According to the Belgian law, if an
offender does not commit a fresh offence within the
next five years from the date of his conditional
release, the conditional sentence passed upon him
cannot be proceeded with. If, on the contrary, he
commits a fresh breach of the criminal law within
the specified period he has to undergo the conditional
sentence as well as the fresh sentence for the new
offence. Conditional release has become a part of the
penal institutions of Australia and New Zealand, and

an Act, based on the lines of the English and Belgian laws, was passed in the French Chambers in 1891. In Germany the principle of conditional release is being gradually introduced. It now exists in the form of royal pardon for juveniles in Prussia, Saxony, and some of the smaller German states.[1]

Belgium is the only European country which has extensively resorted to the system of conditional release. According to the Belgian criminal returns for the year 1892, rather more than 10 per cent. of the offenders convicted before the various Belgian tribunals since the law of conditional condemnation came into operation were conditionally released. As a testimony to the success of the new law it is stated that only about 3 per cent. of those liberated offenders have so far been re-convicted. Results of this description are no doubt highly encouraging, and as far as they extend would seem to show that a sentence of imprisonment hanging over the head of an offender, but yet remaining unexecuted during good behaviour, is of a more deterrent character than a sentence of imprisonment which is actually carried into effect. As far as first offenders are concerned this result is intrinsically probable. A first offender who has had no experience of the interior of a prison regards imprisonment with an amount of dread and apprehension which usually vanishes once he has been inside prison walls and subjected to the routine of prison life. It is probable that this feeling of dread and apprehension is more vividly before him

[1] "Der Mitteilung der Internationalen Kriminalistischen Vereinigung." Funfter Band, 1896.

when he recollects that he has been sentenced to a
term of imprisonment, that the punishment is merely
suspended and will become a reality if he again
commits the slightest offence.   On the other hand,
it is to be remembered that the law of conditional
liberation has as yet been in operation for a very
short period of time, as far as Belgium is concerned,
and it is therefore possible that the exceedingly
favourable results which now appear to flow from
its operation may have to some extent to be dis-
counted in the light of additional and more prolonged
experience.   As a matter of fact additional experience
of almost all new methods of dealing with criminal
offenders by merely repressive measures has generally
been in the direction of showing that the originators
of these methods based too high expectations on
their prospective efficiency, and it is possible that
the hopes at present resting on the recorded results
of the system of conditional release may have to
be somewhat modified by the lessons of a fuller
experience.

CHAPTER X.

FINING.

MANY offences committed by juveniles are of such a
character or are committed under such circumstances
that it is impossible to deal with them by a resort to
admonition in any of its forms. A mere admonition
or a sentence of conditional discharge is in some
cases an inadequate penalty, or is at least considered
to be an inadequate penalty, for certain kinds of
offences committed by juvenile offenders. When
such circumstances arise the requirements of justice
are satisfied and the protection of the public is often
amply assured by the imposition of a fine. Of all
forms of punishment fining is undoubtedly one of the
best and most effective. It is almost the only form of
punishment which is not irremediable. Where corporal

punishment is resorted to, or where a sentence of imprisonment is imposed, it is almost impossible to repair the injury to the individual if it is afterwards discovered that he has been unjustly convicted. But where a fine is inflicted it is easy to make reparation when there is a miscarriage of justice by restoring the amount. Fining is a mode of punishment which might be made even more effective as an instrument of social defence if the proceeds of the fine were more largely utilised as a means of reparation to the sufferers from the crime. Certain practical difficulties are involved in the adoption of such a principle on an extended scale. Still these difficulties are not insuperable, and it is very probable that in the near future some sort of reparation to the victims will form part of the criminal law in all civilised communities.

It is satisfactory to observe that the practice of fining is being more and more used as a substitute for imprisonment. It is largely owing to the fact that fining is being increasingly substituted for imprisonment that the permanent prison population in English jails has decreased so considerably in recent years. I have frequently had occasion to call attention to the significance of this fact, and it is satisfactory to note that it is at last recognised in the criminal returns published in 1895. According to these returns, in the year 1882–3 in every thousand convictions for indictable offences tried before courts of summary jurisdiction 226 of the offenders were fined. In 1893 the number of offenders fined amounted to 270 per thousand. In other words, the practice of fining for the class of offences which has just been mentioned has increased considerably in ten years. An increased tendency to resort to fining instead of imprisonment is observable in criminal courts of all descriptions ; it constitutes a part of the general tendency to minimise punishment and to confine it within the limits absolutely necessary to secure the public safety.

One of the objections sometimes raised to the use of fining as a method of dealing with the delinquent juvenile population is the circumstance that penalties of a pecuniary character fall upon the parent rather than the child. This is to a certain extent the case, but it is to be recollected that in all forms of punishment a considerable portion of the penalty falls upon others besides the person who has directly incurred it. If the father of a family is sentenced to a period of imprisonment the punishment often falls as severely upon his innocent wife and children as it does upon himself. They participate in his disgrace and have to bear a part of the burden of it. In addition to this they have to endure the material discomfort which accompanies the loss of the breadwinner from the home. In many cases they become absolutely help-less and destitute, and pass through a greater amount of real privation than the delinquent himself. "We are members one of another," and it is impossible to object to the fining of juveniles on the ground that a part of the punishment has to be borne by the parent.

Imprisonment is the usual alternative to fining, and it is a matter of fact that the imprisonment of their children is more acutely felt by the majority of parents than the parting with a certain sum of money

in payment of a fine.   During the time the sentence
of imprisonment lasts the parent passes through all
the mental suffering and anxiety which arise from
the knowledge that his child is in prison.   It is true
the mental suffering and anxiety are not accompanied
by the material loss of so many pounds, shillings, and
pence.   But in most instances parents would far rather
endure this material loss than have their children
subjected to the degradations of prison life and the
stain upon the character which imprisonment involves.   The objection to fining is an objection which
applies with equal, if not greater, force to imprisonment.   In fact, it is an objection which applies to
punishment of all kinds.   There are very few people
in the world who are not bound to others by the ties
of home, kinship, or affection, and wherever these ties
exist the innocent suffer with the guilty, and in many
cases more than the guilty.

When fining is resorted to as a means of dealing
with juvenile offenders all the special circumstances
arising from the fact that the delinquent is a juvenile
require to be taken into consideration.   It is obvious,
in the first place, that weight should be given to the
circumstance that the offender is in a condition of
immaturity, and is not to be treated with the same
severity as if he were an adult.   Again it has to be
remembered that the amount of the fine has in most
instances to be paid by the parent, and should to
some extent be measured by the earning capacity of
the parent, and the calls which are made upon his
resources.   Other things being equal, a parent in
receipt of thirty shillings a week is not so able to pay

a fine as a parent in receipt of two pounds a week. And two parents in receipt of the same amount of weekly wages are in a very unequal financial position if the one is the father of a family of six children and the other has only two children. These are some instances of the circumstances necessary to be taken account of in apportioning the amount of a fine. It is of course impossible to lay down a rule applicable to all cases, inasmuch as no two cases are exactly alike. At the same time it may safely be said that the fact of an offender being a juvenile should have the effect of considerably reducing the proportions of the fine and facilitating the conditions under which it has to be paid.

One of the simplest ways of rendering the payment of a fine less burdensome is to accept the amount in instalments. Many parents who are distressed at the prospect of their children going to prison are at present obliged to let them go because the fine which has been imposed as an alternative will not be accepted in instalments. There are no doubt certain practical difficulties in the way of accepting payment of fines by instalments, and when the person who has to pay the fine is the offender himself these difficulties are sometimes of an insuperable character. But where the fine has to be paid not by the offender himself, but by his parents, the circumstances of the case are at once altered and simplified, and it ought not to be a matter of great practical difficulty to devise arrangements calculated to meet these circumstances. It is possible, for example, to utilise the Post Office as a receiving place for fines requiring to be paid by instalments. Almost all the machinery is already in existence at the Post Office for doing work of this character, and it would be very much simpler for the class of people who are under the necessity of paying fines by instalments to pay them at an office close to their doors than to have to transmit them to a distant police-court.

Cases are frequently coming under one's personal observation of men and women who attribute their descent to a life of habitual crime to the fact that their fathers or mothers were unable to pay the fine arising out of their conviction for a first offence. The alternative of imprisonment had to be accepted and endured. As a general rule imprisonment, no matter how mild it is made, is a demoralising experience. It is the severest blow which can possibly be aimed at a young person's self-respect, and if it is inflicted at a time when the mind is peculiarly sensitive to the opinion of the world, it is no wonder that it leads to disastrous results of a permanent kind. To have been in prison is a stigma of which the erring juvenile can never get rid. This he dimly and even sometimes clearly apprehends. It often has the effect of making him seek the society and companionship of others who have been in a similar plight. Among them he will not be looked down upon or upbraided, among them accordingly his · lot is henceforth cast, and the career of an habitual criminal is begun. It is safe to say that among the combination of conditions which tend to produce the habitual criminal a first experience of prison occupies

a considerable place. In many cases this first experience might be avoided as far as juveniles are concerned if some method of paying fines by instalments
were in practical operation on lines which can be
easily worked and understood by the class of people
who have to pay these fines.

Another useful method of dealing with juveniles,
and in fact with adults as well, is to combine fining
with imprisonment. According to the existing provisions of the criminal law an offender who is fined,
let us say twenty shillings, or twenty days' imprisonment, must pay the whole amount of the fine, even
if he has spent five, ten, or fifteen days of the alternative sentence in prison. It very often happens that
a convicted man or his family is unable to collect the
money for the fine till he has spent a certain time in
prison. In cases of this kind the sentence, instead of
being a penalty of twenty days or twenty shillings,
becomes a sentence of ten or fifteen days' imprisoment
and a fine of twenty shillings in addition. In other
words, the severity of the sentence is increased, as
the case may be, one-quarter, one-half, or even three-
quarters, owing to the temporary poverty of the
offender. In some cases it may be increased even
more, but in every case it is increased when a portion
of the alternative sentence of imprisonment has been
served before the fine is paid. When a magistrate
passes a sentence of so many shillings fine or in
default so many days' imprisonment, it is not his
intention that the convicted person should be imprisoned part of the time and likewise fined the full
amount. But under existing statutes the magistrate

has no option.   He is powerless to prevent a mode
of punishment from being inflicted which he did not
decree, and which is more severe than the punishment
he did decree.

It would be easy to remedy such an anomaly in
the criminal law.   The amount of imprisonment endured should count towards the reduction of the fine.
If this simple expedient were adopted a man who is
sentenced to a fine of twenty shillings or twenty days'
imprisonment would have the period of detention reduced by one-half on payment of one-half of the fine.
Assuming that the punitive equivalent of twenty
shillings is twenty days' imprisonment, it is only
reasonable and just that the payment of ten shillings
should diminish the duration of imprisonment by ten
days.   This was the conclusion arrived at by a
departmental committee appointed by Sir George
Trevelyan, when Secretary of State for Scotland, to
inquire into the best means of dealing with habitual
delinquents.   The report of the committee states
that "prisoners committed to prison in default of
payment of a fine should be permitted to work out
their sentences by a combination of fine and imprisonment.   It should not be necessary for them, having
worked out half their term of imprisonment, to remain in prison for the full term unless they pay the
entire fine.   They should be liberated on any day of
their imprisonment on payment of such proportion
of their fines as the term of imprisonment still to be
undergone bears to the entire sentence."   "We are
informed," continues the committee, "that this system
was at one time prevalent in Scotland, but it was

given up because it was found to be illegal. So far as the committee is concerned, it is but fair to give the entire credit of the suggestion to Mr. Napier, governor of Greenock prison."

As an illustration of the hardships of the existing law the committee mention the case of a woman who was sent to Greenock prison for thirty days in default of payment of a fine of forty shillings. After she had been twenty-one days in prison her husband died. Her husband belonged to a burial society. In order to procure her liberation her friends borrowed forty shillings on the security of the sum she was entitled to from the benefit society, and the fine was paid. "Had that woman when convicted," says the report, "possessed forty shillings she would not have gone to prison at all, and would probably have experienced a more improving and refining influence in ministering to the wants of her dying husband. But being moneyless at the time of her conviction, she had ultimately to expiate her offence by payment of the full fine imposed, and three weeks' imprisonment into the bargain. Now the law in imposing a fine as a penalty for an offence, and prescribing imprisonment only in default of payment, evidently meant to mitigate and not to aggravate the punishment."

The Scotch committee, with the thoroughness which characterised all their proceedings, put their suggestions to a practical test. Mr. Napier received five pounds, with instructions to apply it in illustration of his scheme. The following are the cases with which he dealt :—" W. J. C., a case of assault, committed for five days in default of payment of seven shillings and sixpence. After being three days in prison succeeded in raising three shillings, and the balance of four-and-sixpence being provided out of the fund, he was liberated, and two days of his imprisonment was saved. J. S., a case of assault, committed for ten days in default of payment of a fine of twenty shillings. After five days' imprisonment raised ten shillings, and the balance being paid out of the fund, five days' imprisonment was remitted. E. M., another case of assault, committed for twenty days in default of payment of a fine of forty shillings. After five days' imprisonment raised thirty shillings, and the balance being paid out of the fund, fifteen days' imprisonment was remitted. At a cost, therefore, of twenty-four shillings and sixpence to the fund, forty-three shillings was collected in the shape of fines which would never otherwise have been got, and the State was saved twenty-two days' maintenance of a prisoner in jail. Mr. Napier thought that it would be waste of money to continue the experiment, as to secure it full justice it would be requisite that the system should be generally known. But he expressed his belief that if it were known that less than half the fine imposed would be accepted, a large number of prisoners, probably one-half, would take advantage of it."

One of the immediate results of increasing the elasticity of the criminal law in the direction of combining a fine with imprisonment in the manner just indicated, would be to reduce the proportions of the prison population. According to the Scotch committee's report, close on 35 per cent. of the

prison population in Scotland are incarcerated because of inability to pay in full the fine imposed
upon them. If, as is estimated, one-half of these
prisoners took advantage of a provision which enabled
them to reckon imprisonment as wiping out a part of
the fine, the prison population would be diminished
to this extent. Inasmuch as each prisoner costs the
country twenty-five pounds a year for maintenance,
a decrease of the prison population means a corresponding decrease of public expenditure on penal
establishments. A reduction of the average daily
prison population to the extent of one thousand
ultimately means a reduction of expenditure on
prisons to the extent of twenty-five thousand pounds
per annum or thereabouts. This is a consideration
not to be lost sight of in estimating the advantages
to be derived from adding to the elasticity of our
present methods of imposing and collecting fines.
It is also to be recollected that the additional fines
collected, if the system here advocated were in
operation, would amount to a very considerable sum.
This sum would also go towards reducing criminal
expenditure.

In short, the proposal to combine fining with
imprisonment instead of merely using the one as
the alternative of the other, as is done at present,
is in the happy position of possessing a maximum of advantages with an almost entire absence
of corresponding defects. These benefits may
be summed up as consisting of a reduction of
expenditure on crime, a reduction of the number
of people shut up in prisons, a rational adjustment

15

of substitutionary penalties, and a diminution of punishment unaccompanied by a decrease of social security. The application of this system to juvenile offenders would enable many poor people who are unable to pay the full penalty imposed upon their children to shorten their detention in prison by paying a part of the fine. In this way the law would afford a legitimate satisfaction to parental affection and solicitude which it now unmeaningly refuses; it would afford this satisfaction without in any way compromising the public interest.

Compulsory labour without imprisonment is not an unknown punishment in some continental countries. It is a method of dealing with petty offenders which is or has been in operation in France, Italy, some of the cantons of Switzerland, and several of the German States.[1] In the canton of Vaud an offender who is merely fined and cannot pay the amount has his name put upon the books of the State receiver for employment on public works. A notification of this fact is sent to the surveyor of the district, and to the nearest inspector of forests. The offender is then called upon to work at the maintenance and construction of roads, or to work in the woods. In this manner the amount of the fine is worked off at the rate of from three to six francs a day according to the man's industry and the value of his labour. In cases where the offender will not perform the work assigned to him, the fine is transformed into a sentence of imprisonment. It was stated by M.

---

[1] "Zeitschrift für die gesamte Strafrechtswissenschaft." Neunter Band, pp. 764–70.

Correvon, one of the Swiss delegates at the International Prison Congress held at Rome, that the operation of the law was not altogether satisfactory. But he did not regard the difficulties connected with it as insurmountable. It is easy to foresee the obstacles which would surround the working of a law of this character when applied to adult offenders. In a considerable number of instances the sentence to compulsory labour would be disregarded. This would at once involve the necessity of re-arresting the offender and committing him to prison after all. At the same time there are no doubt many offenders to whom a sentence of compulsory labour without imprisonment would be quite practicable. Many offenders could get sureties who would bind themselves to see that the sentence to compulsory labour was not evaded. In all cases where sureties were forthcoming a sentence of this description would be likely to work well, even if applied to adult offenders. But it would undoubtedly work better if applied to juveniles living under the parental roof, and subject to parental supervision and control. It would be distinctly to the parent's interest to take care that a sentence of compulsory labour was carried into effect. If a law relating to compulsory labour were in force, the parent would be well aware that unless this law was complied with in the case of his child, the penal alternative would be fining or imprisonment. Either of these alternatives is more severe than compulsory labour. Compulsory labour would naturally be the form of punishment he would select for his child.

Something very much akin to the principle of
compulsory labour is already in existence in Great
Britain, in the day industrial school system. Most
of the children in our day industrial schools are
committed to these institutions by the magistrates.
In these schools the children are detained from eight
o'clock in the morning till six o'clock at night.
According to the reports of the Inspector of Industrial Schools, the attendance is not all that could be
wished. At the Leeds Day Industrial School, for
instance, there were nineteen cases of truancy during
the year ended September, 1893. On the day of
inspection the school population amounted to 124
boys and girls. When the class of children committed to day industrial schools, and the homes from
which they come, are taken into consideration, nineteen cases of truancy during the whole year in a
school of 124 children cannot be regarded as very
high. Of these schools as a whole the inspector says
that they are " without exception going on well, and
do really good useful work at very little cost to the
Treasury. It is always a pleasure to go into these
schools and to see the order apparent everywhere ;
and the children almost invariably look bright and
cheerful." If compulsory detention and compulsory
labour is so successful when applied to children committed to day industrial schools, there is considerable
reason to believe that a system on somewhat similar
lines would be equally successful if applied to children
convicted of certain kinds of petty offences. Children
of this class are, as a rule, the product of large cities,
and it is in large cities that some form of compulsory

labour without imprisonment could be most easily put in force. If a penalty of this nature became a part of the criminal law, and was fairly successful in its operation, it would possess many distinct advantages. It would still further reduce the number of children who are at present committed to prison. It would be an alternative to imprisonment in cases where the parents were too poor to pay a fine, and the penalty would fall directly on the offender.

CHAPTER XI.

CORPORAL PUNISHMENT.

Prevalence of corporal punishment—The punishment of death—
The death penalty in the case of juveniles—Flogging and
whipping—Whipping in continental penal codes—Whipping
in England, Scotland, Ireland, and the Colonies—Balance of
international opinion hostile to whipping—Opinion in England
on corporal punishment—Opinion in Scotland—Whipping as
an alternative to fining—Methods of inflicting whipping in
Scotland—Imprisonment or whipping for girls—Opinions
adverse to whipping—Whipping or Imprisonment—Conclusion.

CORPORAL punishment is the oldest and most primitive method of dealing with criminal offenders,
and it is only within a comparatively recent period
that it ceased to be the principal method among
modern European communities. It is not worth
while to describe in detail the almost infinite variety
of ways in which corporal punishment was inflicted ;
in fact, some of these punishments were of such a
diabolical character that it is revolting even to
mention them. Any one wishing to draw up an
indictment against humanity will find material for
this purpose to his heart's content in the atrocious
punishments formerly in the statute-book, and in the

still more atrocious manner in which these punishments were carried into effect. Death, torture,
branding, mutilation, flogging, were the favourite
methods of maintaining such social security as
existed in the olden days. The European conscience
has revolted against torture, branding, and mutilation : these forms of punishment have disappeared,
but the penalties of death and flogging are still
regarded as essential instruments of social protection
among many civilised communities. The punishment of death is still retained in France, Germany,
Austria, Russia, Spain, Great Britian, the Colonies,
and in most parts of the American Union. It has
been abolished in Italy, Holland, and in the states of
Michigan, Rhode Island, Wisconsin, and Maine. In
Switzerland it is a punishment which is left to the
discretion of the various cantons ; and although it is
not formally abolished, no capital punishment has
been inflicted in Belgium since 1863, nor in Finland
since 1826.

In countries where the death penalty forms a part
of the criminal law the tendency is to confine its
operation within the narrowest possible limits.
Wilful murder is almost the only crime for which
the penalty of death is in actual operation, and
even in cases of wilful murder capital executions are
slowly diminishing. Wherever there is the least
justification for doing so, extenuating circumstances
are admitted either during the trial or after conviction as a ground for commuting the death penalty to
a sentence of imprisonment. Immaturity is one of
these extenuating circumstances, and in some penal

codes (the German penal code, for example) juveniles are expressly excluded from the punishment of death. In their case the punishment takes the form of a sentence of from three to fifteen years' imprisonment. Among communities where a provision of this character does not exist in the statute-book a somewhat similar principle is acted upon in the actual administration of justice. In practice capital punishment has passed away as a method of dealing with juvenile offenders, and as there is no probability of its restoration it is unnecessary to discuss it.

On the other hand, corporal punishment, in the shape of flogging or whipping, is in active operation in the treatment of juvenile delinquency. But it is far from being universally recognised as a legitimate form of punishment. It does not exist, for instance, in the penal codes of France, Italy, Germany, Austria, Russia, Switzerland, and Sweden. The exclusion of flogging from the criminal legislation of these great communities is a proof of the extent to which civilised opinion is divided on the subject of corporal punishment. Flogging in some form or other forms a part of the criminal law of England, Scotland, Ireland, Norway, and Denmark, and several of the colonies. In Norway whipping is a very common form of punishment for children between ten and fifteen years of age. In Denmark whipping is used for girls up to the age of twelve, and for boys up to the age of fifteen ; in addition to this, flogging is resorted to for youths between the ages of fifteen and eighteen if they are medically certified as fit to endure it. As far as I am aware Denmark is the only civilised community where the whipping of girls is a punishment admitted by the criminal law. [1]

In the year 1893 the number of children sentenced to be whipped in England by courts of summary jurisdiction amounted to 2,858, and it is probable that a few more were sentenced at assizes and courts of quarter sessions. In Scotland in the same year 335 boys were sentenced to be whipped ; in Ireland whipping is very rarely resorted to, and in the Colonies it is a mode of punishment which is very seldom inflicted on the young. In the colony of Victoria, for instance, only forty-four juveniles were corporally punished in the seventeen years prior to 1890, and in New South Wales no case occurred in 1890 in which juveniles were ordered to be whipped by courts of summary jurisdiction. [2]

It must be admitted that the corporal punishment of juveniles as it exists in Great Britain is surrounded by a considerable number of safeguards. Where a child is supposed to be in delicate health a medical man must be consulted before the sentence can take effect. When a child is under ten years of age the birch rod used for executing the sentence must be lighter than the instrument employed for older offenders. The number of strokes is also regulated by Acts of Parliament. Where a child is under twelve the number of strokes must not exceed six, and where he is under fourteen the number must not exceed twelve. The whipping takes place privately.

[1] See " Le Droit criminel des États Européens," Berlin and Paris, 1894.

[2] See Official Year Books of Victoria and New South Wales.

It is administered by a constable, but another constable of higher rank must be present to witness it, and the parents or guardians of the child may also be present if they wish.

The absence of whipping from the penal codes of so many important European peoples is a fact of great significance, and compels us to consider how far it is calculated to serve the ends which punishment has in view. In so far as the statute-books are to be taken as an index of the deliberate judgments of civilised communities, it must be admitted that the balance of international opinion is hostile to whipping. As has already been stated, the only countries which retain this form of punishment as a judicial penalty are Denmark, Norway, and the United Kingdom and its offshoots. All other civilised nationalities are hostile to it. On a matter of this nature a distinct preponderance of international opinion is worthy of serious consideration. There is an international as well as a national conscience. When the international conscience condemns flogging and whipping as legitimate instruments of social defence it is incumbent on the upholders of these modes of punishment to re-examine the grounds on which they rest in the light of this condemnation. It is true the decisions of the international conscience are not decisive in relation to questions of penal law. Penal law, as well as all kinds of law, is, and must always remain up to a certain point, national in its character. But where principles of punishment are involved which are within the scope of penal law as a whole, these principles, if they have become merely national in their application, must be justified by special reasons before the bar of international opinion.

In England and Scotland national opinion, so far as it finds expression, is on the whole in favour of retaining corporal correction as a means of dealing with juvenile offenders. Most of the witnesses examined before the Royal Commission on Reformatory and Industrial Schools expressed their belief in the utility of whipping. Sir Godfrey Lushington, late permanent Under-Secretary for the Home Department, stated in his evidence that all that was needed for certain classes of young offenders was to order them to be whipped and sent about their business. Mr. Rogers, assistant-inspector of reformatory and industrial schools, was of opinion that children might be whipped. Captain Brooks, of the Feltham Industrial School, advocated whipping in cases of truancy, and Mr. Whitwill, a Bristol magistrate of great experience, believed in whipping in cases of stone-throwing, window-breaking, and boyish delinquencies of a similar character. Another witness, Mr. Rathbone, gave it as his opinion that the neglect and rough treatment to which some children are subjected are infinitely more severe than any corporal punishment the magistrate would inflict. On the other hand, Mr. Cook Spens, sheriff substitute for Lanarkshire, objected to the criminal courts ordering a whipping. In their report the Royal Commissioners agreed with the majority of the witnesses. In all cases of offences by children under fourteen they recommended that the magistrates should have power to order boys to be whipped.

Sir Charles Cameron's committee are in substantial agreement with the Royal Commissioners as to the advisability of whipping for juveniles. "We are of opinion," they say, "that in police-court cases, where punishment of some sort must be inflicted, whipping is infinitely preferable to imprisonment, and that the age up to which it is competent might with great advantage be extended." In addition to advocating an extension of the age at which whipping might be administered, Sir Charles Cameron's committee were also of opinion that it should be utilised as an alternative to fining. At present it is a matter of considerable doubt whether a magistrate has the power to order a juvenile to be fined, or in default to be whipped. The usual alternative to a fine is so many days' imprisonment. The question therefore arises whether it would not be expedient to enlarge the discretion of the magistrate in the selection of alternative penalties. The disastrous results of imprisonment are so manifest that an enlargement of the catalogue of legitimate alternatives is one of the necessities of the hour. According to the wording of existing Acts of Parliament it is doubtful whether magistrates have any alternative besides imprisonment when a fine is not paid. It is the opinion of Sir Charles Cameron's committee that all doubt on this subject should be removed. It should be made perfectly clear that whipping may be used as a substitute for the non-payment of a fine.

Whilst advocating the retention and even the extension of whipping, Sir Charles Cameron's committee were very well aware of the disinclination of many magistrates to adopt this mode of punishment in dealing with juvenile offenders. It is no use putting laws upon the statute-book if these enactments are so repugnant to the administrators of justice that they will not make use of them. Many magistrates have a rooted objection to whipping under any circumstances, and many others whose objection to whipping is not of so absolute a character are yet opposed to the instrument with which it is at present inflicted. For all practical purposes magistrates who are hostile to whipping on principle, as well as magistrates who are hostile to the way in which it is administered, belong to the same class. Neither of them will use it as a mode of punishment. In order to meet the difficulties of those magistrates who are not opposed to the principle of whipping, but object to the birch rod as a suitable instrument for administering it, the Scotch committee propose that the " tawse " should be permitted as an alternative to the birch rod, and that the punishment should be administered on the hand of the offender. "To meet the widespread objection to the use of the birch," says the report, ' it might be well to allow magistrates to order the punishment to be inflicted on the hand of the offender with a leathern tawse, an implement to the innocuous yet deterrent effects of which many of them will be able to testify from personal experience."

We have already pointed out that in Denmark whipping is in use for girls up to the age of twelve. The Scotch committee consider that the results of sending young girls to prison are so lamentable that they are prepared to recommend something of a similar character for Scotland. "Whipping with a birch," they say, "is not a suitable punishment for girls, but so lamentable does your committee consider the results of sending young girls to prison, that they venture to recommend in cases similar to those in which whipping can be inflicted on boys, girls might be subjected to a punishment which is meted out to them at public schools, and which has been sanctioned in the case of female industrial schools, namely, strokes on the hand with a leathern strap or tawse. Such a punishment would meet the case of boisterous conduct in the streets or a petty theft of coals much more fitly, and with infinitely less disastrous results to the girl's future, than a sentence of imprisonment."

It will be seen from the numerous quotations which have just been made from experts, Royal commissions, and committees, that the drift of opinion is at present running in the direction of substituting whipping for imprisonment in the case of juvenile offenders, and that one committee has even ventured to recommend a mild form of corporal punishment for girls. On the other hand, we must not omit to mention that some authorities are of opinion that imprisonment is the more effective punishment. In his evidence before the Reformatory and Industrial School Commission the late Mr. Lloyd Baker said, " I consider a short imprisonment very much better than a whipping. Whipping is cheaper and more readily done, but it has not the same effect upon boys. The violent pain is very soon over, and the boy does not like the chance of getting it again, but that is almost all; whereas a week or a fortnight in prison gives a boy time for meditation, and he thinks over what he has done, and it takes a hold upon his mind, and he is far less likely to go wrong again than after a whipping. A whipping will do a great deal of good the first time, but I do not think that whipping a second time does good, and I think that a whipping a third time generally does mischief." In proof of these statements Mr. Baker produced a letter from Mr. Wheatley Balme, an experienced Yorkshire magistrate. In this letter Mr. Balme said, " As a young magistrate four and thirty years ago I was strongly in favour of birching. My faith was shaken by observing in the Black Book at quarter sessions how frequently a whipping appeared at the beginning of a long list of re-convictions. This led me to inquire further, and I got Mr. Shepherd, the governor of Wakefield prison, to go very carefully into a large number of cases of juvenile crime re-corded there. We found that while on the average about 30 per cent. of juvenile offenders sentenced to ordinary imprisonment were re-convicted, of those on whom a whipping had formed part of the sentence no less than 60 per cent. were re-convicted."

In estimating the value of these statistics it is to be borne in mind that juveniles sentenced to a combination of whipping and imprisonment are of a more hardened class than juveniles sentenced to imprisonment only. It is probable that this fact would account, at least to a considerable extent, for the much higher percentage of re-convictions among such offenders. Where offenders have become habituated to a life of crime, the effect of punishment upon their future conduct descends to a minimum, and it is very likely that the twofold punishment of whipping and imprisonment was dealt out to juveniles of this description. But, even admitting this to be correct, it is no doubt significant that re-convictions are much higher among juveniles corporally punished than among the same class of offenders who are merely imprisoned. It would, however, be rash to infer from Mr. Baker's statistics that prison is more calculated to deter than corporal punishment. In order to test the comparative efficacy of these two methods of punishment it would be necessary to have statistics on a larger scale, and covering a wider area.

In the meantime it is perfectly safe to remark that neither imprisonment nor corporal punishment possesses much value in preventing a repetition of the offence unless other conditions of an entirely different character are brought into operation. Unless punishment is accompanied by an amelioration of the individual or social conditions out of which the offence has sprung, the offence will be repeated. It is an amelioration of the conditions which produce the offence which prevents its repetition; and in cases where it is not repeated it is fallacious to assume that the cure has been effected either by corporal chastisement or a short period of imprisonment. An examination of individual cases at once exposes the fallacy of such an assumption. When such an examination is undertaken it will almost always be found that the offence is repeated if the juvenile returns after his punishment to the same miserable social circumstances in which he lived before. But in a considerable proportion of cases the offence is not repeated if the social circumstances of the young offender are ameliorated after punishment. Facts of this character conclusively show that it is not the punishment which prevents a recurrence of the offence. Its recurrence is prevented by removing the adverse circumstances out of which it arose.

CHAPTER XII.

IMPRISONMENT.

Punishment involving loss of liberty—Slavery—Banishment—
Banishment in modern penal codes—Local banishment in
France and Italy—Transportation in Great Britain—Interdiction—Imprisonment—Imprisonment in antiquity—Imprisonment in the Middle Ages—Imprisonment arose as a reaction
against more severe punishments—Houses of correction for
petty offenders—Treatment of offenders in houses of correction—Houses of correction used for serious offenders—The
modern prison based on the ancient monastery—The cellular
system—Filippo Franci, Pope Clement XI., Vilain, Benjamin
Franklin—Continuous solitude—The Pennsylvanian system—
The Auburn system—The progressive system—Archbishop
Whately—Captain Maconochie—Prison life hinders the working
of the progressive system—Prisons in disrepute—Causes of this :
recidivism—Old offenders—Short sentences and old offenders
—Improved methods of detention—Substitutes for imprisonment—The reaction against imprisonment as seen in the treatment of juvenile offenders—Effect of imprisonment on the
young—Age at which children are liable to imprisonment—
Age of penal responsibility in continental criminal codes—Age
of penal responsibility in English law—Committal of children
to prison before trial—Detention of children before trial—The
police cells—Police-court missions—Detention in the workhouse
—Children after conviction—Sir J. Stephen on juvenile responsibility—A knowledge of right and wrong is not an adequate test
of penal responsibility—Prison treatment of juveniles—Prison
dietary—Prison often the final stage of a series of privations—
The discharged prisoner—Prison discipline should be synony-
mous with industrial discipline—The prison cell—Its effects on
the mind—Short sentences and industrial occupations—The

juvenile prisoner's relations with the outside world—Prisons not constructed for juveniles—The supervision of imprisoned juveniles—The liberation of juvenile offenders—The preparations for liberty—Conditional liberation.

WE shall now proceed to the consideration of punishments which involve the loss of liberty. Punishments of this character may be divided into three classes—slavery, banishment, and imprisonment. Educational institutions for juvenile offenders, such as reformatory and industrial schools, are also accompanied by a partial loss of liberty, but inasmuch as these establishments exist for educational rather than punitive purposes, it is better to treat them as a distinctive class. Loss of liberty in the form of slavery was a common form of punishment among the nations of antiquity. It was also in use among partially civilised or uncivilised races, such as the Aztecs of Mexico and the people of Oceania, and is at present in operation among some of the Indo-Chinese populations. As a method of dealing with criminal offenders it does not exist in modern European communities. The Western conscience has decisively turned its back upon the institution of slavery. As a punishment for crime slavery merely possesses an historical interest as far as the West is concerned. It is therefore needless to discuss it here.

Banishment is one of the very oldest and most widely spread forms of punishment. It has existed in all stages of civilisation and among almost all races as an accredited instrument of social displeasure and defence. Among the uncivilised tribes of Africa and the scattered communities of the

southern seas, banishment is a portion of the
unwritten criminal code. It is a legal institution
among many of the races in the Far East, and if
we travel back into antiquity it will be found in-
scribed in the surviving fragments of ancient Egyptian
law.[1]   Banishment is a familiar weapon in Greek and
Roman jurisprudence, and it exists in one form or
another in the penal codes of several modern communities. In Russia banishment is a very common
method of punishment. It exists in three forms :
deportation with hard labour, or, as it is called in
Russia, *katorga ;* deportation with obligatory residence in Siberia ; and simple deportation. Simple
deportation consists in sentencing the offender to
exile in Siberia, or to exile in one of the more remote
provinces of the empire. Punishment of this description is only applicable to the privileged classes. In
France banishment is also a portion of the criminal
code, and, as in Russia, it assumes three distinct
forms. For political offences of a secondary character
the offender may be banished from French territory
for a period of from five to ten years ; for crime
against the common law criminals may be sent to
French Guiana or to New Caledonia. In addition
to these penalties a sort of local banishment exists
in France consisting of certain special restrictions
with regard to residence and liberty of movement.
Offenders liberated, as we should say, on ticket-of-
leave are, instead of being placed under police
supervision, sometimes subjected to these special

---

[1] See "Grundriss der Ethnologischen Jurisprudenz," von A. H.
Post., Zweiter Band, p. 284, Oldenburg und Leipzig, 1895.

restrictions. They are forbidden to live in certain localities, such, for instance, as the large cities of Paris, Marseilles, Lyons, and Bordeaux. The new Italian penal code has also a sort of local banishment somewhat similar in character to the French.

Restrictions upon liberty in the shape of compulsory deportation to another country do not exist in the United Kingdom or in the United States. As a means of dealing with adult criminals it undoubtedly produced grave abuses in the past, but it is questionable whether these abuses are inevitable accompaniments of the system, or whether they arose from the defective manner in which it was administered. The best of systems if badly administered will produce bad results. The evils of the old system of transportation arose to a large extent out of the atrocious severity with which the convicts were treated. Some of the officials exhibited the ferocity of wild beasts in the treatment of the prisoners committed to their charge. One of the fundamental rules of efficient prison management is that a severe example should be made of every official convicted of inflicting illegal and excessive punishments. It was unquestionably owing to a neglect of this wholesome precaution that transportation was often attended with such deplorable results. As far as the treatment of juvenile offenders is concerned, it is unnecessary for us to discuss the question of transportation. Transportation is hardly applicable to persons in a condition of immaturity. Before the offender has attained the full measure of physical and mental development, it is only in the rarest cases that it would be either wise or just to expel him permanently from the society in which he has been born.

The case is somewhat different when we come to consider the expediency of interdicting the juvenile offender from living in certain specified portions of the realm. In a preceding chapter it has been pointed out that large cities are the hotbeds of juvenile crime, as well as of criminality in general. That liberated prisoners are often forbidden to live in large cities such as Paris and Lyons is a proof that the same opinion is entertained in France. The principle of interdiction is undoubtedly a sound one. If crime is from five to ten times more rampant in some districts than it is in others, a juvenile who has been once convicted is much more likely to become an habitual offender if he goes to reside in a place where the percentage of crime is above, rather than in a district where the percentage of crime is below the average. At the same time it is to be remembered that many sound principles are of little practical utility owing to the difficulty of putting them into effective use. A sound principle is one thing, its application in the midst of existing social conditions is often quite another thing; and for purposes of penal legislation a principle must not only be sound, it must also possess the merit of being adaptable to practical needs. To put an interdict upon certain places of abode can only be effectively applied when the individualisation of punishment has assumed a much more prominent position in the administration of justice than it does at present. In certain cases of juvenile crime the utility of the French and Italian law of interdict is unquestionable, and the application of such a law would undoubtedly be productive of the best results. But before it could be put into operation all the circumstances of the offender would require to be taken into the most careful consideration in order to ascertain whether the proposed penalty was suitable to the concrete individual case. The individualisation of punishment—in other words, the adaptation of punishment to the individual circumstances of each offender—is one of the most pressing requirements of the time in the domain of criminal jurisprudence. It exists as a sort of embryonic principle in all criminal codes, and it is to a certain extent resorted to in practice. But until it becomes a fundamental part of all criminal proceedings, many valuable reforms in criminal law must remain in abeyance, or if enacted can only produce imperfect results.

We now come to the last kind of punishment which involves the loss of liberty—namely, imprisonment. Imprisonment is a less primitive method of dealing with offenders against the law than slavery or banishment. It is for this reason that we do not find any traces of its existence among many uncivilised races. Even among communities standing as high in the scale of social development as the Chinese, the practice of imprisonment does not exist as a penalty for crime. Chinese prisons are merely establishments for the safe custody of offenders awaiting trial or awaiting punishment.

It is also a well-known dictum of Roman law that prisons in the Roman empire are to be used for the

safe custody and not for the punishment of the
prisoner. In practice this principle was acted upon
by most European communities till about the period
of the Reformation. Before that period cases sometimes occurred, especially in Italy, in which an
offender was committed to prison as a punishment.
But as a rule imprisonment in the modern sense of
the word occupied a very obscure place on the list of
pains and penalties, and, except among the monastic
orders, had hardly come into existence as a regular
means of dealing with serious crime. In the reigns
of Henry VIII. and Edward VI. several enactments
of a severe character were passed against "sturdy
vagabonds, valiant beggars," and other offenders
against public order, but the usual penalties attached
to these offences were whipping, mutilation, slavery,
or death.

Towards the end of the sixteenth century and
the beginning of the seventeenth we witness the
commencement of a reaction against these punishments. In England, Holland, and Germany, a new
form of penal treatment in the shape of houses of
correction came into prominence. In the reign of
James I. it was enacted that houses of this description should be established in every county. At first
these houses of correction were principally used for
the punishment of petty offenders against public
order. These people are described in the quaint
language of the time as "rogues, vagabonds, idle,
loitering, and lewd persons, and masterless men and
women." In the thirty-first year of the reign of
Queen Elizabeth the justices of the peace for the

county of Suffolk assembled at Bury St. Edmunds and drew up a number of orders, rules, and directions for the treatment of such offenders. These rules and regulations enable us to form some sort of idea of the manner in which houses of correction were then conducted. " It is ordered and agreed upon," say the justices, " that every strong or sturdy rogue at his or her first entrance into the said house shall have twelve stripes upon his bare skin with the said whip provided for the said house, and every young rogue or idle loiterer six stripes with the said whip. And that every one of them without fail at their first coming into the said house shall have put upon him, her, or them, some clog, chain, collar of iron, ring, or manacle, such as the keeper of the said house shall think meet, so as he may answer for every one as well for his forthcoming, as also that they shall be quiet and do no hurt for the time they shall continue in the said house." From the wording of this order it appears that it was the custom to whip every prisoner committed to a house of correction, and in order to secure his safe custody to put him in chains. Severities of this acute description would now be regarded as intolerable, but as a set-off it appears that the inmates were abundantly supplied with food. " It is ordered," say the justices, " that every person committed to the said house shall have for their diet the portions of meat and drink following, and not above, namely, at every dinner and supper on the flesh days bread made of rye eight ounces troy weight, with a pint of porridge, a quarter of a pound of flesh, and a pint of beer. And on every fish day

at dinner and supper the like quantity, made either
of milk or pease or such like, and the third part of a
pound of cheese, or good herring, or two white or red,
according as the keeper of the house shall think
meet."   Well-conducted prisoners had an extra
allowance of food.   "It is ordered that such persons
as will apply their work shall have allowance of beer
and bread between meals."   But, on the other hand, it
is ordered "that they which will not work shall have
no allowance but bread and beer only until they will
conform themselves to work."

The establishment on an extensive scale of houses
of correction for petty offenders gradually led to
their being used for persons convicted of serious
crimes.   It was in the course of the seventeenth
century that the original purpose of these penal
establishments was enlarged, and criminals of all
sorts began to be found within their walls.   One of
the first results of this change was the promiscuous
association of all classes of delinquents, and in order
to counteract the inevitable evils of indiscriminate
association it was essential that prisons should be
constructed upon a principle which would effect this
object.   A hint was taken from the methods of
punishment in use in the monasteries.   It was a very
old practice in these institutions—a practice dating at
least from the sixth century—to condemn the re-
calcitrant monk to a period of detention and isolation
in his cell.   In many of the monastic institutions
special cells were set apart for this purpose.   In the
Rule of St. Benedict, who founded the monastery of
Monte Casino, near Naples, in the year 529, it is laid

down that delinquent inmates of the cloister shall be shut up in their cells as long as the abbot considers it expedient. In the same century St. Columba prescribes a period of complete isolation in a cell for excommunicated nuns. St. Cæsarius of Arles also made regulations to the effect that offending brothers shall be confined in a dark and solitary cell. In fact, almost all the monastic orders resorted to cellular confinement in one form or another as a mode of punishment and of enforcing monastic discipline.

One of the first recorded instances of the application of cellular imprisonment to ordinary offenders dates from the year 1667. At that period a Florentine priest named Filippo Franci became the head of an institution at Florence established for the purpose of reclaiming abandoned and delinquent juveniles. Cellular separation was one of the methods adopted by Franci in the organisation of his charitable work. The children were admitted to his institution at night so that no one should see them enter, and each time an inmate left his cell he had to wear a sort of mask so that no one should be able to recognise him. The system adopted by Franci at Florence was shortly afterwards followed in its main outlines at Rome. In the beginning of the eighteenth century Pope Clement XI. opened the celebrated juvenile prison of San Michele (1704). In this establishment the inmates worked in common during the day and were subjected to cellular separation at night. From Italy the cellular system found its way to Belgium. Here it was applied not merely to juveniles but to offenders of all ages. There may be no direct evidence of the

kind which Mr. Wines in his interesting book on
" Punishment and Reformation " asks for to show that
Vilain, the founder of the prison at Ghent (1772), was
aware of the experiment made in Italy about a
century before.   But it is exceedingly unlikely that a
man of his wide intelligence was unacquainted with
the institutions on the cellular principle which had
been established in the south of Europe.   But whether
Vilain was acquainted with these experiments or not,
it is in any case the fact that it was he who gave the
most important impetus to the cellular system of
imprisonment.

Largely under the influence of Benjamin Franklin
this method of prison treatment was transplanted
across the Atlantic and established at Philadelphia
in its most rigorous form.   Neither Vilain nor Pope
Clement had dreamt of keeping the prisoner in perpetual solitude.   Both these eminent reformers were
quite content with enforcing the rule of cellular separation at night and labour in common under careful
supervision during the day.   But the Quakers of Pennsylvania, in their zeal for separation, devised a plan of
rigid and unremitting solitude both day and night,
and unaccompanied by work of any kind.   The
terrible isolation and monotony of an existence under
such conditions rapidly enfeebled the bodily and
mental health of the wretched prisoners, and the
system proved a failure.   The legislature of New
York fell back upon the method in operation at San
Michele.   The prison at Auburn was administered
on the principle of separation at night and work in
common under the rule of silence by day.

In the first half of the present century commissions of inquiry were sent over to the United States by England, France, and Prussia, to examine into the working of the prison systems in operation in Pennsylvania and New York. As a result of these investigations modifications of the Pennsylvanian and Auburn systems of prison treatment were introduced into Europe. Australia also had its lessons to teach. Among the convicts undergoing sentences of transportation a method was introduced of mitigating the severities of detention, and of shortening its duration as a reward for good conduct. This system was considered to produce such excellent results that it was ultimately adopted in English and Irish prisons, and it is now in operation in the majority of prison establishments throughout the civilised world. It is usually known as a progressive system of prison treatment. The principle at the bottom of it is that the treatment of the prisoner when under detention, and the duration of the detention itself, shall in a certain measure be made dependent on the manner in which the prisoner conducts himself while in confinement. We owe the enunciation of this principle to Archbishop Whately, and its practical application to Captain Maconochie, who was for some time head of an Australian penal settlement. It would be an ideal principle if good conduct in prison could be accepted as a guarantee of good conduct in the ordinary relations of life. But unfortunately this is far from being the case, and there is a large amount of truth in the familiar paradox that the good prisoner is a bad subject. The reason of this is not

far to seek. The qualities which are requisite to
make a good prisoner are very different from the
qualities required to make a good subject. The good
prisoner is the man who can accommodate himself
most easily to conditions of existence which have no
counterpart in the outside world. His life in prison
is an unceasing round of silence, solitude, isolation,
and mechanical docility. He is continuously under
the dominion of a highly artificial set of regulations.
All the elementary needs of existence are provided
for him as if he were a child. In most cases he has
become a criminal because he has been unable to
provide himself with these elementary requirements.
When he enters a prison, food, shelter, and clothing
are immediately supplied to him without any effort
of his own, and his conduct in prison affords very
little evidence that he will be able to supply them for
himself when he is once more admitted into the
atmosphere of freedom.

In order that good conduct in prison may become
a rough sort of test of the manner in which a man
is likely to act when he again secures his liberty, the
conditions of prison life must be assimilated as closely
as possible to the conditions of ordinary existence.
How far this process of assimilation can be carried
is a matter of administrative detail, and would require
to be considered point by point. But it is perfectly
certain that it can be carried much further than it is at
present. Prison discipline, if it is to be of any use at
all as a means of adjusting the prisoner to social life
in the outside world, must become practically synony-
mous with industrial discipline. The further it departs

from this ideal the less likely it is to be successful as an instrument of reformation or social protection. It is because the conception of prison discipline as a discipline in industry is sacrificed to an unnatural compound consisting of monasticism and militarism that the good prisoner is so often the bad citizen. The virtues of the monastery and the barrack-yard are undoubtedly of the highest value in their proper place. But it must be admitted that they are not the characteristics best calculated to adapt a man to the conditions of existence which prevail in a competitive and industrial community.

It is no doubt the more or less conscious recognition of this fact which has brought imprisonment into so much disrepute in recent years. The criminal returns of almost every country in Europe show that the percentage of well-conducted prisoners in penal institutions was never higher than it is at the present time. But unfortunately the same returns also show that the proportion of prisoners who return to a life of crime after their release was never so great as it is now. If good conduct in prison were a trustworthy test of the enduring efficacy of imprisonment its effects would be exhibited in the after-life of the discharged prisoner. But a reference to the after-life of the discharged prisoner shows that his behaviour in prison is in far too many cases no assurance whatever of the course he will pursue when he is again at liberty to follow the bent of his own inclinations. Conclusive evidence of this fact is to be seen in the number of persons who are discovered to be old offenders when placed upon their trial.

In a recently published Blue Book dealing with the subject of habitual criminals it was pointed out that in Lancashire, the West Riding of Yorkshire, and the county of Stafford about 70 per cent. of the prisoners tried were known to have been convicted before. In Liverpool, Bradford, and Birmingham the proportion of old offenders was as high as 79 per cent. In other parts of the country the ratio of old offenders was not so high, but this is to be accounted for merely on the ground that they escape identification. With facts of this character before us it is not far from the mark to say that the proportion of old offenders amounts to about 70 per cent. of the convicted population.

It is sometimes suggested that the increase in the proportion of old offenders in prison is to be attributed to the circumstance that sentences are now shorter than formerly, and that the old offender, being more frequently at liberty, has more opportunities of returning to prison than he had in days when a long period of detention was the penalty for a comparatively slight offence. It is possible that this theory may contain a certain modicum of truth. But it is hazardous to attach much value to it in view of its rejection by a very experienced committee which recently reported to the Secretary of State for Scotland on this very subject. It is the opinion of this committee that the shortening of sentences in Scotland by one-half within the last thirty years has had nothing to do with the increase of re-committals to prison, and that to double the duration of the present sentences would not diminish the proportion of old offenders who repeatedly return to prison.

It is also suggested that the increase of old offenders is perhaps more apparent than real. Our methods of detecting old offenders are now much in advance of what they were a generation ago, and the ratio of old offenders is apparently greater because more of them are now detected than used to be the case. That our methods of detection have considerably improved is no doubt true, but, on the other hand, it is to be recollected that the difficulties of detection have also materially increased within the last twenty years. Within the last two decades the population of our large cities has become much vaster, and it is universally recognised to be the fact that the larger the city, and the denser the population, the more difficult it is to detect the old offender. The value of improved methods of identification is practically neutralised by the increased difficulty of detecting the offender at all. In view of considerations such as these it is difficult to attach much importance to the theory that the increase of old offenders among the convicted population is to be attributed to the shortening of sentences or to the effect of improved methods of identification.

The very limited success of imprisonment as a method of dealing with the criminal population has led to a considerable diminution of its application. It is being supplanted as far as possible by other penalties. Fines, sureties, the probation of first offenders, institutions for delinquent juveniles, are now being resorted to in a vast number of cases

17

which used to be dealt with by imprisonment. But it is only within certain limits that these substitutes can be applied. For all offences of a serious character imprisonment, in one form or another, is, in the present condition of public feeling, the only practicable method of treatment. In these circumstances the problem to be faced is—How to make imprisonment a more efficient instrument of social security.

The reaction against imprisonment is most clearly exhibited in the changes which have recently taken place in the treatment of juvenile offenders. In England, notwithstanding the increase of population, the number of juveniles committed to prison has diminished more than one-half within the last twenty years. In Scotland the number has diminished more than one-third. On the Continent one of the questions which is agitating the minds of social reformers is the question of an effective substitute for imprisonment in the case of juveniles. The diminution in the number of committals of young people to prison in Great Britain is not to be attributed to a corresponding decrease in the amount of juvenile crime. It is in great measure owing to an alteration in our methods of dealing with delinquent juveniles. Experience has shown that imprisonment is a very ineffective method of dealing with the youthful offender. Once he has seen the inside of a prison his dread of it is apt to disappear. The feelings of awe and mystery which surround his ideas of prison life are lost as soon as he has had a few days experience of its realities. Imprisonment ceases to have an intimidating effect upon his mind, and the check which punishment is believed to exercise upon the tendency to crime is gone. " The fact is that the life of many children of the class from which criminals chiefly spring is a very hard one, and when they find that in jail they are regularly fed and comfortably housed in warm cells, that they are not starved, or kicked, or beaten, or even sworn at, and that, for children at least, there is no hard work or harsh discipline in Scottish prisons, the terror vanishes with which, when known only from the outside, the prison is regarded, and the salutary deterrent effect disappears." These are the words of the Scotch committee appointed to inquire into the best methods of dealing with young offenders, and they undoubtedly represent the facts of the case.

Inasmuch as imprisonment is such an ineffective method of penal treatment for the young, it follows that children of tender years should be committed to prison as seldom as possible. Admitting this to be established, the question naturally arises—At what age should children be legally liable to imprisonment? A good deal of diversity exists upon this point in the criminal codes of civilised communities. According to Canon law and the later Roman law a child was not punishable till he had completed his seventh year. In the Italian penal code a child cannot be punished till he has completed his ninth year, and ten is the age of penal responsibility in Norway, Denmark, Austria, and Holland. In the German Empire the juvenile must have completed his twelfth year before he is criminally responsible. In France and Belgium no age is mentioned in the penal code at which a child is necessarily irresponsible. The question of responsibility or irresponsibility is left to the discretion of the judge. Ministerial circulars were, however, issued to the French judiciary in 1855 and 1876 to the effect that children between seven and eight years of age should not be prosecuted. By the general law of England a child under the age of seven is regarded as incapable of committing a crime. Between the ages of seven and fourteen a child is still presumed to be irresponsible. But he may be proved to have sufficient knowledge of right and wrong to make him responsible. And, as a matter of fact, a certain number of children under the age of fourteen are annually sent to prison in Great Britain both before trial and also after conviction.

Children are committed to prison before trial with a view to their safe custody until the preparations for their trial have been completed. In many cases these preparations can be completed in a very short time, but cases sometimes occur when a juvenile may have to be detained for a considerable period. These cases usually arise when the offence is of such a serious character that it cannot be dealt with by a court of summary jurisdiction. It can only be tried before a superior court, and inasmuch as the higher criminal courts only sit at considerable intervals the juvenile has to stay in prison till these sittings commence. When a child is accused of a grave crime, a crime which cannot be adjudicated upon by an ordinary magistrate, it is difficult to see how imprisonment before trial can be avoided. Happily the number of children charged with serious crime is exceedingly limited, and it is only on rare occasions that juveniles under the age of fourteen have to appear before the higher criminal tribunals.

When children under the age of fourteen, or even under the age of sixteen, are charged with petty offences which are within the competence of courts of summary jurisdiction, it is of the greatest importance to the child's future welfare that he should not be committed to prison pending the indispensable preparations for his trial. Although there may be a difference of opinion as to the deleterious effect of what is sometimes called the prison brand on the character and future prospects of a young person, there is entire unanimity as to the desirability of keeping him out of prison as long as it is possible to do so. Imprisonment should always be the last resort. In these circumstances the question arises as to what is to be done with juveniles charged with petty offences during the time which must elapse between their arrest and their conviction or acquittal. In every instance a certain amount of time must elapse between the apprehension of an offender and his trial. In some cases it may only be a few hours, in other cases it may be several days. Where is the accused to be detained in the inevitable interval? This question is a very pressing one, for it cannot be said that our present methods of dealing with children under remand are altogether satisfactory.

In large cities where courts of summary jurisdiction are in the habit of sitting every day, or almost every day, it is a very common plan to detain the young offender in the police cells till the charge is heard.

When this method is adopted, and in many cases it is the most convenient method, the utmost care should be taken that the child is not placed in the same cell with other prisoners awaiting trial. Association of this undesirable character is not an un-known thing. At the sixth conference of the national Association of Industrial and Reformatory Schools an experienced reformatory school manager mentioned cases of it which had come within his own experience. " I once had a boy," he said, " who was committed to a police cell. I visited him and found him in the same cell with a thorough ruffian—a man charged with manslaughter, but which amounted almost to murder—and my boy was incarcerated with this man day and night. I had another instance in which a boy on licence was committed to a police cell, and he was in company with two persons who had been convicted. He was also supplied with spirits by his mother while in the cell." Abuses of this serious character are probably of rare occurrence, but it is deplorable to think that they have taken place at all. The police station has at times to be used as a place of detention for children before trial, but when it is used for this purpose it should be an absolute and imperative rule that the accused juvenile shall be placed in a separate cell.

In cases where an accused child is of respectable parentage and is amenable to parental control it is frequently sufficient to place him in the hands of his natural guardians, and to make them responsible for his safe custody till the day of trial comes round. This method, no doubt, entails serious responsibility upon the parent, but it is a responsibility which parents who have the welfare of their children at heart are perfectly willing and even anxious to bear. Unfortunately in many instances it is a method which the magistrate cannot resort to, inasmuch as a considerable proportion of children who are charged with petty delinquencies belong to a section of the population who have bad parents, or incapable parents, or perhaps no parents at all. Where, for one reason or another, children under accusation cannot be placed in the custody of their parents, it is sometimes expedient to place them in charge of charitable societies connected with the police courts, such as police-court missions. These excellent societies might at the same time be utilised for prosecuting inquiries into the circumstances and antecedents of the child. In some cases a constable, or a private person of known respectability, is fit to be entrusted with the care of children under remand. But before such a course is adopted it is essential to ascertain that such persons possess proper accommodation. Truant schools are sometimes mentioned as suitable places of detention for children under remand. But these institutions are too few in number to be universally suitable for such cases. Besides, it would be inadvisable to introduce children to these establishments until it had been ascertained that they are free from infectious disease, and this is a proceeding which often requires time.

When children under remand cannot be taken charge of by parents or the police or by a charitable society, the workhouse is at present the only alternative. Committal of these cases to the workhouse is sometimes objected to on the ground that workhouses are institutions for the poor and not for persons accused of offences against the criminal law. This objection would no doubt possess considerable force if the accused persons were adults and if the offences with which they are charged were of a serious character. But inasmuch as the accused are only children, and as the charges against them are of a comparatively trifling character, the objection to their temporary detention in the workhouse loses much of its force, and can hardly be regarded as a fatal objection. Another objection to the workhouse as a place of remand is that many of the guardians object to its being used as a sort of prison. But this objection cannot be looked upon as serious when it is recollected that it is used as a place of temporary detention for vagrants and casuals. If children under remand for petty offences were not destitute and practically friendless they would remain at liberty on bail till their cases were disposed of in the courts of justice. But the fact that they are destitute and friendless should not and cannot be used as a reason for shutting the workhouse doors against them. It is, on the contrary, the most powerful reason why these doors should be opened.

In workhouses which are used for the detention of children under remand a special ward and properly qualified attendants should be provided. In several workhouses this is what is done. " In the Kensington Union," says a well-informed correspondent of the *Times* newspaper, " the guardians, recognising the

duty imposed upon them of detaining these children
in safe custody and at the same time the danger of
evil association with adult paupers, have built special
quarters for this class. The boys have a sleeping-
room and day-room, &c., and are supervised by an
official assisted by a respectable elderly pauper;
they have no communication with either adults or
boys waiting to be sent to school. The girls have
a day-room off the nursery, where a paid and
trusted nurse can keep an eye on them." Unfortunately all unions are not administered upon
these principles. On visiting a London workhouse
two members of the Poor Law School Committee
found children under remand living under the
following conditions. " In one room fourteen or
fifteen feet square and eight or nine feet high we
found six boys. There were no tables, no chairs, and
they were eating their dinners on the floor. There
were no books, pictures, or playthings. Only six
beds, which during the day are turned up on end.
For washing purposes a pail was brought in. The
door of the room was locked, the area outside being
railed in at the top to prevent the boys from escaping.
They were attended night and day by a young pauper
man, who had been an inmate for two weeks, and
was frequently in and out. In this room the boys
live, wash, eat, sleep, sometimes for three weeks,
sometimes for longer. Last week there were fifteen
lads there, and then the matron told us they slept
three in a bed. On visiting the girls we found they
shared the receiving ward with the women. In a
room smaller than that occupied by the boys we

found a young dissolute-looking woman, still in her rags, who had just come in from the streets. Besides her there was a poor, half-witted creature who had been in the receiving ward a month, because she made 'a bother' in the body of the house. These, with others, were the companions of the remanded girls, aged twelve, nine, and ten, who slept, ate, and lived in such companionship."

In some workhouses the authorities have so little accommodation for children under remand that they are obliged to take their clothes off and put them to bed to prevent them from absconding. One of the principal causes of this unsatisfactory condition of things is that there is no provision in the Poor Law Acts which has in view the treatment of children under remand. It is only since the Industrial Schools Act of 1866 came into operation that magistrates possessed the power of sending children to workhouses under remand. And in some cases the guardians of the poor do not consider it is their duty to take charge of children remanded under the provisions of the Industrial Schools Acts. Most of these children are brought before the magistrates at the instance of the school boards, and in the opinion of the poor law guardians it is the school board authorities which should undertake the responsibility of detaining them till the cases have been finally adjudicated upon by the courts. But whether the custody of these children is ultimately entrusted to the poor law or to the school board, it is of the highest importance that they should be properly taken care of in the interval which must elapse between their apprehension and their trial before the magistrates.

Thus far we have been discussing the various methods of dealing with children before conviction ; the question of the treatment of children after conviction still remains to be considered. According to English law, as has already been stated, a child under the age of seven is regarded as incapable of committing a crime. It is looked upon as not having reached such a stage of mental maturity as would justify society in holding it responsible for its acts. In such cases imprisonment, or any other punishment by a public tribunal, is out of the question. It may be a fitting case for a truant school or an industrial school, but it is not a case for penal measures. When a child is over the age of seven it is in the eye of the English law a fit subject for punishment, and may even be committed to a prison if it can be shown that it understands its own acts and has a sufficient knowledge of right and wrong. "Between the ages of seven and fourteen," says the late Mr. Justice Stephen, " a child is presumed to be irresponsible, but may be proved to have sufficient knowledge of right and wrong to make him responsible. In practice this rule is tacitly passed over. A child of ten or twelve would be unusually dull if it did not know that it might be punished for stealing."

It is perfectly true, as Stephen observes, that most children between the ages of ten or twelve are aware that they may be punished for stealing ; but a wide experience of children who have been committed to prison for stealing convinces me that a large pro-

portion of them, after they have passed the age of
twelve, do not realise that they will be committed to
prison for stealing. These children in all cases know
that the act of stealing is wrong, but in many cases
they do not know that it is criminal. They have
only the dimmest notion that it will place them in
the hands of a policeman, that it will bring them
before a judge, and that it will involve them in a
period of imprisonment. The distinction between
what is wrong and what is criminally wrong does not
exist in the minds of many children till they have
passed the age of fourteen. Few juveniles are able
to discriminate very clearly with respect to the comparative gravity of offences, and in many instances
they do not grasp the difference between what is
merely wrong and what is a crime. In their minds
all offences are classed under the general heading of
things that are forbidden. But that certain forbidden
things will entail the most serious consequences on
their future career if they are committed does not
enter into their calculations, and is in fact beyond the
reach of their faculties. They do not realise, for
instance, the damaging and perhaps fatal effect which
imprisonment may have upon their prospects in the
world. The only point in connection with imprisonment which at all touches them is its immediate dis-
comforts. To be shut up in a strange place, to be
compelled to live among strange surroundings, to be
separated from their home or their family, are the
only things which concern a child who is committed
to prison. He does not look, and is incapable of
looking beyond the moment of his release. The

remote consequences of imprisonment in the shape of casting suspicion on his character and lessening his chance of employment do not give the young prisoner a moment's uneasiness. Taking these facts into consideration, it cannot be said that juveniles under the age of fourteen have an adequate knowledge of right and wrong, inasmuch as they do not realise the disastrous consequences in which a criminal act will involve them.

Before leaving the subject of juvenile responsibility another point also requires to be noticed. Intellectual maturity precedes moral maturity. The growth of moral ideas and sentiments is almost always later than the development of intellectual perceptions. A child accordingly acquires the knowledge of right and wrong before it acquires the corresponding power of moral restraint. In these circumstances a mere knowledge of the difference between right and wrong is not in itself a sufficient test of criminal responsibility in the case of the young. Before criminal responsibility can be established there must be moral as well as intellectual maturity. "*Malitia supplet ætatem*" is a well-known maxim in criminal jurisprudence, but the fact that moral ideas are of considerably later growth than intellectual perceptions renders this maxim of comparatively little value in estimating the penal capacity of the young.

In connection with the imprisonment of children under fourteen it is to be observed that these children are still of school age, and it is an exceedingly undesirable thing that children, after suffering a sentence of imprisonment, should have to return to the elementary school. A child who has been in prison is always an object of curiosity and often of admiration to his school companions. Even if the young ex-prisoner exercises no evil influence personally, the effect of the fact that he has been in prison has a sort of fascination on the minds of his schoolmates, and it is fortunate if his exploits are not imitated by some of them. Among many young people the desire to imitate is an almost irresistible impulse, and from this point of view alone it is highly inexpedient that children under fourteen should be committed to a prison.

If it is necessary in the interests of public security that juveniles over the age of fourteen should be liable to imprisonment, it is equally essential that prison treatment should not be the same for them as for adults. Adults have reached a period of life when bodily and mental maturity is complete, but this cannot be said of juveniles between the ages of fourteen and eighteen. In most cases these young people are even below the average development of juveniles of their own age and sex, and most of them become delinquents owing to an unhappy combination of adverse individual and social circumstances. A short time ago I had occasion to point out to a committee appointed to inquire into the administration of English prisons, that the majority of young prisoners between the ages of sixteen and eighteen are below the average in weight and stature of artisan population in towns, as well as of the general population. It is also certain that many of these young people fall into criminal habits because they are unable to do an ordinary day's work. On this account employers of labour often discharge them, and if they live in towns and find themselves without the elementary means of subsistence they very soon drift into prison. In their case what is wanting is a physical foundation which will enable them to perform the ordinary duties of industrial life. If they are defective in this respect, and if prison dietary is framed on such a scale that it is calculated to subvert their physical capacity, the effect of imprisonment is certain to be disastrous.

When mere physical weakness is the cause of social failure and the origin of offences against the criminal law, surely the way to put a stop to these offences does not consist in making the offender still more unfit for the stress and strain of industrial life. Imprisonment unquestionably has this effect in all cases where the imprisoned juvenile is underfed. Whatever form punishment may take it ought not to take the form of underfeeding the prisoner to such an extent that he is too weak to do a day's work when he is restored to liberty. Punishment of this character defeats its own ends. It appeases the desire for retaliation and revenge, but it accomplishes no other result. All forms of punishment which reduce the physical strength of the prisoner directly tend to transform him into an habitual criminal. These punishments cripple his efforts to re-enter the ranks of honest industry. The only way in which a juvenile released from prison can live in honesty is by manual labour and as a rule it is only the hardest and the roughest kind of manual labour which such a youth can obtain. In three cases out of four he has not been taught the rudiments of a trade, and if he has it is exceedingly difficult for him to get employment at it after he has suffered the disgrace of imprisonment. This means that he has to begin life again as a day labourer at some unskilled employment. Employ-ment of this kind involves a severe strain on the physical energies, and if the severities of imprison-ment are calculated to unfit the prisoner for enduring the strain of a hard day's work, it has the inevitable effect of forcing him back into the ranks of crime.

It is not enough, as is sometimes supposed, to send a juvenile away from prison in the same physical condition as when he entered it. In the sad history of the young offender imprisonment is often the final stage of a long series of privations. Often homeless and friendless, thousands of these young people pass through all sorts of bitter trials and hardships before they ultimately reach the criminal court and the prison cell. In most cases they are not actually suffering from disease, but they are often feeble, listless, and emaciated, and if they are allowed to leave the prison in the same wretched condition as when they entered it, it will be physically im-possible for them to do a hard day's work even when it is offered them. Among the causes which are augmenting the proportions of recidivism and turning such a large proportion of occasional criminals into habitual criminals, an important place must be assigned to the feeble physical condition in which so many short-sentence prisoners leave the prison cell. It is possible that a prison system which is conducted on the principle of giving an inadequate supply of food to offenders under short sentences might be unobjectionable if the prisoner had a home to go to and friends to support him for a week or so after his release. In such circumstances the discharged prisoner would have a little time to recruit before he again resumed his ordinary occupations. But, as a matter of fact, a large proportion of ex-prisoners have no home to go to and no friends to assist them when they leave the prison gates. If they are not to drift back into prison they must not only be able to get work immediately but also be fit to do it.

It is often stated by employers of labour that discharged prisoners are not fit to do an ordinary day's work. Many of the cases which are recorded as failures in the proceedings of discharged prisoners' aid societies are failures owing to the physical incapacity of the released prisoner to do the work in an efficient manner which has been procured for him. In some instances no doubt it is the want of will rather than the want of power, but in a considerable number of cases the real cause of failure is physical and not mental incapacity. It is often assumed in connection with the discharged prisoner that the only difficulty to be contended against is the difficulty of finding work for him. This undoubtedly is a great difficulty, and it is not always easy to overcome it; but it is a mistake to suppose it is the only difficulty. After the difficulty of procuring work for a discharged prisoner has been solved it is to be recollected that a

18

certain percentage of them are unable to work. Many of those who are hastily classed as unwilling are in reality unable.

Inability to work arises from several causes. Many ex-prisoners are unable to work because they have never been accustomed to a life of steady and continuous occupation. Habits of industry, it is well known, are the product of time, and large numbers of prisoners grow up to maturity without acquiring these habits. Unless they are acquired in youth it is difficult to acquire them at all. And the reason many an ex-prisoner cannot keep in work is owing to the circumstance that he has never been exercised in regular, settled, industrial habits in his early days. The regularity, the punctuality, the mechanical sameness of a settled occupation are more than he has been accustomed to endure and more than he can endure. He prefers the uncertainties and privations of an unstable, irregular, unsettled existence. This is the kind of existence in which he has grown up to maturity. When the yoke of industry is put upon him it is often too late in life. He finds it intolerable, and drifts back into crime. Cases of this kind are usually looked at from a superficial point of view, and are sometimes referred to as instances of innate criminal perversity. I am not concerned to deny that cases of innate criminal perversity may exist and probably do exist. But these cases are not so numerous as is often supposed. A careful examination of the early records of a criminal career often shows that the hardened, habitual criminal who persists in a criminal mode of life has never had any industrial discipline in his youth. This discipline proves too galling for him when he becomes a man. It upsets all his previous habits of existence. Tracing back the evil to its ultimate source, we see that such a man has become a criminal because he has not passed through a regular course of industrial discipline at the period of life when habits are formed. The responsibility for this neglect does not rest upon the criminal but upon those whose duty it was to prepare him for the tasks of life. The responsibility rests upon their shoulders but the retribution falls upon him, and regarded from this point of view he is to be pitied as much as blamed.

The want of industrial discipline being one of the reasons why the liberated prisoner cannot retain work after it has been procured for him, the only way to remedy this defect in the case of juveniles is to make prison discipline, as far as practicable, the counterpart of industrial discipline. The juvenile during the period of his detention in prison should be subjected to the same hours of labour, the same habits of industry, the same kind of industry, in short, the same sort of regulations and occupations as prevail in well-ordered manufacturing and commercial establishments in the outside world. If this principle was made the basis of the prison treatment of juveniles it would give them an opportunity of acquiring habits and capacities calculated to enable them to perform an average day's work and to retain employment when it had been found. It is no doubt true that habits acquired under compulsion are not quite the same as habits acquired in an atmosphere of freedom. It is possible that such habits are more likely to be discarded when the pressure of compulsion is removed. At the same time it is to be remembered that an element of compulsion is connected with the acquisition of almost all civilised habits. No matter under what conditions habits of industry have been acquired, the acquisition of them is the paramount object, and must have a wholesome effect on character and conduct. The probability that industrial life will be honestly and strenuously embraced by the ex-prisoner is vastly increased when a life of this description is no longer strange and irksome to him.

If these principles of prison treatment were put into operation the character of imprisonment would be considerably altered and imprisonment would become a much more severe discipline to the young offender than it is now. The prison cell, with its blankness, its silence, its monotony, its almost complete exclusion of the external world and its realities, reproduce in a truly marvellous way the blankness, the deadness, the immobility, the lethargy of the prisoner's own mind. It is, in fact, an outward representation of the prisoner's inward mental existence. It nurses and accentuates the class of defects which characterise so large a proportion of the criminal population, and which must be got rid of if the prisoner is to become a useful member of the community when his term of detention has expired. Cellular imprisonment is not the sort of detention which the majority of prisoners would deliberately choose if they were allowed the opportunity of choice in such a matter. But inasmuch as it is such a close reproduction of the listless, aimless, mindless, apathetic existence in which the offender lives in the outside world, it does not affect him with an acute feeling of discomfort, and he passes away his time in a kind of waking dream. A course of industrial discipline would be the very opposite of all this. It would stimulate and rouse and animate the sluggish mental and physical faculties of the prisoner. It would quicken the dormant activities of the hand and brain. It would compel mental energy to run into new channels, and physical energy to manifest itself in new modes of activity. All this is highly distasteful to the average juvenile prisoner. It involves effort and exertion on his part in entirely new directions. The necessity for being attentive, observant, industrious, is a new and a painful experience. It is a far more severe discipline to the young delinquent than the most rigid cellular confinement. It produces a far keener sense of discomfort than the mere negative existence of the prison cell.

It is of course impossible to do much in the way of providing industrial occupation for juveniles committed to prison for very short periods. But in this connection the question arises whether it is wise to send juveniles to prison at all when the offence is so trifling that it can be purged by a few days' or a few weeks' imprisonment. In such cases it would be well to adopt some different kind of penalty. It is true the existing substitutes for imprisonment soon become exhausted, and the magistrate is compelled to resort to it although he is aware that it is of little or no use. But surely it is not beyond the power of

criminal jurisprudence to add materially to the
number of substitutes for imprisonment. It is often
supposed that the manifest failure of short sentences
is an argument for longer sentences. But this is not
the case. The failure of short periods of detention
in prison is an argument against imprisonment
altogether and the substitution of some other
penalty when the offence is of a trifling character.
Very nearly 40 per cent. of the total committals to
prison in England and Wales consist of cases in
which the offender is sent to prison for a week or
less. A considerable proportion of these short-sentence cases is composed of young people. This
arises from the circumstance that juveniles are often
unable to pay a fine and are obliged to submit to the
alternative of a few days' imprisonment. If the
criminal law provided a greater variety of alternative
penalties for slight offences a vast number of petty
cases would not require to be dealt with by imprisonment at all. Imprisonment under the very best of
systems is accompanied by a certain number of
inevitable dangers while it lasts, and is followed by
serious drawbacks after it has expired. Wherever
an alternative penalty can be adopted as a substitute
it is a clear gain to the community as well as to the
delinquent.

When imprisonment has, unfortunately, to be
resorted to in the treatment of the juvenile offender
it is of the utmost importance that he should not
be cut off for prolonged periods from all communication with his relatives in the outside world. In
cases where the delinquent juvenile is not absolutely

friendless and homeless it is very often found that his downward career has begun by breaking off all communication with his home. In large cities young people, when they reach the age of sixteen, and sometimes before reaching that age, become economically independent of their parents. Their wages are sufficiently high to enable them to maintain themselves. The result of this is that when disputes and disagreements arise at home these juveniles readily leave the parental roof and cut themselves adrift from the restraining influences of family life. They thus find themselves in the wide world without friends or counsellors, or a temporary retreat if work for a time should happen to fail them. Juveniles in this perilous position often get into contact with undesirable companions. They sink down in the social scale, irregular habits are contracted, employment is lost, desperate courses are resorted to, and they ultimately find themselves in prison.

One of the first steps to be taken in the restoration of these young people is to induce them to enter once more into cordial relationship with their families. To reconcile them to their father or mother, or to reconcile the father or mother to them, is practically to save them from a broken life and often from a career of crime. Impediments in the shape of prison regulations which forbid, or practically forbid, communication for prolonged periods between parent and child in circumstances of this kind are nothing short of iniquitous. Regulations of this kind betray a complete want of knowledge of the effect of prison life upon the young. The adaptability of the young mind to altered circumstances is such that long before three months have passed away the juvenile prisoner has become quite accustomed to his surroundings. Prison routine has been learned, prison habits have been formed, the worst has been endured, the prison has ceased to terrify or alarm. When this state has been reached, and it is wonderful how quickly it is reached, the young prisoner resumes the mental attitude towards his family which he had before he was convicted ; the favourable moment for effecting a reconciliation between him and them has passed away.

The most favourable opportunity for work of this kind is the moment when imprisonment begins. It is at this moment that self-confidence is shattered, that the feeling of dejection is deepest, that the desire to seek relief and consolation by renewing the ties of home is most keenly felt. But, strange to say, this is the very time when some prison systems practically forbid communication with home. All communication is forbidden in deference to a mere doctrinaire idea that every prisoner shall be subjected to the severest possible hardships when he first enters the prison cell. Common sense and experience teach us that the sacred memories of family life are most vivid in times of trouble and distress. It is at those times that the bonds of family affection become the most powerful instruments of moral and spiritual reform. But the use of these highly moralising agencies is not allowed in deference to an absurd pedantry which knows nothing of the workings of the human heart. In all establishments where a considerable number of human beings are collected together it is impossible to manage affairs without regulations of some kind. But in cases where the treatment of human character is concerned the regulations should consist of a few general principles which are to be observed ; they should never assume the form of hard-and-fast commands.

One of the difficulties of dealing successfully with juveniles committed to prison is that prisons are primarily constructed for the detention of adults. Prison regulations, prison labour, the prison staff, prison buildings, are all intended in the first instance for grown-up people. Modifications of the system are introduced to meet the case of juveniles, but these modifications do not alter its fundamental character. In all its essential features the prison still remains a place for grown-up people and not for the young. The general tone and temper of the administration is not adapted to the young, and in the end the effect of imprisonment for good or evil is not to be measured by rules drawn up on bits of paper, but by the spirit in which these rules are administered. The existence of this state of things constitutes a plea for special places of detention for juveniles. No doubt this would be the best solution of the matter if the practical, or rather the financial, difficulties were not so great. In the very largest centres of population, such as London, it would be possible to have establishments constructed for juveniles, and for them alone. But, except in these very huge centres, establishments of this character would not be feasible, owing to the fact that the juvenile portion of the prison population is too limited to warrant the expenditure which such a plan would necessarily involve.

In most cases juveniles and adults must continue to be committed to the same prisons. The only way to mitigate the evils involved in this condition of affairs is to separate the two classes of prisoners as far as possible, and to assign the care of juvenile prisoners to specially selected officers. It would be the special duty, and wherever possible the exclusive duty, of these officers to supervise juvenile prisoners. Where prison officers are to-day entrusted with the task of looking after men and to-morrow with the task of looking after boys the best results do not ensue. In dealing with men, what may be called a disciplinary attitude has to be exhibited ; in dealing with juveniles, an educative temper is required. It is difficult for the ordinary official to change suddenly from the one temper to the other. It is not often that the same man has sufficient mental flexibility to combine both. On this account, as well as for other reasons, the young prisoner should as far as practicable be placed in charge of officers exclusively devoted to the task. These officers should be carefully selected, and should, as a rule, consist of men who have children of their own. A proper classification of the prison population is one of the supreme objects of all modern prison treatment. But this object is practically defeated unless the classification of prisoners is accompanied by a corresponding classification of the prison staff. The classification of the prison population involves the specialisation of the prison staff. If this fundamental principle is overlooked classification becomes comparatively worthless

The end of imprisonment is liberty, and the most perilous period in a young prisoner's life is the day on which his detention expires. All prisoners of whatever age look forward with a feeling of joy to the hour of their liberation ; it is, nevertheless, a most critical time for them, and is beset on many sides by peculiar trials and dangers. As long as a prisoner is shut up within the narrow compass of his cell he is protected against the temptations which have proved so fatal to him in the outside world. But as soon as he is at liberty these temptations reappear in all their old vitality, and the liberated prisoner is in a very bad condition for resisting them. To a person who has been subjected even for a short period to all the artificial restraints of prison life, and whose liberty of action has been cramped in so many directions, it is a trying ordeal to be suddenly exposed to the full light of unrestricted liberty. It is a well-established axiom that servitude in whatever form has the effect of unfitting men for freedom. A condition which has such disastrous results on the ordinary man is even more fatal to a prisoner. He is usually a person of feeble will and character, and the sudden acquisition of liberty after a course of galling bondage is more than his nature can endure. The sudden transform-ation unbalances him, intoxicates him, dazes and bewilders him. He reels to and fro like a drunken man. His powers of self-restraint are temporarily paralysed, and before he can recover the normal attitude of a freeman he again finds himself in the clutches of the criminal law.

It is the first few weeks of liberty which is the period of greatest danger for the juvenile prisoner, and in fact for all prisoners. If he is able to pass through this critical period in safety it is probable that he may afterwards settle down into a law-abiding citizen. It is imperative that these facts should be taken into consideration in determining the nature of prison treatment. Imprisonment should never be conducted on such a footing that it unfits the prisoner for liberty. It fails in one of its most essential purposes if it terminates in such a deplorable result. Imprisonment should be a gradual preparation for liberty. It should be organised on such a principle that the contrast between detention and liberty will not be too great when the day of liberation at last arrives. The tension of restraint should be relaxed as time goes on. The circle in which the prisoner is allowed to move at will should be gradually enlarged. If this principle is acted upon the faculties which the prisoner requires in a state of freedom will have some preliminary exercise. In prison these faculties are practically dormant, and when the prisoner is liberated and the need has arisen for using them they will not respond to his call.

In the treatment of a prisoner, and in the regulations affecting him, the fact is not sufficiently borne in mind that he is a person who will one day be at liberty. If he is treated in prison in such a manner as to render him unfit for liberty, the punishment inflicted upon him is altogether out of proportion to the offence. The sentence of the judge may only be a sentence of six months' detention, but if a prisoner during that period is unfitted for liberty at the moment of his release the sentence is not a sentence of six months' detention, it is a sentence which dooms the man to the life of an habitual criminal. The severity of a sentence depends upon its nature as well as upon its duration, and a short sentence, owing to the manner in which it is carried into effect, may mean the transformation of a comparatively harmless offender into a criminal for life. It must never be forgotten that the habitual criminal is in far too many cases a product of prison treatment, a victim of vicious and unsound methods of dealing with the convicted population. The value of prison regulations is not to be tested, as is too often assumed, by the behaviour of prisoners within the prison walls. The value of these regulations must be tested by their beneficent effect upon the prisoner when he is restored to liberty. In other words, prison treatment is successful in so far as it results in preventing the ex-prisoner from returning to a life of crime.

In order to minimise the evil effects of prison life and gradually pave the way for liberty the principle of conditional liberation should be extensively utilised in the treatment of juvenile offenders. Conditional liberation bridges the gulf between imprisonment and absolute liberty. It minimises the rebound from servitude, and provides the prisoner with an opportunity of regaining his mental balance. If this system is conducted upon proper principles it reduces the risk of the discharged prisoner relapsing into crime. One of the principal causes which hampers the efficiency of societies for assisting prisoners on release is the absence of a properly constituted system of conditional liberation. Under existing circumstances a prisoners' aid society has no control over the discharged prisoner at the moment when control is most required. The society may have provided him with work, with tools, with clothing, in short, with every industrial requisite, but if the ex-prisoner should suddenly leave his work or pawn his tools the society which has done so much to set him on his feet is absolutely helpless. It has no legal hold upon him. His punishment is over. His period of detention has expired. He is at perfect liberty to give up his work, or sell his tools, or do whatever he chooses so long as he refrains from committing a fresh offence against the criminal law. Under a properly organised system of conditional liberation it would be impossible for an ex-prisoner to undo the work of these charitable societies with impunity. Instead of being liberated absolutely he would only be liberated on condition that he submitted himself to control for a certain period after his release from prison. If the conditions on which liberation was granted were not fulfilled it would be in the power of the society which assisted him to procure his rearrest. In reformatory schools conditional liberation, or liberation on licence, as it is called, has been in operation for many years, and works, on the whole, with excellent results. The managers of reformatory schools possess the power of liberating a juvenile before the legal duration of detention has expired, and of placing him in the hands of a trustworthy and respectable person who is willing to take charge of him. A somewhat similar power should be placed in the hands of a competent authority for the conditional liberation of young prisoners. There is every reason to believe that such a system would work as efficiently in the treatment of young prisoners as it now does in connection with the treatment of juveniles committed to reformatory institutions. If conditional liberation is applicable to the reformatory boy it is equally applicable to the juvenile prisoner. If it can be worked in the one case, it can be worked in the other. The power of supervising and controlling the conditionally liberated juvenile would be in the hands of the society which undertook to find him occupation. It would in many cases be necessary to extend the power of supervision beyond the limits of the sentence to imprisonment. But this is no novelty to the criminal law. It is a common occurrence for an offender to be sentenced to a definite period of police supervision, to begin when his imprisonment has expired. In the case of juveniles the supervision of a charitable society would be substituted, and it is certain that if such a society were to exercise its powers with vigilance and discretion it would succeed in rescuing hundreds of young people who are otherwise destined to become habitual criminals.

CHAPTER XIII.

CORRECTIVE INSTITUTIONS.

Crime cannot be suppressed by intimidation—The certainty of
punishment does not suppress crime—The experience of punishment does not deter—Why punishment is ineffective—Punishment does not remove the conditions which produce crime—
The ameliorative method of dealing with juvenile crime—
The principle on which it rests—The practical application of
the principle by voluntary societies—The practical application
of educative methods by the State — State institutions for
juvenile offenders in Great Britain—Population of these institutions—Cost of juvenile institutions—Effect on crime of institutions for juvenile offenders—Prison population—Committal to
prison—Cases of Scotland and the United States—The increase
or decrease of crime is not entirely dependent on the juvenile
population—Large cities produce crime—Economic vicissitudes
produce it—Crime may increase in spite of institutions for
juvenile offenders—How to measure the worth of juvenile
institutions—Percentage of inmates who do well in after-life.
—Reconviction the test of well-doing—Value of the returns
relating to reconvictions—Value of juvenile institutions—Corrective institutions a necessity—Cases for committal to these
institutions—The committal of first offenders—The committal
of young children—Committal of children to day industrial
schools and truant schools—Cases for day industrial schools—
Training in day industrial schools—Truant schools—The object
of truant schools—Dull and defective children—Treatment of
children in truant schools—Individualisation in truant schools
—Punishment in truant schools—The treatment of juvenile
offenders over sixteen in England—In the United States—Dr.
Appelius and Professor Stoos on the treatment of offenders

under eighteen—The age of maturity—Maturity and intelligence—Age of admission to corrective institutions—Report
of the Prisons Committee on the subject—Classification of
corrective institutions—Classification in Great Britain—Classification according to age—Children of different ages subjected
to too uniform treatment—Classification according to offence—
Difficulties of classification—A proper system of classification
—The supreme authority over dependent and delinquent
children should be the Education Department—Classification
of institutions must be supplemented by individualisation of
inmates—The size of corrective institutions—Small schools—
The New York Conference on the care of dependent and
delinquent children—The Poor Law Schools Committee on
large schools—Size of schools for juvenile offenders in Great
Britain—Physical and mental examination of children committed to corrective institutions — This examination should
be repeated at frequent intervals—Physical examination of
delinquent juveniles in France—Liberation from corrective
institutions—Liberation after a short period of detention—
Evils of detention for prolonged periods—Principles regulating
the release of juveniles—Conduct in the school—Nature of
offence — Habit of offending — Destination of offender —
Michigan system.

IN the preceding observations on the repression of
juvenile crime we have been discussing and appreciating the value of methods which are primarily
punitive in character. The fundamental defect of all
punitive measures which ultimately terminate in the
liberation of the delinquent is that they are in the
main intimidatory. They do not touch the individual
and social conditions which produce the criminal
population. The scope and purpose of penal methods
is almost exclusively confined to operating on the
sense of fear. It is not to be denied that the fear of
punishment exercises a deterrent effect of some sort,
but the criminal returns of every civilised community
point with remarkable unanimity to the conclusion

that the restraining influence of fear on criminal tendencies is much more limited than is generally supposed. It is perfectly certain that if the terrors of the criminal law could have stamped out crime it would have disappeared long ago. Punishments of the most appalling severity existed until a comparatively recent period in every criminal code, and what is more, these punishments were regularly and systematically resorted to in dealing with criminal offenders. Hanging, branding, burning, mutilation, was the fate which awaited the perpetrators of what would now be regarded as trifling offences. Yet there is no evidence to show that these severities had the effect of putting a stop to crime. On the contrary, as far as it is possible to get information on the subject, the proportion of criminal offences to the population was as high a century ago as it is to-day.

It is generally believed that the value of punishment as a deterrent depends as much, and perhaps even more, upon its certainty than on its severity. Within the present century punishments of a penal character have diminished in severity to a remarkable extent. The penalty of death has been abolished in practice for every offence except the crime of wilful murder. The practice of sending criminals to penal servitude has materially diminished, the duration of imprisonment has been shortened, and in a great many cases penalties of a lighter description have been substituted for committal to jail. Side by side with this movement for diminishing the severity of punishment there has grown up a corresponding movement to increase its certainty. The principal

and most conspicuous feature of this movement consisted in the establishment and organisation of a
vast and minutely ramified system of police. The
result of the establishment of this force has probably
been to secure a greater degree of certainty in the
detection of crime and criminals. I have been repeatedly told by old criminals that it is now a much
more difficult thing to escape the clutches of the law
than it was prior to the establishment of the police.
This is no doubt an accurate statement of the case.
It may therefore be safely accepted as a fact that
while punishment has decreased in severity during
the present century it has at the same time increased
in certainty. The probability that a criminal will be
apprehended and convicted is now greater than it was
when punishments were more severe. But the increased probability of detection and conviction has
not put a stop to crime, or even perceptibly diminished
its volume and intensity. According to the official
returns of every civilised state, offences against the
criminal law are steadily increasing in number; it is
sometimes maintained that they are diminishing in
seriousness, but the apparent diminution in this direction arises from alterations of judicial procedure of a
mitigatory character, and from a growing unwillingness among the public to prosecute.

It might be supposed that if the fear of detection
and the fear of punishment are of so little efficacy the
actual experience of punishment would at least have
a salutary result. Punishment in the shape of committal to prison or to penal servitude is a severe and
humiliating ordeal. During the time it lasts the

person who has to endure it is in the abject position
of a slave. His liberty is taken from him, his freedom
of movement is confined within the narrowest limits :
he cannot choose what he will eat or where he will
sleep or what he will put on. His will is obliterated,
his powers of decision and action are reduced to a
nullity. A considerable part of the satisfaction which
we derive from life consists in observing the wide world
around us, and in watching or participating in the
changing and dramatic incidents with which it is
filled. The prisoner is completely cut off from all
these sources of interest ; for the time being the
world is dead to him ; he has no outlook upon
external things ; he is shut up within the narrow
horizon of his own disordered imaginings ; he lives
and breathes in a polluted atmosphere of monotony,
solitude, and gloom. In addition to these privations
his social sympathies are repressed and starved.
Society, friendship, affection, the pillars on which
human happiness repose, are demolished. The
friendly greeting, the solace of companionship, the
consolations of affection, are practically excluded
from a prisoner's life. The human element in it is
reduced to a minimum ; he is only allowed to retain
the instincts and faculties which he has in common
with solitary birds and beasts of prey.

A single experience of imprisonment would constitute an effective check on any future tendency to
crime if punishment possessed the efficacy which it is
generally believed to have. But the ordinary view of
the efficacy of punishment is largely an illusion. It
is not supported by facts. A period of detention in

prison produces very little change on the future conduct of the convicted population. As a proof of this it has only to be remembered that among every hundred prisoners more than one-half have been in prison before. And a large percentage of these prisoners have been recommitted, not once or twice, but five, ten, or twenty times. In face of facts of this character it is folly to imagine that punishment is an effective remedy for crime. When we come to look at the reason why punishment involving the loss of liberty is so ineffective, we find in the first place that it aggravates the conditions which tend to make a man a criminal. Nearly all the people who are committed to prison are somewhat deteriorated either bodily or mentally before they come within the clutches of the law. Crime is usually the result of this condition of deterioration. If the deterioration which has set in before imprisonment is made worse by the conditions of prison life, it is impossible for punishment in the shape of imprisonment to prevent the offender from repeating the offence. According to the Royal Commissioners of 1879 and the Prisons Committee of 1895, the conditions of prison life are of this adverse character. Imprisonment, they pronounce, "not only fails to reform offenders, but in the case of the less hardened criminals, and especially of first offenders, it produces a deteriorating effect." In other words, imprisonment defeats the very purpose for which it is supposed to exist. Instead of operating as a deterrent and a check on the criminal population, it deteriorates the offender and increases the probability that he will continue to be a criminal for the remainder of his life.

When we look behind the elaborate machinery of penal codes and penitentiary establishments at the criminal himself, the failure of mere punishment as an instrument of social security at once becomes apparent. An inquiry into the individual and social circumstances of the criminal when he begins his career of crime reveals the fact that in nearly every instance these circumstances are of an abnormal character. As far as individual conditions are concerned it is found that a considerable percentage of the juvenile criminal population are either physically or mentally below the average. As far as family life is concerned it is found that the juvenile offender, as a rule, has either no home or else a bad one, has either no parents or else bad parents. Again, when his economic circumstances and opportunities are reviewed, it is seen that they are of an adverse and abnormal character. It is obvious that the connection between abnormal circumstances of an adverse kind and an abnormal or criminal mode of life is not a mere accidental coincidence. It is in the main a relation of cause and effect. It is the abnormal circumstances which produce the abnormal conduct, and the abnormal conduct will continue, and as a matter of fact does continue, till the abnormal circumstances are removed. When the question as to the best method of dealing with the criminal population is looked at from this point of view it immediately becomes evident that neither punishment nor the fear of punishment will remove the conditions which make men criminals. The penal law, with its formidable looking instruments of retaliation and intimidation, does not so much as touch the permanent causes of crime. All that it succeeds in doing is to inflict an immense amount of suffering and misery. It is the more or less conscious perception of this fact which has diverted men's minds from the penal to the educational treatment of juvenile offenders.

The principle at the root of the educational method of dealing with juvenile crime is an absolutely sound one. It is a principle which recognises the fact that the juvenile delinquent is in the main a product of adverse individual and social conditions. From this fundamental fact it draws the obvious conclusion that the only effective treatment of juvenile crime must consist in placing the juvenile in the midst of wholesome material and moral surroundings. The practical application of this principle commenced about three centuries ago in Holland and Germany, and has since slowly extended to all civilised communities. It is only within a comparatively recent period that the State has formally recognised the value of the ameliorative as compared with the punitive process of dealing with juvenile delinquents. Till the middle of the present century the establishment of institutions for dealing with these offenders was in the main a matter of private initiative. Long before the State took any action it was perceived by private individuals all over Europe that the causes of juvenile crime originated in the miserable conditions of the juvenile criminal. It was seen that as a rule the juvenile

offender was sunk in moral and material wretchedness.   His offence was the natural outcome of the
deplorable circumstances in which he had to live.
The perception of these facts led to the conclusion
that he was to be regarded with pity rather than
resentment.   He was a victim of circumstances over
which he had little or no control.   The terrors of the
penal law were powerless to alter these circumstances.
The State, through its criminal machinery, was
striking at the offence and not at the offender.   Men
began to see that this method would have to be
reversed.   Alter the conditions of the offender, they
said, and the offence will cease.   Remove him from
his miserable surroundings.   Instruct him.   Put him
as far as possible on a footing of equality with the
rest of the population.   Give him the same economic
opportunities as other men, the same habits of
industry as other men, and he will in the vast
majority of cases act like other men.   These were
the principles on which the individuals and voluntary
associations devoted to the reclamation of juvenile
offenders commenced and carried on their work.

The success of these principles ultimately attracted
general attention in Europe and America, and public
opinion began to demand the application of them on
a more extended scale.   It was felt that private
initiative, however admirable, was unable to cope
with the vast problem of juvenile delinquency.   The
dimensions of the evil necessitated the co-operation
of the community in its collective capacity.   In
Europe, France led the way, and in 1850 special laws
were passed in the French chamber relating to the

treatment of juvenile delinquents. In 1854 England followed in the wake of France. In the two decades between 1850 and 1870 almost every state in Europe had passed laws or organised establishments for the reclamation of juvenile offenders. The new world was as active as the old. In the rational treatment of the young offender many states of the American Union have borne an honourable and conspicuous part. The New York House of Refuge, chartered in 1824, was established by the state of New York many years before any European government had given its attention to the value of reclamatory methods of dealing with juvenile delinquency. Since that date the number of institutions for young offenders has steadily increased, especially in the North Atlantic states. According to the census bulletin, the total number of inmates in juvenile reformatories in the United States in 1890 amounted to nearly fifteen thousand. The population of these establishments increased nearly 30 per cent. in ten years.

The principle of dealing with juvenile offenders in special institutions has been most widely applied in Great Britain. According to the report of the inspector of reformatory and industrial schools for 1894 the number of children under order of detention in reformatory, industrial, truant, and day industrial schools amounted to 33,521. During the last twenty years the number of children sent to reformatory schools has remained almost stationary. This stationary condition of the reformatory school population has arisen to a considerable extent from the fact that until recently it was obligatory that every child

destined for a reformatory should first undergo a
preliminary sentence of imprisonment. Magistrates
became more and more unwilling to pass these
sentences, and many of the children who used to
be committed to reformatories were sent to industrial
schools. In the case of committal to an industrial
school a period of preliminary imprisonment is not
required. Partly as a result of this fact, and partly
from other causes, the number of committals to these
schools has been increasing by leaps and bounds.
In 1870 the number of children in industrial schools
in Great Britain amounted to 8,778; in 1880 this
number had increased to 16,446; ten years later it
had risen to 22,735; and according to the last returns,
1894, the total number of children in industrial schools
is 24,683. Day industrial schools are a class of institutions in which children who have been before the
magistrates are detained during the day but are
allowed to return to their homes at night. These
schools have been in operation for the last eighteen
years. There are now more than twenty of them
in the large towns of England and Scotland. The
population of day industrial schools has increased
from little over a thousand in 1880 to more than
three thousand in 1894. The expenditure on juvenile
institutions of all sorts is now a considerable sum.
According to the latest returns on the subject it at
present amounts to over half a million sterling per
annum. The larger part of this amount is paid by
the central government. A certain amount is derived
from local taxation and voluntary subscriptions, and
about twenty thousand pounds per annum is paid

by the parents of the children who are under detention.

What has been .the effect of these institutions on
the general movement of crime? Has crime increased or decreased as a result of their establishment? These are questions which are very often
asked, and an answer is usually sought by a reference
to the prison population. During the last ten years
or so the number of persons in prison in England
and Wales has on the whole tended to diminish,
notwithstanding the growth of the general population.
The diminution of the prison population is an interesting fact, but it does not necessarily mean a
diminution in the amount of crime. As has already
been mentioned, the prison population in England and
Wales has been diminished by a variety of causes
which are quite unconnected with the decrease of
crime. It has been diminished, in the first place, by
the shortening of sentences. It is notorious that the
tendency in recent years has been to sentence convicted men to much shorter periods of detention than
used to be the case. Crimes for which offenders used
invariably to be sent to penal servitude for long
periods are now considered to be purged by comparatively short terms of imprisonment. If sentences
are shortened in this manner the population in prison
will diminish although there has been no corresponding diminution in the amount or gravity of crime.
A reduction in the duration of sentences by one-half
has the immediate and inevitable result of reducing
the inmates of prisons by one-half. In short, the size
of the prison population depends on the duration of

sentences, and not on the amount of crime. It is
therefore useless to appeal to the dimensions of
the prison population as a proof of the success or
failure of the reformatory and industrial school movement.

Another test of the criminal condition of the
community which is sometimes resorted to is not
the number of persons in prison on a certain day,
but the number of cases committed to prison in the
course of the year. The value of this test is also
very much affected by changes in judicial procedure.
Within the last twenty years there has been a
strongly marked disinclination on the part of judges
and magistrates to commit offenders to prison. In
the case of adult offenders fining, sureties, conditional
sentences, admonitions, have been largely substituted
for imprisonment; and, as regards the young, in
addition to these methods committal to certified
schools and voluntary homes has in a vast number
of instances taken the place of the prison. If penalties of the kind which have just been mentioned are
substituted for imprisonment the number of persons
sent to prison is certain to be reduced. In these
circumstances a decrease in the numbers sent to
prison in the course of the year is not to be con-
founded with a corresponding decrease in the amount
of crime. It may be merely the result, and as far as
England and Wales is concerned it is unquestionably
the result, of alterations in our methods of punishment. Whether, then, we look at the daily average
prison population or the annual total of committals
to prison we find that they are unsatisfactory stan-

dards for measuring the fluctuations of crime. These standards cannot be used as tests of the value of our existing educational methods of dealing with juvenile offenders.

The case of Scotland is an additional proof of the fallacy of attempting to gauge the worth of the educational institutions by a reference to the number of committals to prison. There is every reason to believe that establishments for juvenile offenders in Scotland are just as efficient as institutions of the same character in England. The inspector of reformatory and industrial schools speaks of them in as high terms of approval, and as far as figures go they appear to present as high an average of successful results. But if these institutions were to be tested by the number of committals to Scotch prisons they would have to be condemned as a comparative failure. Within the last thirty years—that is to say, within the period which coincides with the rise and growth of these schools —the number of committals to prison in Scotland has on the whole tended to increase. The United States is in exactly the same position as Scotland. According to the United States census of 1890 the number of convicts in penitentiaries has increased to the extent of 27 per cent. in ten years, and the number of prisoners in county jails has increased nearly 54 per cent. On the other hand, the population of the American Union has only increased about 25 per cent. during the decade. In other words, the prison population is increasing faster than the general population. But it would be absurd and unjust to draw any conclusions from these figures as to the value of the child-saving institutions of the United States.

The fundamental fallacy at the bottom of all comparisons between the prison population and the growth of institutions for delinquent juveniles is the assumption that the movement of crime is entirely dependent on the juvenile population. A community which has a considerable proportion of young people who are morally and materially neglected will undoubtedly tend to produce a corresponding proportion of criminals. But it is to be remembered that crime is produced by other conditions besides the neglect of the young. Neglected youth is an important condition, but it is not the only one. It is merely one among many causes. Another most important cause in the production of crime is the concentration of population in large cities. It has already been pointed out that a densely crowded population produces a larger quantity of criminals in proportion to its numbers than a thinly peopled district. Among the inhabitants of such vast cities as London, Paris, and New York there is a much larger proportion of criminals than there is among an equal number of the population in the country districts around them. This arises from several circumstances. In the first place, large cities have a tendency to attract the criminal elements in the community. Notwithstanding the presence of a huge police force it is easier for a criminal to escape detection in a large city than in a thinly peopled district. A large city also offers the criminal greater opportunities of plunder, owing to the immense concentration of property which always takes place within it. In addition to these causes the artificial conditions of existence in large cities produce a large degenerate class. Many members of this class are almost forced into a career of crime by their wretched moral and material surroundings. The material conditions among which they are born and have to live are of the worst description. They are huddled together by the thousand in gloomy and squalid streets and alleys. It would be a mockery to call the dens in which they live by the name of home. Even in these dens they are often packed together in numbers which make decency impossible. No doubt there are exceptional cases in which people who have been brought up under such conditions rise superior to their surroundings and exhibit many of the characteristics of orderly citizens. But these cases are the exception. As a rule a man is shaped by the surroundings in which he has been born and is obliged to live. If these surroundings are all calculated to injure him and to degrade him he will sooner or later degenerate, and become a drunkard, a pauper, a lunatic, or a criminal, or, as not infrequently happens, a combination of all.

Economic vicissitudes are another important element in the production of crime. The relations between poverty and crime are not, perhaps, so intimate as is commonly supposed. A poor population may be, and very often is, an exceedingly honest and orderly population. But a population which is exposed to severe economic crises is a

population in which criminal propensities are sure
to be strongly developed. Whenever a wave of
industrial depression sweeps over a population it
is always followed by an increase in the number
of offences against property. And the worst of it
is that when the wave ultimately recedes it has so
demoralised certain sections of the community that
they do not resume their ordinary occupations.
They have become criminals in bad times and they
continue criminals when times are good. Economic
stability, even if the standard of material comfort
is comparatively low, is infinitely preferable, from
the point of view of public security, to an industrial
system in which considerable masses of the people
are subjected to violent economic ups and downs.
Many other causes of crime might be mentioned
besides economic vicissitudes and the concentration
of population in large cities ; but a reference to these
two causes is sufficient to show that crime is produced by other conditions besides neglect of the
young. There are circumstances in which these
conditions may be working more powerfully for
evil than child-saving institutions are working for
good. When this is the case crime will increase
in spite of the best juvenile institutions imaginable.
It is therefore useless to estimate the worth of these
institutions by a reference to the general movement
of crime.

The real test of the value of institutions for
juvenile offenders is not the rise or fall of crime,
but the percentage of children who do well in the
world after they have left them. The rise and fall

of crime, as we have seen, is dominated by a variety
of conditions over which juvenile institutions have
exceedingly little control. All that can reasonably
be claimed for these establishments is that if they
are successful in the work of juvenile reclamation
they prevent crime from assuming the proportions
which it would otherwise possess. But it would be
absurd to contend that the movement of crime is
entirely regulated by their failure or success. Crime
in its totality is the product of a multitude of
social and individual conditions of which juvenile
delinquency is only one. To suppose that its
dimensions can be regulated by juvenile institutions
alone is to assume that it is entirely produced by
the adverse circumstances attending neglected youth.
This, as we have shown, is not the case.

Let us, then, examine the worth of these institutions by the only proper standard of their worth—
namely, the amount of success which attends their
efforts in reclaiming the children committed to their
care. When the children who have been in reformatory and industrial schools go out again into the
world it is the duty of the institutions where they
have been confined to keep in touch with them, and
to report upon their conduct for the first three years
after their liberation. In these reports the children
are divided into four classes. The first class consists
of juveniles who are doing well after their liberation,
the second consists of those whose conduct is doubtful, the third of those who have been again convicted,
and the fourth of those whose whereabouts are un-
known. According to these returns it appears that

20

three-fourths of the children committed to reformatory schools in Great Britain do well after their discharge. The remaining fourth are either lost sight of or are doubtful cases or have been reconvicted. Industrial schools receive a younger, and on the whole a less criminal, class of children than reformatory schools. We should therefore expect a somewhat higher percentage of success among them. According to the returns about five in every six are recorded as doing well after their liberation. The amount of success attending the operation of day industrial schools is not so easy to estimate. If, however, children who have been in these schools and are afterwards reconvicted and sent to reformatory and industrial institutions are to be regarded as failures, it would appear that one in every seven of the juveniles committed to day industrial schools are afterwards recommitted to reformatory and industrial schools.

In appreciating the value of these returns of success and failure it is to be remembered that the definition of doing well is a somewhat lax one. The absence of reconviction is practically the test of welldoing. This test, it must be admitted, is not all that could be wished. A juvenile may succeed in escaping the meshes of the criminal law for three years after he is set at liberty, yet in many cases it is only by a stretch of imagination that he can be said to be doing well. He may be successful in keeping out of prison, yet he may be living an idle, aimless, worthless existence hovering on the borderland between pauperism and crime. On the other hand, it is only fair to recollect that many cases which have to be put down in the returns as failures are not really failures in the long run. Some juveniles after their terms of detention have expired are temporarily intoxicated by their newly acquired liberty, and as a consequence find their way into prison. But this relapse, although of evil omen, is sometimes merely a disastrous incident. It is not always to be taken as a sign of ultimate failure. It is not to be regarded as a proof that the youth means to follow, or actually does follow, settled habits of crime. After a time he rights himself and becomes an honest and industrious member of the community. Cases of this description have several times come within my own observation, and I should not like to say that the training a juvenile has received is wasted, or that he should be for ever classed in the category of failures on the ground of a solitary reconviction for some trifling offence.

As a matter of fact, tabulated returns relating to the success or failure in after-life of children who have been under detention can never be altogether accurate, and must be regarded in the light of mere approximations. They are not a complete representation of the actual facts. They leave much to be considered which cannot be reduced to statistical formulæ, and cannot be expressed in the nomenclature of figures. Assuming, however, that these figures are the most precise expression of the worth of educational institutions for juvenile offenders which it is possible to find, can they be described as altogether satisfactory? If the whole of the children subjected to detention in these institutions

would otherwise have become criminals of the
habitual type, it must be admitted that a system
which saves three-fourths or even one-half of them
from such a disastrous fate is not to be lightly condemned. On the other hand, it is a large assumption
to suppose that all the children committed to corrective institutions would have become criminals if
these institutions had not been in existence to rescue
them. It is practically certain that a fair proportion of the inmates of establishments for juvenile
offenders would ultimately do well in the world even
if they had not been committed to these places of
detention. But, admitting all these facts and making
all reasonable deductions on account of them, it must
still be maintained, to use the words of the Royal
Commission appointed to inquire into them, that the
work of these schools is important and beneficial.

In view of the failure of imprisonment as an effective means of dealing with juvenile offenders, the
community is bound to resort in a greater or less
degree to the practice of committing certain classes
of juveniles to corrective institutions. In these circumstances the only question which remains for
consideration is the principles on which these institutions should be conducted, so as to achieve the best
possible results. The primary purpose of these
institutions is to deal in the first place with children
who have actually committed offences against the
criminal law, and in the second place with children
whose conduct and surroundings are of such a
character that offences against the criminal law are
in all probability only a question of time and oppor-

tunity. The case of children who have actually fallen into crime is comparatively simple, and it is not as a rule difficult for a magistrate to arrive at a decision as to whether a child of this description should be committed to a corrective institution or not. If such a child is living under adverse parental circumstances, and if the offence with which he is charged is the result of deep-seated moral obliquity, then it is clearly advisable in the interests of public security that the juvenile should be removed from his surroundings and placed in the midst of more wholesome moral conditions. On the other hand, it is as a rule inadvisable to commit children to corrective institutions who are living under normal parental conditions, even if these children have become offenders against the criminal law. The discipline of a somewhat inferior home is always better than the discipline of an institution, and the efforts of parental solicitude are much more likely to be effectual in the ultimate reclamation of a wayward child than any kind of State machinery.

It is sometimes suggested that first offenders should in no case be committed to corrective institutions. Where the offence is actually a first offence, and where there are no circumstances calling for exceptional treatment, it is a wise principle to act with every possible indulgence. But the difficulty of applying this principle in its entirety arises from the fact that a first offender is sometimes an old offender in reality. His first appearance before the criminal courts is not always to be accepted as a proof that he has just begun to offend against the criminal law. It is only a proof that he has so far succeeded in escaping detection. He may in reality be an old offender, although it is his first appearance before the criminal courts. Circumstances of this kind have always to be taken into consideration in dealing with juvenile offenders. Appropriate methods of treatment can never be arrived at by the application of any hard-and-fast rule. Each case presents peculiarities and distinctive features, and it is only after all circumstances have been allowed their proper weight that a wise judgment is in the end attained.

As a rule it is undesirable that very young children should be committed to corrective institutions. According to the returns for 1893 forty-seven infants under six years of age were committed to industrial schools in England, and 347 boys and girls between the ages of six and eight. Some of these little ones were, it is true, sent to day industrial and truant schools, but a considerable proportion of them were committed to the ordinary industrial school. No doubt there are cases in which other circumstances beside the element of age have to be taken into consideration in dealing with little children. Evil habits arising from constant contact with vicious or criminal surroundings are sometimes developed at a very tender age. But as a rule these habits are not deep-seated, and when this is the case it is a mistake to commit little children to ordinary industrial schools. The rules, the daily duties, the whole arrangements of these institutions are designed for older children. The younger ones have in the main to conform to a set of regulations which is not in the first instance intended for them, and the result is that a strain is put upon them which they are not always able to bear. According to the evidence given before the Commission on Secondary Education, children under eight years of age, if they are to be kept in health, should have five meals a day and from eleven to twelve hours' sleep. But where corrective institutions are worked upon hard-and-fast regulations very little attention is paid to the dissimilarity of treatment required for children of dissimilar ages, and the younger children are in danger of being sacrificed to the older ones. Many of the children committed to industrial schools are really cases for poor-law schools, or cases in which judicious boarding out would be the best specific. As a rule children under the age of ten should not be committed to an ordinary industrial school. Where children under this age are committed they should not be subjected to the regulations in force for older boys.

Children may be committed to day industrial and truant schools at an earlier age than is desirable in the case of children sent to the ordinary industrial school. Day industrial schools should as a rule be used for children who are unable on account of poverty to attend the ordinary national school. In our large centres of industry there is a considerable proportion of children in such wretched material circumstances that it is undesirable to place them amongst the ordinary school population. Children are very keen to detect differences between themselves and others, and an ill-cared for and poorly clad child is apt to be subjected to treatment from his fellows at an ordinary school which makes school life a misery and burden to him. For children of this class a day industrial school is a most useful institution, and inasmuch as the children in these schools are at home in the evening, the tie between the parent and the child is not broken. It cannot be said that the industrial training in day industrial schools is conducted on satisfactory principles. In some schools too much time seems to be occupied in wood-chopping, mat-making, and work of an analogous character. What most of the children in day industrial schools require is a sound training in the elements of knowledge. Many of these children are too young to be subjected to industrial discipline of a serious kind, and it is a mistake to assimilate the routine of these schools too closely to the system which prevails in the ordinary industrial school. The children committed to truant schools are, as a rule, backward children who are unable, from natural incapacity or from irregularity of attendance, to keep abreast of children of their own age. The principal cause of truancy is backwardness, and the primary object of a truant school should be to bring the child into line educationally with children of a similar age. As soon as a child is able to hold his own in class with other children he is no longer afraid of school, and the chief cause of truancy disappears. But until a child is placed in this position school life will always be a source of terror and apprehension to him. According to the late Inspector of Reformatory and Industrial Schools, a child often goes to the truant school " discouraged and hopeless, and the object of the school is to establish the boy in his standard and to give him confidence and assurance as to his own ability, so far as it goes." It should be a comparatively easy matter for truant schools conducted on sound principles to deal satisfactorily with children who are backward merely owing to irregularity of attendance. Assiduous attention to the educational defects of these children will soon be rewarded by an improved standard of efficiency, and everything at the truant school should be subordinated to securing this supreme end. It is a much more difficult problem to deal effectually with children of dull and defective capacity. The child population of the country contains a certain percentage of this unpromising material, and there are cases where it is quite impossible to put such children on an educational level with their equals in years. But until this is done the great cause of truancy will remain, and with it will remain the temptation for the child to absent himself from school. Where the truant school has to deal with children of this description, it is often safer in the interests of society that the child should be detained till the period of school age is over. In the truant school the juvenile will at least be taught those habits of order and regularity which are essential to success in industrial life, and which will stand him in good stead when he is old enough to begin to earn his living in the field, the factory, or the workshop.

Children, as a rule, are detained from three to four months in truant schools, and in several of these institutions they are subjected to treatment which in the opinion of competent observers is too strict and

severe.   According to the official returns the children
in some of these schools are only allowed half an
hour's play during the whole day, there is an excess
of corporal punishment, too little recreation, and no
incentive to industry in the shape of reward for good
conduct.   Sometimes the children admitted to truant
schools are unwell when they arrive, and in many
cases it is to be feared that the cause of truancy is in
reality ill-health as much as anything else.   In such
circumstances it is most essential that truant schools
should be managed with the utmost discrimination,
and that the children should be individualised and
not dealt with in the mass.   In these schools the dull
child, the sickly child, the neglected child, the wayward child are all collected together.   Each of these
classes of children requires treatment adapted to its
individual characteristics, and the success of the
school as an instrument of social security will depend
upon the extent to which this individualising process
is carried out.   In each case inquiry must be made
as to the set of circumstances which have made the
child a truant, and the efforts of the management
must be directed towards removing these adverse
circumstances wherever it is possible to do so.   In
cases where the adverse conditions cannot altogether
be removed, then attention must be directed towards
the best means of mitigating them.

As truant schools are at present conducted there is
reason to fear that the inmates of some of them are
treated too much as if they were criminal prisoners.
Classification according to the causes which have produced truancy, and individualisation, based upon classi-

fication, are the only sound principles of dealing with children in truant schools. In these institutions too much reliance must not be attached to mere repression. Severity of treatment will never remove the conditions which produce truancy. In most cases this kind of discipline has a hardening and brutalising effect ; it deadens the sensibilities of the young heart, and when this is the result the truant very often degenerates into a criminal in after years. The cellular punishments which are resorted to in some truant schools are an admirable preliminary preparation for the prison cell, and it will generally be found that the class of children who take kindly to the isolation of the prison cell are children who have already had experience of a similar kind of punishment in the truant school. No surer method can be adopted of utterly destroying any deterrent effect which imprisonment may possess than the method of accustoming children in corrective institutions to cellular confinement. Among children who have passed through this ordeal imprisonment is accepted with indifference ; in their minds the terrors of the law have practically ceased to exist.

While the English law allows children to be committed to corrective institutions at an exceedingly tender age, it forbids any juvenile offender who has passed the age of sixteen to be committed to establishments of an educational character. England has no place of detention for juveniles over sixteen except a prison, and even in prisons all juveniles over the age of sixteen are treated as if they were men. A very different method of dealing with young offenders exists in the United States. In the state of New York offenders who have become criminals for the first time may be committed to reformatory institutions between the ages of sixteen and thirty. In the Massachusetts reformatory at Concord the average age of the inmates is twenty-two. In the state of Pennsylvania the industrial reformatory at Huntingdon receives offenders between the ages of fifteen and twenty-five. In the state of Minnesota the average age of the inmates is about twenty-two, and in Illinois the range of age is between sixteen and twenty-one.

Wherever we look for expressions of opinion on the subject of juvenile crime, it will be found that the tendency of the present time is to raise the limits of age at which a juvenile may be committed to educational establishments. In an admirable report presented by Dr. Appelius to the International Union of Penal Law it is recommended that juveniles should be allowed the benefits of educational institutions up to the age of eighteen. In the proposed penal code for the Swiss Confederation which has been drafted by Professor Stoos at the request of the Swiss Federal Council, it is proposed that juveniles under the age of eighteen may be committed to corrective institutions. Professor Stoos justifies his proposal on the following grounds : "It is only by degrees that a juvenile acquires physical and mental development. The period of transition falls as a rule between the fourteenth and the eighteenth year. During this period a juvenile possesses penal capacity, but he ought not to be dealt with as if he were an adult.

Up to the present time, and under the influence of French legislation, the degree of discernment exhibited by a juvenile has always been the chief point for consideration. But what is lacking in a juvenile is not so much the faculty of discerning whether his conduct is wrong and deserves punishment, *as the power to conform to what he knows to be right,* the power to resist the solicitations of evil—in a word, what a juvenile lacks is maturity of character."

Maturity of character is largely dependent on physical maturity, and, according to the evidence of Dr. Roberts before the Secondary Education Commission, the children of the poorer classes do not attain physical maturity till they have reached their twenty-fifth or twenty-sixth year. " The size of the body," says Dr. Roberts, " as determined by stature, weight, and chest girth, has definite relations to precocity and dulness of intellect in children. When we examine children anthropometrically we find that the more intelligent classes are taller and heavier at corresponding ages than the less intelligent, the most favoured classes than the less favoured classes. Full growth in stature is attained in the professional classes about the twenty-first year, but in the poorer classes not before the twenty-fifth or twenty-sixth year. Thus just as girls attain maturity earlier than boys of corresponding classes, so the better class boys attain maturity earlier than boys of the poorer classes. When I state, therefore, that big boys are more precocious than small boys, I am stating in another way the fact that big boys are more developed than little boys mentally as well as physically,

and more work both mental and physical may be
required of them." If the investigations of Dr.
Roberts are correct (they are accepted by other
investigators of equal eminence) as to the age when
bodily and mental maturity is attained among the
poorer classes, our existing penal laws and our
present methods of administration, in so far as they
relate to juveniles over sixteen, are at once cruel and
absurd. American legislation is, on the whole, based
upon much more defensible principles, and it is along
the lines laid down by the American people that
European legislation will sooner or later have to
move.

A tendency to move in this direction has been
exhibiting itself in England for several years, but
so far without any practical results. The managers
and superintendents of reformatory schools have
been contending that they are quite able to deal
with juvenile offenders admitted into their establishments at the age of eighteen. The report of the
Departmental Committee on Prisons recommends
that the age of admission to reformatories should be
raised to eighteen, and the ultimate limit of detention
to twenty-one. This Committee also recommends
that the experiment should be tried of establishing
a special penal institution for offenders under the age
of twenty-three. "The initial cost of this experiment," says the Committee's report, "would not be
great. It might lead to the closing of one or two
prisons occupying sites in large towns, an effect
desirable in itself ; and we do not hesitate to believe
that it would draw upon the main source of habitual

criminality to a very considerable extent. We look upon this plan in conjunction with the raising of the age of admission to reformatories as the best proposal that is open to us for the rescue of young offenders. Under the present system numbers of them come out of prison in a condition as bad or worse than that in which they entered it. They go out with the prison taint on them. The available prison staff and the rigid system of prison discipline, without any fault on the part of the officials, preclude the possibility of bringing to bear on the prison population the moral suasion and the healthy practical advice which we think could be exercised by a trained and selected staff in a penal reformatory." It will be seen that these recommendations point to the adoption of a system of dealing with the older class of young offenders on principles somewhat similar to the system which is in operation in several states of the American Union. The fundamental idea at the root of this system is that remedial agencies should play a large part in the treatment of offenders until maturity of character has been attained, and among the class from which the bulk of the criminal population is recruited maturity of character is not reached till the age of twenty-five.

In order that society may derive the utmost possible benefit from corrective institutions it is essential that these institutions should be properly classified. In a proper system of classification the age, the sex, the individual and social circumstances of the offender, as well as the offence which he has committed, should all be taken into careful considera-

tion.   If all sorts of offenders are mixed up together,
and all are subjected to precisely the same kind of
regimen, a certain dead level of uniformity in external
demeanour will be obtained, but comparatively little
effect will be produced upon the springs of conduct,
and when a juvenile growing up under such conditions is again let loose in society, he will be in
danger of returning to habits which have been
temporarily repressed, but never eradicated.   In
Great Britain the classification of corrective institutions which at present exists is a classification in
name rather than in reality.   We have day industrial
schools, truant schools, ordinary industrial schools,
reformatory schools, all certified by government, and
in addition a vast number of voluntary homes for
juveniles which are not in any way under government
control.   The classification of the children committed
to these schools is of a very rudimentary character.
Classification according to sex prevails in most of
them, but a matter of quite as great importance,
classification according to age, exists to a very limited
extent.   In reformatory schools children under ten
years of age are associated with youths of eighteen
and twenty.   In industrial schools infants under six
are sometimes mixed up with boys of fifteen and
sixteen.   Except in schools such as the institution
at Redhill, where the inmates live in different houses,
it is impossible to deal with children varying so
much in age in a satisfactory manner.

Even at some of the best-conducted institutions it
will be observed that the time-table for the boy of
twelve is exactly the same as the time-table for the

boy of eighteen. In other words, the life of the boy of twelve is mapped out on exactly the same plan as the daily life of the youth of eighteen. Both boys, though differing so much in age, have to rise at the same time in the morning, and retire at the same time in the evening to rest. Both boys are allotted the same time for work, food, and recreation. As far as it is possible to gather from the time-table, children of twelve are treated as if they possessed the same physical and mental development as youths who are approaching maturity. According to the teachings of physiology, not to mention the teachings of common sense, a boy of twelve should not be subjected to the same regimen as boys considerably his senior in years. The younger boy requires more sleep and rest, he requires more time for meals, he requires more play, games, and exercises, and he should have less school and industrial work imposed upon him. But in institutions where boys cannot be classified in different houses it is difficult to arrange a variety of time-tables adapted to the ages of the inmates. To work smoothly the institution must be administered as closely as possible upon a uniform plan. But in order that uniformity may not be purchased at the expense of efficiency, it is essential that classification according to age should prevail in corrective institutions.

Classification of juveniles according to offence is also largely overlooked in juvenile institutions in Great Britain. Children who are orphans and deserted, and are merely suffering from want of parental care, are often mixed up in the same establishment with children charged with offences against the criminal law. A number of the children at present confined in ordinary industrial schools are the children of parents who, according to the Education Acts, habitually and without reasonable excuse, neglect to provide efficient elementary education for their offspring. These institutions also contain a certain number of children charged with theft and other offences of a criminal character. In reformatory schools children who are found begging and sleeping out, or who have committed some offence against the regulations of the poor-house, are classed together with juveniles convicted of such serious crimes as burglary and housebreaking. It was the original intention of the framers of the Industrial and Reformatory School Acts that industrial schools were to be used for children who were in material and moral danger of becoming criminals, whilst reformatory schools were to be utilised for juveniles who had actually committed offences against the penal law. As a matter of fact, this distinction has been to some extent lost sight of, and in practice reformatory and industrial schools have tended to become in many respects institutions of a very similar character.

In the classification of juveniles it has been pointed out that the age of the offender and the nature of the offence are two questions which should always be taken into consideration, but it would be unwise to classify children in accordance with age and offence alone. Other circumstances also require to be considered, such as the character, the constitution, and the parental condition of the child. One child convicted of begging or wandering may be much more depraved in character than another child convicted of theft, and sometimes a boy of twelve is at a lower moral level than another at sixteen, although the offences committed by both are exactly the same. In deciding on the kind of institution to which a juvenile should be committed it will be seen that the judge or magistrate has a delicate and difficult task before him. He has not only to take account of such obvious facts as the age of the offender and the nature of the offence, but all the more remote individual and social circumstances surrounding the offender. But the duties of the judicial authorities would be very much facilitated if corrective institutions were classified on clearly defined principles.

A proper system of classification, for instance, would confine the operation of the day industrial school to cases where the child was unable through poverty to attend the ordinary board school. It would confine the truant school to cases in which the child, either through his own fault or the fault of the parents, or from a combination of both circumstances, was habitually absent from school. On the other hand, the distinction in name between industrial and reformatory schools should be abolished, and both sets of institutions should receive the common appellation of industrial schools. They should be restricted in their operations to the reception of juveniles who had actually fallen into crime. If these principles of classification were adopted many children of the type which is now to be found in industrial schools would have to be provided for in another manner. Some of them would be provided for in truant schools, others would be provided for in day industrial schools ; the remainder would be provided for in poor-law schools, or judiciously boarded out, or remain, as in Massachusetts, with their parents, subject to the supervision of a special agent.

What all these children require, to whatever class they may belong, is moral, mental, physical, and industrial education. The supreme authority in charge of delinquent and dependent children should be the Education Department of the State. So long as these children are looked at as at present through the eyes of the Criminal Department, or through the eyes of the Pauper Department, they will not receive the humane consideration to which their miseries entitle them, and society will be punished for refusing them this consideration by seeing an ominous percentage of them relapsing into a life of habitual criminality, and becoming a permanent danger to the community.

A classification of corrective institutions is, as has been said, the first step towards a more efficient method of dealing with juvenile offenders. But classification will fall short of its ultimate end unless it is supplemented by individualisation. All that a sound principle of classification can effect is to enable a juvenile to be sent to the right kind of institution. It is individualisation which ensures that he shall receive the right kind of treatment after he has been admitted. The object of classification is

to facilitate the task of individualisation. Each child
has a certain number of characteristics in common
with other children of the same age and with childhood as a whole. But he has also a group of
characteristics which are peculiar to himself. It
is these characteristics which constitute his individuality. Classification can never be made so
complete or proceed so far as to take account of
individuality. It must at best stop short at similarities such as age, sex, and so on, which do not go
down to the roots of personal character. Behind
these similarities are fundamental idiosyncrasies of
mind and temperament which are peculiar to each
individual. These idiosyncrasies can be modified
and moulded by education and surroundings, but in
every rational system of dealing with the young
they must be considered and respected.

The only way in which it is possible to individualise
the treatment of juvenile offenders; to deal with each
child in accordance with its personal characteristics
of mind and temperament, consists in working
corrective institutions on a comparatively small
scale. The results of all recent inquiries as to the
best methods of dealing with children in institutions
are unanimous upon this point. The report of the
Reformatory and Industrial Schools Commission
says that "it is in the smaller schools that the
personal influence of the superintendent can be
applied with the most satisfactory results to every
individual boy or girl in the school, and to those
who having left it can still benefit by the watchful
guidance and sympathy of a superintendent who has

acquired a knowledge of their characters and an influence over them for good. The difficulty of acquiring such a knowledge and influence increases in direct proportion to the numbers of the school. And seeing that in most cases the neglect of the parent has been the cause of the committal of the child, and that this neglect must be repaired by the influence of those who stand in *loco parentis*, there are strong reasons for keeping reformatories and industrial schools as small as local circumstances will allow, so that each boy or girl may receive as much personal care and interest as can be given in an institution which is necessarily an imperfect substitute for home." These remarks are in substantial agreement with the opinions of a Select Committee of the House of Lords on the operation of the Poor Law. " There are serious disadvantages," say the Committee, " which are inseparable from any system under which a number of children are brought up together without any home influence or any contact with the outer world, but we cannot doubt that they are much aggravated by the overgrown size of the metropolitan district schools."

Similar expressions of opinion as to the desirability of smaller institutions, so as to secure greater individuality of treatment, reach us from the United States. At a conference held in New York in 1893 on the care of dependent and delinquent children, Mrs. Charles Russell Lowell said that " thousands of children who ought to receive the training of family life are, on the contrary, living in the unnatural isolation of a crowd of children like themselves, and subject to institution training which must destroy in almost all the capacity to meet the difficulties and temptations to which they will be exposed as soon as they begin life for themselves. What preparation for independent action can be found in a life the one necessity of which is absolute dependence upon and conformity to rule? What room is there for the development or exercise of energy or invention in a life where everything is ready to hand and prepared by machinery? What chance is there for a child to learn the value of property or the difference between *meum* and *tuum* where everything, even the clothing, belongs to no one individual but to the whole community? What sense of personal love or care can be felt when the child is one of a thousand or even of a hundred marshalled and drilled in companies, from getting up in the morning until going to bed at night? Fancy the stultification of mind and soul which must follow from such conditions. Yet these conditions are, I believe, inevitable even in the best of our institutions, for there are only four on the whole list of those of which I am speaking which have less than a hundred inmates."

The impossibility of individualisation in large schools and the serious evils arising out of the absence of it are strikingly illustrated in the report of the Committee appointed to inquire into the administration of Poor Law Schools in London. "It is impossible," says one witness, "in those large schools for anybody, no matter who they are, to manage them so as in any way to touch the

children as individuals, even to know their names.'
" When children are not touched as individuals
it is necessary," says the report, " to maintain a
rigid system of discipline as well as an effective
quarantine, and thus it becomes impracticable to
vary the life of the inmates by walking out, shopping,
returning to their homes or friends for short holidays,
and mixing with the outside world. The children
under such conditions have a tendency to become
dull, sullen, and mechanical, and to lose interest alike
in work and play. The standard of health among
them is lower than that of children living under
ordinary conditions. The use of machinery and
other appliances for the performance of domestic
duties is so extensive that the children never see the
simple methods of ordinary homes and do not learn
to manage for themselves."

It is only right to mention on behalf of the institutions in existence in Great Britain for juvenile
offenders that very few of them contain the vast
number of children which are sometimes to be found
in poor-law schools. None of the reformatories for
girls, either in England or Scotland, contain an
average population of a hundred inmates. In the
reformatories for boys the aggregation of the inmates
is considerably higher, but none of these institutions
reach an average population of three hundred. Most
of them have a population of less than one hundred,
and a considerable proportion range between one and
two hundred under detention. In industrial schools,
and more particularly in industrial school ships, the
average child population sometimes exceeds three

hundred. But a large number of these schools are also of comparatively small dimensions. In cases where corrective institutions contain a large number of inmates it is essential that such institutions should be divided into sections, and that each section should be placed in charge of a superintendent who will be able to acquire a thorough knowledge of the capacity, disposition and aptitudes of every individual child. It is only in this way that the dangers of aggregation can be minimised, and perhaps to some extent obviated.

In order to facilitate the delicate and difficult task of individualisation all children admitted to corrective establishments should be submitted to a careful examination. This examination should take the form of a thorough inquiry into the bodily and mental condition of the child. It has already been pointed out that a considerable percentage of the juveniles under detention in corrective institutions are below the average of the general juvenile population of the same age and sex. They are more stunted in growth and are lighter in weight, they suffer from a larger proportion of defects of development, they exhibit a higher percentage of mental dulness. At present the tendency of institutional life is to aggravate the physical and mental defects of the juveniles who reside in them.[1] This is not an inevitable accompaniment of institutional life. It arises from the fact that the children are dealt with too much in the mass. The only way to remedy

[1] See Report on the Mental and Physical Conditions of Childhood, p. 55.

this fundamental evil is to submit the children to such an examination as will enable the persons in charge of them to know what they can do and what they cannot do. If children are forced to pass through a course of discipline which they are either physically or mentally unfitted for, the result of such a system is certain to intensify and aggravate their congenital or acquired defects. Another serious evil arising from a want of knowledge of the bodily and mental capacities of children in corrective institutions is that they are in danger of being subjected to mistaken harshness. Actual want of ability is mistaken for idleness, carelessness, or want of will, and punishment is inflicted when it is out of place.

In order to keep in the closest possible touch with the capacities of juveniles in corrective institutions the bodily as well as the mental examination of the inmates should be repeated at stated intervals. At the present time the greatest amount of stress appears to be laid on the progress made in intellectual acquirements, but it is to be recollected that the future of these children on liberation will depend quite as much on their capacity for bodily exertion as on their mental knowledge. It is by hard manual labour that most of them will have to earn a living, and physical vigour will be as indispensable to them as mental vigour. Unless they possess material backbone they are only too likely to fall back into the ranks of the criminal population, no matter how anxious they may be to do well when they start again in the world. In France the importance of periodically examining the physical condition of juvenile offenders is adequately appreciated by the central administration. "The object of the law," says M. Raux, an eminent penitentiary official, "is to liberate the pupils of the State from corrective institutions sound and robust in body as well as in mind. Our duty is to utilise every method calculated to maintain health and to assure a maximum of development to all the organs." In order to give practical effect to this purpose M. Raux says that the central administration requires the heads of all establishments to subject the inmates to a careful physical examination every six months. It is only in this way, he tells us, that it is possible to detect sudden stoppages of development and to find out the causes of them. The result of these inquiries is to show that a certain percentage of juveniles under detention hardly develop at all. They have suffered so many hardships before admission that it is impossible to restore their prematurely exhausted forces. Their members are atrophied, and a life of privation has paralysed their powers of growth. With material of this description it is impossible to do much, but the duty of the State towards these unhappy victims of heredity and surroundings is just as great as its duty towards the robust and normal. Its first and most imperative duty is to know in what proportions this class of children are to be found in corrective institutions. The only way in which they can be known is by means of a periodical examination of the physical condition of all the inmates. A system of this kind would tend to prevent many feeble children from being subjected to unmerited hardships when under detention, it would lead to a more individualised method of treatment for such cases, and it would prevent some of them when liberated from relapsing into habits of crime. From a wide experience of juveniles who have failed after being dealt with in correctional establishments I feel sure that one of the causes of failure is the want of sufficient individualisation during the period of detention, and this want has the most disastrous results in the case of juveniles who are somewhat anomalous in physical or mental constitution.

The classification and individualisation of juveniles in corrective establishments in accordance with definite and intelligible principles would immensely facilitate the task of conditional liberation. It has already been mentioned that juveniles committed to industrial or reformatory schools may be liberated conditionally, or on licence, as it is technically called, long before the full term of detention has expired. Juveniles liberated in this manner are committed to the care of some trustworthy person, either in this country or the colonies, who is willing to take charge of them. The power of licensing a juvenile offender may be exercised at the expiration of twelve or eighteen months' detention, but it is seldom resorted to at such an early period. It is contended that children who are let out of corrective institutions at the end of comparatively short periods of detention relapse in greater numbers than children who have been subjected to the discipline of these institutions for a greater length of time. In the Quartier

Correctionnel at Lyons it was found that juveniles liberated in less than a twelvemonth after admission exhibited a higher percentage of failures than juveniles detained for longer periods.

Whilst liberation after a brief detention is probably a mistake it must, on the other hand, be pointed out that it is possible to go to an extreme in the contrary direction, and to make too little use of conditional liberation. This appears to be the danger in England at the present time. According to the returns the vast majority of juveniles in reformatory and industrial schools are detained between three and four years before being released on licence for the first time. In some of the industrial schools the children are detained for five, six, or even seven years. It is said that one reason why juveniles are kept away from the ordinary realities of social life for such prolonged periods is the difficulty of procuring suitable people to take charge of them. The labour which these juveniles are able to give in exchange for their maintenance is not enough to remunerate (in this country at least) the persons who would offer them a home. Even with the addition of a small sum from the institutions from which they are conditionally released, the task of keeping them is said to be an unremunerative one. In these circumstances the only people willing to receive such children are their parents, and the parents are in many cases the last people into whose hands they should be placed. These are difficulties in the way of licensing children at a comparatively early date which deserve consideration and must not be overlooked.

At the same time the principle of liberation before the full sentence of detention has expired is such a sound one that every effort should be made to overcome the practical obstacles which at present stand in the way of its application.

In connection with the release, whether conditional or absolute, of juvenile offenders there are certain general principles which it is always well to bear in mind. Juveniles whose conduct has been indifferent during detention cannot be liberated with safety until a considerable portion of their sentence has expired. At the same time it does not always follow that a juvenile whose career in a correctional establishment has not been altogether exemplary should be set down beforehand as necessarily doomed to failure when he re-enters the world. In cases where individuality is strongly marked, and also in cases where developing faculties are late in acquiring equilibrium, it is found that juveniles succeed in actual life who have been more or less failures in institution life. Although this is often exemplified in experience, the only safe principle to act upon in connection with the conditional liberation of refractory inmates is to detain them for longer periods in the hope that the nearer approach of maturity will be accompanied by a greater measure of mental and moral equilibrium.

Another principle to be recognised in connection with conditional liberation is that juveniles convicted of offences against the person are more likely to do well in after-life than juveniles charged with vagabondage and offences against property. Juveniles of

the former class may accordingly he conditionally liberated sooner than juveniles of the latter. There are
fewer relapses among children whose antecedents are
good, and among children whose homes are good,
than among children more unhappily circumstanced in
these respects. Consideration should be given to these
facts in deciding at what period a juvenile should be
conditionally liberated. It is also to be recollected
that children sent to the country when conditionally
liberated are more likely to do well than children
sent to the towns. The destination of the liberated
juvenile is a consideration to which the very greatest
weight must be attached, and juveniles destined to
return to the temptations of city life cannot be
liberated at such an early date as those whose
characters will not be subjected to so severe a
strain.

When conditional liberation takes place the juvenile
offender, though differing in age, is in a somewhat
similar position to the poor-law child who is
boarded out. His future depends to a considerable
extent on the character of the person into whose
custody he is entrusted. In the first volume of the
American Journal of Sociology Mr. C. D. Randall
gives an interesting account of the measures taken
in the state of Michigan for securing proper homes
for juvenile offenders after liberation. All delinquent
and dependent children are under the charge of a
State Board of Corrections and Charities. This
board has agents in every county, and their duties
relate to both dependent and delinquent children.
"The agents," says Mr. Randall, "all inspect and

report on all proposed homes for dependent or delinquent children, and none of either class are placed in families by indenture or adoption unless the agent approves. And when he finds after indenture that the home is not adapted to the child, or that the child is ill-treated, it is his duty to report the case at any time to the school which placed the child. The county agency is very necessary to a well-ordered system. The applicant for the child lives in the county of the agent. He can readily learn whether the home is suitable, and when the child is placed he soon hears if it is not well-treated. He is where he can see and learn all, and protect the child, and guard its every interest. The agency is not expensive. It is largely a labour of love and self-sacrifice when the duties are well discharged."

If the care of dependent and delinquent children were placed in the hands of the County Councils in England under the supreme supervision of the Education Department a system such as prevails in Michigan, and which Mr. Randall says works so well there, would be of immense assistance in the placing out of juveniles on conditional liberation. The managers and heads of corrective establishments do their best to keep a watchful eye on juveniles who have left their hands, but the task under existing circumstances is an exceedingly difficult one. It cannot be doubted that a more efficient system of "after care" would materially minimise the risks at present connected with conditional liberation. Too much credit cannot be attached to the statements of juveniles who find their way into prison after passing through industrial and reformatory schools. But careful examination of many cases of this unfortunate description convinces me that the good effect of the schools is sometimes obliterated by the bad effect of an unsuitable home or situation after discharge. It is certain that the percentage of failures would considerably diminish if it were possible to bestow more attention on juveniles when they leave correctional establishments. It is during the first two years that the risk of failure is greatest, and the utmost pains should be taken to enable a youth to retain his balance during this perilous and trying period.

THE END.